Commodore Hilty's
Second Act

Also by Thomas Corcoran

The Flag List
Waiting for V-J Day
Decoration Day
The Hobbledehoy: Stories

Commodore Hilty's Second Act

a novel by

Thomas Corcoran

Bernice Feigenbaum and Company
Philadelphia ~ 2023

This is a work of fiction, set in the imagined past, occasionally depicting historical figures and places.

ISBN (HC): 979-8-218-24991-5
ISBN (PB): 979-8-218-24992-2

First Printing

Epigraphs from T. Lucretius Caro, *The Nature of Things,* translated by A.E. Stallings (New York: Penguin, 2007), p. 71; Victor Hugo, *Ninety-Three,* translated by Frank Lee Benedict (New York: Carroll & Graff, 1988), p. 377; and F. Scott Fitzgerald, *Notes for The Last Tycoon, an unfinished novel* (New York: Charles Scribner's Sons, 1970), p. 163.

For Linda

Now the old farmer shakes his head and groans again and again / That the hard labours of his hands have turned out all in vain.

—T. Lucretius Caro

Your Republic weighs, measures, regulates man; mine lifts him into the open sky. It is the difference between a theorem and an eagle.

—Victor Hugo

There are no second acts in American lives.

—F. Scott Fitzgerald

Contents

The End of Act One

Decommissioned, Sold, Renamed, Forgotten

People had it wrong about homecomings, of course: they were harder than departures. A sailor home from a long cruise had to discover what his sweetheart had become without him, and she had to do the same.

If thirty years of naval service, most of it at sea, could be thought of as a long cruise, then Bradford Hilty's six years as a civilian living with his wife, Madeleine, was essentially a homecoming. In that light, each had discovered that the other had become a stranger—though strangely familiar—and their life together was no longer a pleasure.

They felt this through short-lived disputes and protracted silences and frequent irritating mannerisms that had once seemed endearing. Other than in their fantasies, they never spoke about the problem, which would have made it a real thing to be dealt with. In fact, other than the end-of-day report, in which each showed more interest than they felt, they didn't have much to talk about at all.

While they chafed, their marriage was effectively on autopilot. Their two children were grown, and in characteristically different ways both parents were on good terms with them. Their house was renovated, and they worked together to be efficient owners. They had the same values. They generally felt the same way about books, music, and TV—though Mad was quick to point out any differences. They thought alike politically (a blessing in that era). They treated each other with respect and kindness and occasionally with the old humor. But all from habit.

For example, when he received an invitation to the decommissioning of the destroyer he had once commanded, affectionately known as "Plumpy," and the invitation momentarily knocked him off-stride, being so unexpected and calling up so many powerful memories, Madeleine, in a stratagem easily penetrated, offered to go with him.

Easily penetrated, that is, given her present attitude toward the service. At one time she had known all the knots and splices; had wept at "Anchors Aweigh" and sung the national anthem in ceremonies.

"You hate these things," he said.

"But it must be sad for you. Your ship, all you put into her. Of course I'll go if you want me to."

Not having seen him for a few hours, she had looked into his study. Men his age (but he was only sixty) were sometimes found dead over a favorite book. In recent years she had lost her affectionate ways, but she would always do her duty as a wife. He was sitting at his desk, and she was in the chair that any petitioner for the favors of the squire must occupy. Not that he was that or there were many petitioners anymore. In the high school where he taught American history, a few of his students—usually the same students—would come into his classroom after hours. No one came to his house. Any visitors were contractors or friends of Mad.

"They're decommissioning three destroyers, all in good shape," he said. "I don't understand."

"Yes, I heard it on NPR. They're being sold to Taiwan. It's a big deal. China's making threats."

"I imagine so. That would be a redline for them."

He thought it might be instructive if he recited the history of China's declarations about the Aegis technology, the most advanced in the world, but he wasn't up to giving a lecture, and her eyebrows asked only if she should go with him.

"No need. Any old shipmates I see, we'll be telling sea stories. You've got your own life to live."

"I'm happy to do this, Bradford."

"But you don't really want to."

"I'm happy to."

"It's not the same. If we were lying in bed now and planning our day and I asked, 'What would you most like to do, Madeleine?' would you say, 'Well, we haven't been to a decommissioning in a while'?"

[4]

"When did we last lie in bed—I mean that idle?"

"All right, let me make it real. Scale of one to five?"

"What is one?"

"Wild horses couldn't drag you."

"Three point seven." At this she got up and moved among the bookshelves straightening the books. Once or twice she glanced over with burning cheeks.

"I don't believe you. Which would you rather do: go to this decommissioning or to a faculty party?"

She turned. "Who would be the faculty?"

"Decommissioning or another visit to Cooperstown?"

"Apples and oranges. That trip takes several days."

"Decommissioning or read my essay on the fallacy of the Lost Cause?"

"Unfair. I did read it once—and praised it, remember."

"Or watch *Citizen Kane.*"

"Ugh! The decommissioning."

"Very well, at last we've found bottom."

The invitation had arrived three weeks before the event, which was proper, and the ceremony was to be on a Friday, which was traditional. Sailors never put to sea on Friday if they can help it, but in port almost every kind of ceremony is scheduled for that day, even when Saturday might be more convenient for guests. He entered the particulars into his calendar: Friday 8 June 2018, Pier 22, Naval Station Norfolk. For him that Saturday would have been more convenient because school was still in session. But the students would be taking final exams then, and someone else could act for him as proctor.

This being an official occasion, he might have worn his uniform (which still fit him after six years), but he didn't want to seem like one of those retired officers who still think—who still wish—that they mattered. He dressed in a summer suit with an open collar and, because there would be saluting, a lightweight English cap.

[5]

The ceremony was held at the head of the pier (the seaward end, King Neptune's view of it), where the three ships were moored in a nest, beam to beam. Exactly aligned, they looked like triplets brought out for inspection. Plumpy was the inboard ship, her captain being senior.

The day threatened rain under heavy motionless clouds, and the forecast gave it a seventy percent chance. Sitting in his reserved seat, he kept one eye aloft. So did the other guests and, more discreetly, the high officers on the dais, but each of their weather eyes was on a cell phone. He was satisfied by this fresh evidence that so many sailors were actually lubbers.

The ceremony itself gave him a good feeling. The ships' companies were being called from their unfinished artwork, and they were leaving their home away from home as well. Yet they were proud of themselves, being young they looked to the future, and in all circumstances they possessed the sailor's natural gift of fun.

In his speech the admiral commanding the fleet praised the ships for their fighting qualities and the government's sale of them as a sign of the health of the partnership between Taiwan and the United States. Following his talking points, he didn't call Taiwan a country.

The commodore of the ships' readiness squadron recognized former commanding officers in the audience. Hilty was asked to stand as one of these and also as a well-respected commander of the squadron himself, highly visible on the waterfront. This too felt good.

Each of the outgoing commanding officers then spoke. The first told a story about his crew that reduced everyone to tears. The second astonished the audience by proposing marriage to her boyfriend (who nodded yes). The third, Plumpy's own captain, shared the critical secrets of command, of which Hilty recited two at dinner that night, amid some hilarity:

☞ When the families come onboard after a cruise, they're not interested in shaking your hand.

☞ If you must ski behind the ship, use a long tow-rope and check first for any fins in the water.

After the speeches, orders were read and commands given: all the flags and pennants were hauled down beginning with the American flag; the turbine generator in each ship running simply to make noise, to show that there had been life onboard, was silenced; and the ships' companies marched ashore in files of two. A chaplain gave the benediction, during which the band played "Eternal Father, Strong to Save" in slow crescendo. The master of ceremonies pronounced the traditional, self-evident dismissal, "Ladies and gentlemen, this concludes the ceremony." And Plumpy wore an altered light in his memory.

The one thousand former crew members and their loved ones, the dignitaries in their various lumens of celebrity, and Hilty and the other guests walked down the pier to a reception under a series of tents. The rain was holding off for now. The refreshments attracted many under the canvas but with a periphery outside enjoying the fresh air and the elbow room. White uniforms mingled with the colorful summer clothes, and soon the hundreds of conversations raised a din.

As a nice touch the organizers had roped off three tables for the alumni of the ships, creating spontaneous reunions. These punctuated the talking with the sudden shouts and cries of old shipmates greeting each other.

Plumpy's table had several eras of alumni, of course, but among them were four sailors that belonged to him, including one particular favorite.

His name was Owen Blaylock; he was an engineer. Everyone admired him back then. Young as he was, he thought like a leader, and leadership became him.

Captain Hilty had once overheard him taking an older subordinate to task. He did it well: confirmed the facts, identified the fault, taught the lesson in a clear, resolute voice but without condemnation, and sealed the promise of improvement with a friendly handshake. But when the man got into trouble again and came to Captain's Mast for punishment, and when Hilty asked, as the proceedings required, if Blaylock would speak up for him, he replied, "What can I tell you, Captain? He doesn't care, and he's holding us back. If I were you I'd shit-can him." And so he had, right out of the Navy—that afternoon the masters-at-arms dropped him at the gate with his sea bag.

Since then Blaylock had advanced to senior chief petty officer, had retired on twenty years, and had raised a family: an attractive wife and two precocious daughters about whom he often posted. In retirement he stayed in coveralls as a civilian contractor, becoming a fixture on the waterfront, endlessly making house calls. Hilty had run into him several times and always with pleasure. He was now middle-aged, filled out, even a little heavy, with a man's earned knowledge of the world.

Thus Blaylock. In truth he wanted to connect with all of them. However sentimental it might be, he loved them; loved them as themselves and because he had loved his profession. He moved around the table remembering their names and hearing their life stories. Often at ship's reunions some lubricated sailor will recall his captain's many mistakes. These old shipmates seemed pleased just to be with him again.

It was gratifying to hear how well they were doing. The Navy—and perhaps he—had helped to set them on their courses in life. Kate Harcourt, a radar specialist then, now ran a federal air traffic control center in the Midwest. William Houy managed a team that built towers for a cell phone giant; he had been a boatswain's mate in the ship, where, promoted to chief, he had kept down unheard-of amounts of "truth serum" at his initiation. Donald Franzen, a gunner's mate who had taught the captain's children to fire the M60 machine gun, had bought a semi-trailer truck and hauled loads all over the country until his wife had got the truck in their divorce. Hilty, though the idea of divorce troubled him, acknowledged the comic grimace with one of his own.

"And of course I know what this young man's been up to," he said, gripping Blaylock's shoulder. In return Blaylock exhibited that nice sense that while there was no longer any military obligation between them, he esteemed his former captain for the leader he had been.

They were chatting easily when a portly older man emerged from the crowd.

It was retired Rear Admiral Johnson, who had commanded the naval shipyard when then Commodore Hilty had commanded the readiness squadron; as a civilian now he worked at the shipyard on special projects. Hilty had known him for thirty years. The admiral had been a comfort when he had been passed over for flag.

His face was pink and white, with fat cheeks. His body had gone to fat too—Mad had related from Mrs. Johnson that he suffered from gout. But he had retained the flag officer's assumption that everyone in his presence was waiting for him to speak. "Hilty, there's someone I want you to meet," he said, turning on his heel as soon as his desire had been communicated.

"Better go," Hilty said, getting up.

"R.H.I.P., sir," Blaylock replied.

He followed Johnson into the crowd. Suddenly from nothing the rain fell straight down in a lush tropical stream. With various cries of delight or alarm, the outsiders pressed into the tent, and much of the talking was interrupted. Johnson and he were held up by the crush. Not five minutes later the rain ceased as though a faucet had been shut, leaving a desultory spattering of raindrops. The crowd expanded to its former size, people resumed their conversations, and Hilty heard this behind him:

"Such a nice person," Kate Harcourt said.

Then Blaylock: "I always thought he was full of shit."

[9]

"What do you mean?"

"The Old Man of the Sea. Hornblower at the helm."

"But wasn't he those things?"

"We snipes always knew where the exits were."

Admiral Johnson's expectation of being followed was like a tow line through the crowd. He and Hilty ducked under the edge of the tent, avoiding the chaotic runoff (which could have been regulated by securing the canvas with a few sheepshank bends), and found a place outside, amid the puddles, where two men were standing. The rain had stopped, and the cloud cover, reflected in the puddle surfaces, was thinning. A breath of air on his cheek confirmed the promise of fair weather.

Admiral Johnson presented him—"the officer you had asked about"—to two members of the Taiwan Navy, an Admiral Chen, in civilian clothes, and a Commander Lee, in uniform. "After the sale closes, Hilty, Lee will have your old Plumpy."

"Hornblower never took the helm," he said.

"I'm sorry?" Lee's face was puzzled, regretful that he had apparently missed something of value from a respected senior, and more than anything eager to please.

"No, *I'm* sorry," he said, for Johnson was looking at him weirdly. "A stray voltage in the brain, forgive me. I am very glad to meet you, sir. My heartiest congratulations. She's a great ship."

"A great ship," Lee simpered.

Johnson said to Chen, "He means that all the ships in the sale are capable and well maintained."

"Oh, yes. Of course."

Lee's whole being seemed delighted by his good fortune. Selected to command one of the most advanced warships in the world, he must have become instantly famous, one of the Mercury astronauts of Taiwan. At a closer look he was a man happy from birth, with the kind of complacent temperament toward which good fortune seems to be drawn. He might have been Captain Hilty's reincarnation from 1999. His choker white uniform was similar to the U.S. Navy's, but his shoulder boards, with their three stripes, ended in a many-rayed yellow sun, taken from the national flag, instead of the five-pointed gold star taken from ours. On his chest was apparently a surface warfare insignia but with only two decorations underneath. It must have been a long time since his navy had fought a battle.

Chen too, though his courtly manner was unchanged, had the manner of expecting to be heard. "Commander Lee and I have particularly wanted to meet *you,* Commodore Hilty. You have a fine record, both in this ship and afterwards. Admiral Johnson has told me many accounts, and I was pleased to hear you singled out in the speeches today."

"Thank you, sir. Thank you, both."

"Is it possible that during this turnover you might have some wisdom to share with us?"

"Certainly if I can be helpful. Whatever arrangements have been made in the contract for information transfer," he added glancing at Johnson. "Are you connected to the fleet, sir?"

"I used to be. I was a surface sailor like yourself. First commanding officer of our *Kee Lung,* formerly USS *Scott.* Now I am ashore, sadly. Director of the Integrated Assessment Office at the Ministry of Defense."

"That sounds like an important job."

"They sent me here because of my destroyer background and as a bennie, yes? A bennie?"

Bennie was Navy slang for a benefit, to the service or the individual: *a bennie sug* was a beneficial suggestion, for which a cash reward might be paid; *bennie dudes* might be something like duty escorting a pop diva around your ship.

"You know our vernacular, Admiral."

"I am a 2008 graduate of the U.S. Naval War College. With distinction!" he added, smiling. Turning to Lee: "You should read my paper on Admiral Mahan."

He himself could not help offering: "Mr. Churchill on the Battle of Britain might also be instructive, sir. I understand the sale is somewhat controversial."

But Chen looked doubtful, and Johnson said, "Not at all, Hilty, perfectly straightforward."

"But with the People's Republic of China?"

"Time will tell with them," Chen replied. "For our part we have wanted the Aegis technology almost since you invented it. With some lacunae"—a word that was probably in his War College paper.

"As you may know," he continued, "there are two major political parties in Taiwan: the Kuomintang or K.M.T. and the Democratic Progressive Party or D.P.P. The K.M.T. is the party of General Chiang, who retreated to Taiwan in 1949 with his defeated Nationalist army. In power for many years, through the dictatorships of Chiang and his son, the K.M.T. sought to retake the mainland by force, often sending bombers across the Taiwan Strait. After many years of stalemate and a most regrettable repression of our own citizens in the name of that struggle, its policy has evolved to one of peaceful assimilation within the greater China.

"The D.P.P., now in power in our young democracy, favors a sovereign and independent Taiwan, the first step of which is to secure our islands and our people against any threat. In that goal the D.P.P. has long pressed for this sale, and it now finds the U.S. administration sympathetic, even proactive.

"I support my government, of course. These destroyers will greatly strengthen our defenses and, along with continued support from our U.S. partner, act as a further deterrent to the cruel ambitions of the Chinese dictator."

"And that is more candor than you will hear from any other official of a foreign country—or deserve to hear," said Johnson.

"I understand," Hilty said. "I'm sure they will serve you well, gentlemen. With no threats to a happy first voyage. You'll be sailing soon?"

Before Chen could answer Johnson said, "The ships will have a brief upkeep at the pier, a couple of days of demonstration trials, formal acceptance and transfer of title, commissioning, three weeks of orientation training in the Virginia Capes, a visit to Yorktown to load the armament specified in the contract, and *then* they will sail—on Saturday 21 July, Admiral, is that not right?"

"Assuredly."

It almost didn't matter if he agreed: Johnson couldn't be stopped now. "I happen to know that it's 10,769 miles from Norfolk to Kaohsiung via the Panama Canal. At fifteen knots, an economical speed, that would be thirty days. If my calculations are correct you will arrive in home port on Sunday 19 August—I say Sunday assuming there would be no religious proscription against arriving on the Christian sabbath?"

"None, sir." But Chen's eyes shared with Hilty what Johnson hadn't thought of, that the ships would probably have to stop enroute for fuel: at Pearl Harbor and perhaps at Guam.

"Not counting," Johnson went on, now that apparently candor was in vogue, "the P.R.C. reaction."

"Commander Lee and his fellow captains will be very quiet, very circumspect, very stealthy," replied Chen. "No trouble to anyone. Perhaps you would like to sail with them, Commodore?"

The Goof

"Taiwan?" Gloria Wharton exclaimed at dinner in a tone of astonishment, delight, and ridicule.

"Wrong-o, scupper-lips," Hilty replied, for they were all quite merry by then. "The idea is ridiculous, and he didn't actually invite me. He just mentioned it."

"I'd go," said her brother, Dustin Parke. "In a heartbeat."

"Why not go?" asked Gloria's husband, Harry.

"For one thing, I wouldn't know a word of the language."

"Is it *in* words?" Dustin asked. "Don't they speak in characters?"

"I could be advising them on how to defend against an air attack, and they could be saying to themselves, 'Why, he's a perfect fool!'"

"They'd have that part right," Mad said.

"Or 'Kill the Yankee Dog and throw his body overboard,'" Dustin predicted, at which he and Mad enjoyed a comradely nod.

"Or 'Make him eat our dlunken slimp,'" Gloria said.

Everyone looked the other way. Gloria Wharton was a belle of the Lost Cause, who after a couple of drinks would try out her bigotry. He couldn't count the times over the years when she had gleefully used the *n*-word, amid the groans from her listeners. She and Mad had been friends since the Hiltys' early days in Norfolk. He had never understood this, for Mad, despite her tart tongue, was kind, affectionate, and interested in people from what used to be called "all walks of life." Harry Wharton, despite a tendency to drop names, was a decent enough guy, but he could do nothing with his wife, whose hatreds were both baked in and acquired.

She was not without a heart, for she loved her baby brother. He was in town on a rare visit, and Gloria wanted to show him off. Throughout the evening she doted on him: refilled his drinks, served him first, laughed at his jokes, sat back and admired him.

"Dustin's between gigs," she said. "He's a paparazzo."

Mad nodded as if she understood; as if such a term were perfectly understandable to the meanest intelligence.

Hilty asked, "Is that some sort of porn star?"

The table erupted, and Dustin too laughed. The joke was on him, not the ignorant man across the table. His hands described his own bald blond head, his tubby self. He said, "Fuck yeah! But think of the injuries."

"*O* is the singular form," Harry explained with a smile.

"A freelance photographer," Mad explained with a grin.

"Would I have seen your work?" he asked just as he understood what they were telling him. It wasn't his fault, but the table couldn't take it anymore.

Flinging his arms wide, Dustin upset his wine glass. As Gloria sprang to mop up, he replied, serenely seated, "In your local supermarket. You might remember some of my work on the British royals."

"He did the Sussex wedding," said Harry Wharton, as if Dustin had been court photographer. "The Wales, the Cambridges, Princess Anne: he knows them all."

"What a blast that was," Dustin agreed. "A thousand of us photogs pushing and shoving for a clear line of sight. I did get a good snap of Harry and Meghan making out in their limo, taken standing up in the sidecar of a motorcycle, scared shitless."

"Don't show us!" Gloria shouted as he leapt onto his chair. Lost in the memory, he twisted his hips back and forth to make the chair swivel as he demonstrated how to look through the viewfinder of a high-resolution camera at fifty miles an hour as your every synapse seeks the telling image. "Whoa," he managed to say as the chair went over and he crashed into the corner cupboard, unhooking several cups from the priceless collection of antebellum china on display, china which enslaved persons had probably handled, which dropped from sight with the telltale sound of breakage.

The Goof

Gloria was extremely upset, particularly because he was so immensely pleased by his own clowning; but after the slightest word of contrition she forgave him, as apparently she always would. The Hiltys left their wealthy friends disgusted and entertained respectively. Neither of them thought to hear from him again.

But on Monday, the dinner party having been on Friday, a manila envelope without postage was put in their mailbox addressed to both of them. Inside were an eight-by-ten photo and a letter on graph paper in upright printing with embellished capitals.

The photo, from an aerial view, depicted a man and woman having relations on the deck of a yacht; an inset in the corner showed them to be a celebrity chef and a reality housewife, both of them married to other people. On the back were details of where, when, and how the image was taken, assurances of authenticity and copyright, and a price, *$10,000 or best offer.*

The letter said, "Dear Friends! This is the *ne plus ultra* of celebrity imaging. For a small sum I rent this drone, whose camera the National Reconnaissance Office would envy, and depending upon a reliable network of informants and a modicum of dexterity (I'm the fellow, remember, who stands up in motorcycle sidecars—and dining room chairs ☺), I document the lives of the rich and famous in some of the most beautiful locations in the world.

"Next up: Grand Cayman Island. After that wherever the Beautiful People Breeze may blow. Come join me and my dear sister! The skinny on Madeleine is she's at home anywhere. Harry says you play golf, Brad. For high school teachers it's summer vacation—what else have you got to do? Come share in the fun. Scandal is the opiate of the masses."

"What a goof," he said, looking at her for agreement. They were sitting on the couch in the great room with the envelope and its contents spread on the coffee table in front of them.

Mad studied the photo, which needed no study.

"Chef certainly seems to be enjoying himself—"

"I don't care."

"While she's looking right at the camera."

"You'll send our regrets to Gloria?"

"I suppose you're not interested, then?"

"Why? Are you?"

She was. It was all over her face. He slid away from her.

"Well, why not?" she asked. "Don't be so disapproving."

"It's squalid. He's vulgar."

"You think Dustin's vulgar?"

"Fuck yeah."

With her little hand she waved away his objections. "It's part of the culture, Bradford. Maybe it's not how we were brought up, but there it is. This is how people live."

"It's not how I live."

"No, not you. Everybody else, all seven billion of us. These celebs know the game. This woman's face shows it perfectly: she's making love—in deference to you I won't use the vulgar term for it, although that's what it was— she hears the drone, and she looks for the camera. She lives to be caught by the photogs. Dustin's only giving the public what it wants."

"Celebs," he said. "Photogs."

He and Mad were very different. After thirty-six years of marriage, unconstrained by the conformity that the Navy imposed on them, the differences were plain. But never before had she simply gone off and done what she wanted against his objections. Now, in a burst of activity— impulsiveness? rebelliousness? excitement?—she declined the goof's invitation for him and accepted for herself. Shortly afterwards she went to their house to make plans, and he scarcely saw her after that. She bought new clothes, including several beach ensembles for which an extra-long shower suggested that she was attending to her bikini line. She walked with a spring in her step. An old Navy proverb says not to whistle while packing your sea bag. She whistled. It was excitement.

"Well, I'm off," she said on Thursday.

"Yes you are."

"This will be good for you. You like to be alone."

"As the goof reminds me, what else have I got to do?"

"Don't go to Taiwan, for one thing."

"I won't. Don't get sued by the celebs you spy on."

"I won't. Well." They kissed on the mouth, briefly, and exchanged the man-hug with two pats on the back apiece, and she wheeled her luggage out to the cab, where the goof and Gloria were waiting. For solidarity's sake he waved at them.

Summer Break

In his last years in the Navy, Commodore Hilty and his wife had lived in government quarters. After retiring they had bought a house in an old, refined neighborhood south of the Lafayette River. The house was like the rest of the neighborhood—old, refined, tall, drafty, inconvenient, and badly maintained, so that its restoration had required several years and a not insignificant portion of his retired pay. It was a nice hobby for both of them. After she flew to the Caymans, he carried it on alone.

Summer in the Tidewater area comes early, a particular stillness, hot and humid, with green living things that have managed without notice to run riot between the low gray sky and the olive-gray water. To stave off feelings of emptiness he kept to a strict daily discipline. Every morning after a cooked breakfast, he put on a wide-brimmed hat and a long-sleeved shirt, for he was easily burned, and dug in the salty black soil. He mulched and weeded and thinned the tree branches and refreshed the perennials and planted the seasonals and trimmed the lawn until it was shipshape.

For company he had fat brown worms, which he moved to safety, and for torment a rising layer of mosquitoes. Every year he reacted violently to them at first and then, after he got used to it, allowed them his blood in exchange for their sealing proteins. The one thing he found intolerable was the insinuating buzz. But the world was abuzz with morning, and he was more sensitive to it than usual because her leaving had made him self-conscious.

Among the many things she didn't understand about him, he said in his grousing, was that he preferred *not* to be alone. He liked people and liked being around them. Good Lord, hadn't all the years in crowded ships proved that point? But he was an introvert by nature, an honorable minority of the seven billion though not much valued now. Solitude was a relief sometimes. Only he wished to choose it for himself, not have it thrust upon him. That last kiss, so perfunctory, had left a bad taste in his mouth.

Thus the yard. In the afternoon he did all his required reading for the fall term, taking extensive notes, some of which he might expand into essays, like that of the Lost Cause. He rode his bike—most often on the Elizabeth River Trail but sometimes the Cape Henry Trail in Va Beach or the Dismal Swamp Trail in Chesapeake—keeping records of his distance, highest speed, and heart rate.

For the conscientious there is always something to do. Besides cleaning house according to schedule, he checked off a list of repairs deferred from the academic year. The Navy had taught him the elements of plumbing, electrical, and carpentry, and he put them to good use. By the official start of summer he had worked through the list except for the last item, long desired by both of them, which needed a contractor.

The contractor was going to say whether solar panels would be cost-effective. Trained as a roofer, he had switched to solar from the first news about climate change. He was to be admired for his progressive ideas and forgiven for his self-righteousness. Snapping the metal tape about, he took his measurements and compiled his estimate.

Hilty, as was his wont, soon found its flaws. He questioned the break-even date, which caused offense as if he thought the other too stupid to do the math correctly. Well: the math *wasn't* correct. After handing across the estimate as written, the contractor backed his truck from the driveway, no doubt to visit someone who truly loved the planet.

What have you done to our contractor? Mad emailed him without mentioning her life in the Caymans.

He prided himself on his ability to fit requirements into available shapes of time—and vice versa—the way some people can pack a moving truck (which he also could do).

With his chores well in hand, he foresaw at least a week before Mad might come home: ergo, he would visit his children.

His daughter, Sarah Hilty-Nichols, was an ophthalmologist in Boston, where her husband was a hand surgeon: two extremely busy people who were also parents. Of course he called to ask if a visit would be convenient.

"Absolutely," Sarah said. "The kids will be thrilled. Mom thought you might come. Only, I have to be at a conference that first day. Can you make it one day later?" She would never raise a problem without presenting a solution.

"Or I could spend some time reliving history and come to you for dinner the next day, if you won't be too tired from the conference."

"Perfect. Tell us everything you'd like to see and do. I'm not sure about Phil, but you and I and the kids will go everywhere. School's out. Couldn't be better."

He had always been respectful of the First American Revolution, but his great love was the Second, also known as the Civil War and Reconstruction, whose animating purpose was born here as well. In his imagination now he became an abolitionist. He taught children of color in the Abiel Smith School. Defying an unjust law, he rescued Shadrach Minkins from the slave-catchers. He marched with the 54th Massachusetts to emancipate their brothers and sisters in South Carolina and again with the survivors thirty years later, past the splendid monument to their fallen colonel. On a lovely evening in late June he stood before the monument between the two broken elm trees and wept to see the young resolute faces marching toward freedom, justice, and inclusivity, values that somehow the sculptor had managed to show they knew they would lose again. But not glory. But not faith. And not the most fundamental value of all: *I am a man,* which in that moment felt like enough. He wept. Surely people like him could redeem such a sacrifice!

[23]

"Have you been enjoying yourself?" Sarah asked after they had met up and he had digested her happy family.

"Very much. I'm ready to solve all the world's problems."

"Uh-huh."

"How have you been, darling?"

"Health good. Phil good. Kids good. Work impossible."

"What's going on?"

A small, intense woman, Sarah had been a straight-A student from her first report card. Her MCATs had been in the 99th percentile. She had had her pick of residencies and fellowships. Being such a serious student, she had hardly dated before choosing a prince for her husband. Her children were, in character, temperament, and intelligence, *wunderkinder.* He and she were much alike, yet with so many achievements to make him proud, she had somehow become more distant—more guarded, certainly. As if this too were an act of will.

"They've shortened our appointments."

"Whatever for?"

"See more patients. Make more money."

"And they can justify this—medically, morally?"

"Ours, you remember, is a non-profit hospital. But sometimes I think the CFO has more clout than the chief of medicine. It's gotten to the point of impacting care. I'm upset, Phil's upset. And...yeah. How about you?"

"All's well, keeping busy, doing a bit of writing. Missing your mother."

"Of course. This is your vacation."

"I was wondering if you'd heard from her."

It was the kind of question that intruded on their new boundaries. She was too well-bred to ignore it, but she wore that guarded look.

"Still in Grand Cayman, far as I know. Lots of time hanging out with Gloria."

"Is she spying on celebrities?"

Sarah smiled: he shouldn't joke about such a thing. "That doesn't sound like her. Let me tell you what Phil and I have in mind while you're here."

It was all pleasant, all loving, and all carefully regulated. Every moment they were doing something. They had no conversation except when enroute to the next event, and then it was only superficial and hardly true—certainly there was no unburdening of souls, no regrets, no pain recalled and forgiven. He stayed the weekend and breathed more freely when he was heading south on the interstate.

"Well, what did you think would happen?" he said to the windshield. Sarah had set those boundaries, but he suspected that all his sea duty, his long absences from home, had had something to do with them. She and he were very good at counting the cost of things; unlike him, she had also learned to exact it.

Adam too, in his way, was distant, but in a different way than Sarah's. His father had always been the hero of his life.

At one level this was astonishing. A trained artist, a working sculptor with a growing reputation like a young Saint-Gaudens, he had also wanted to be, in order of penchant, a naval aviator, an FBI agent, a professional golfer, and a member of the foreign service. With each new interest he could count on his mother's full support, emotionally and materially, and he could also count on a cross-examination from his father. Through it all Adam's admiration for his judgmental parent never flagged. A few years and, finally, success and vindication were necessary to show that, while the hero-worship continued, the willingness to listen had been tempered by a kind-hearted conviction that they lived in separate worlds.

He often spoke to Adam in his mind.

I saw Saint-Gaudens's finest work.

Beautiful, isn't it!

Those faces.

He took some flak. None of his models were soldiers.

[25]

You sculptors aren't interested in likenesses now.

Exactly, Dad. Modern art's all about ideas. Of course that allows mediocrity to slip in, if the market's gullible and the artist is good with buzzwords. You're so right. Ninety percent of it is crap.

But there was not in his son's oeuvre a single sculpture from life; not even a bad dream about it, like the Chicago Picasso.

His thoughts raced on and on, elaborating the hypocrisy, until, when he came to the turnoff to Adam's farm in the Poconos, he kept going south, to his own empty house.

A Plea for Help

Among his service friends was a very important person. James S. "Slate" Greene, his subordinate in their first ship, had overtaken him in their profession, eventually becoming his boss; for he possessed the looks, vitality, people skills, and, it must be said, moral flexibility to rise to the top. Not only had he made flag rank, he had been promoted to four stars and command of the Indo-Pacific region, with its vast responsibilities and territorial extent.

A reputation for sometimes exercising a little too much charm prevented Admiral Greene from being appointed to the very highest, most visible positions in the government. (In fact, until his third wife, Julia, had inspired him to reform, he had been a terrible skirt-chaser.) No one had to explain to him the realities of high office. He retired, to be rewarded for his experience and connections by a seat on the board of a major defense conglomerate, headquartered in Chicago. A year or two before now, he and Julia had bought an expensive house on the North Shore and set about understanding how much their civilian lifestyle could claim of their lives.

For Greene the answer lay in his temperament: though he might never join the president's cabinet, he couldn't help acquiring power and using it, for ends that, under Julia's influence, and as he himself grew in wisdom, became ever more altruistic.

Among his other gifts, he had an uncanny ability to know his old friend's moods and circumstances.

"You're lonely, right? Come visit us."

"What makes you think I'm lonely?"

"You're on summer break with nothing to do. Your wife has left you for an adventure in the Caymans. After six years, the thrill of teaching history to teenagers is gone. The last ship you served in has been decommissioned.

[27]

You're not just lonely, you're grieving about your life. I'd better call 911 before you shoot yourself."

He no longer asked how Slate knew these things.

"I don't own a gun."

"Good decision. I had to buy one to make the security folks happy—we also have a panic room—but it's locked away, so you're safe. Come to Chicago, and Julia and I will make you forget all your woes, if that's possible. Plus there are people I want you to meet."

"What's going on with the Company?"

"We seem to have a quality problem," Slate replied.

"That sounds like PR talking. Didn't one of your airplanes crash? What's going on?"

"There's a bug. We finally owned up to it after weeks of violating the first precept of public relations: *bad news doesn't keep.* But the problem goes beyond flight control systems. We've got plenty of policies, processes, safeguards, and exception-reporting in place—all the things Uncle Sam and our other customers require—but they haven't been what the gurus call normalized."

"Adopt Admiral Rickover: two people for every task."

"For critical tasks we do that. But it's not just following a checklist, it's using common sense. When the wing says *No Step* you're not supposed to step there, right? And you don't need a checklist to tell you so."

"This seems like a Slate Greene kind of problem."

"Actually, it's a Bradford Hilty kind of problem, but I doubt that you'd be interested." When he didn't respond, Slate went on: "My sense of it is that most of our folks, loyal folks, arc cutting corners to lower costs. Or we may have gotten to the point that our products are simply too exotic. Or all this might just be a string of bad luck. But bad luck, Lieutenant Hilty always told us, was just a failure to anticipate entropy."

"Quite right, too."

"But your problem isn't entropy, it's loneliness, and I'm here to solve it. Stay with us for a week. We'll do all the things you like except that you'll have to attend the Company Fourth of July picnic and make nice with our senior leadership team. Come to think of it, you can tell them how to normalize higher standards. Seriously, Brad, we'd love to have you."

"Enough, I'm sold," he said with a lightened heart.

In fact they did seem glad to have him, and he was glad to take an interest in their comfortable life in Kenilworth, in the lakeside mansion standing on the bluff with its privileged fellows. After a rocky start Slate and Julia were happy in each other's company, and seeing this was a pleasure too, both in itself and as a reminder that the arc of marriage is not inevitable.

When the Greenes were busy, as they often were during the day, he revisited old haunts and let the memories pour out.

In Northfield, his childhood home, he had tackled a much bigger boy in football, each of whose thighs was as big as his own chest, by hanging on and ignoring the punishment. At Sunset Ridge School his teacher, Mrs. Klass, had been unable to speak the words that the president had been shot. At New Trier High School, in Dr. Johnson's Civil War Roundtable, he found that he liked military history. His first kiss had been in Hubbard Woods, outside the Sweet Shop (appropriately named!), after which he had had no thought but to apologize. In their last time at home together, his father had met him beside his mother's rose garden to tell him of her fatal heart attack, and in the hillside of their church in Winnetka, his ashes had joined hers after ten wasted years of wishing for it.

In emotional value the happiness, embarrassment, regret, or pain that these memories caused him had faded to a dreamlike quality, without the power to move him now. A preternatural sun seemed to be shining down on Young Hilty. His feet seemed to float across the landscape, carried by a slow current. It was enough just to remember: meaning and significance might come later, but they didn't seem to matter now.

Planning for the Fourth of July party took up the last few days of the visit. In this both Greenes showed that knack of leadership that gives general direction, trusting to subordinates while anticipating and drilling down into thorny details, mostly involving the peculiarities of certain guests. He was happy to help with this. As someone who knew the area, he ran errands to various out-of-the way shops to solve emergent problems.

"We have this weird way of receiving people," Julia said to him on the afternoon of the Fourth. "Something Slate picked up from his travels in Asia. It's like pinball. You'll be our third bumper."

Actually, he was their sixth. A valet met the cars and parked them in the area beyond the carriage house. A young man from the Philippines whom he remembered from Slate's Navy staff, wearing a wireless earpiece, pointed the way around the great house to the party in the back. There the guests were announced by a young woman, also with an earpiece but who seemed to know everyone by sight. Slate met them first. After just the right amount of time he sent them to Julia across the way and in her own realm. She performed the same office and sent them to their old friend and houseguest, Brad Hilty, who was generally as overwhelmed as by that first kiss, although he had learned not to show it.

The backyard was wide and deep with a wooden staircase down to a boathouse and a pier on the lake. The buffet was across one corner of the yard and the drinks table across the other. The air was smoky from the multiple grills, each with its obliging chef, and smelled deliciously of hickory and meats. Beyond and below in the crystalline blue expanse were tiny sailboats too far away to give a sense of movement but ideal for a backdrop. The event was so well organized and resourced and its setting so beautiful and privileged that it might have overawed the guests as it did him except that they were rich and knew each other.

After the last had been welcomed, Julia gave him a hug. "Old friends are the best," she said, though they had been friends only for a short time years before, with a long interval afterwards. But he understood.

He had first known her as a disenchanted bride who out of the cloistered world of academia had married into the unfeeling aristocracy of the seat of government. And who had soon discovered that her noble husband was wantonly breaking his marriage vows. But she had seen something in Slate that he never let on, a desire to become a better man, and she had had the strength to confront him, more than once, and the wisdom not to issue ultimata. By now the years of service and the rebuilding of trust after the cessation of unexplained absences had changed both husband and wife. Once accustomed to the high perch, she found much to enjoy in the issues and dramas of state. Standing in this beautiful place co-equal to these powerful men and women, she looked confident, high spirited, relaxed—yes, happy at last.

"I am," she said when he suggested it. "Remember how miserable I was in that empty house on the naval base. And how kind you were?"

"It was you. You figured it out."

"Well, it was *about* me. My problem."

"I wanted so much to...to take the pain away."

"You did help with that. You showed me that the Navy was about service, duty, country, patriotism, the whole ten yards. I could find myself in those values. And I'll always be grateful to you for it."

He had befriended her in the worst of her time with Slate. His intentions had been of the best, but by then, in his grief at being passed over for admiral, he was like a sailor who had lost hold of a running line. Sympathy is easily confused, not that anything had happened, but his feelings had verged on a foolish declaration which must have been plain to Julia, who forestalled it. Mad knew the truth as surely as if she had been there; it caused a tension between them that they woke up with every day.

His sympathy for Julia had not been the only problem. Even as he pondered whether to fire one of his commanding officers, a woman named Robin McGill, who had certainly committed adultery while on deployment, he was fascinated by her—by her charismatic leadership and professional skill but also by her beauty, so easy to confuse with goodness. He wasn't in love with either of these women, but frustrated in his life's ambition, he was ready to be, and it was that prevaricating readiness that had eclipsed his wife's joy in the world, from which crisis their marriage, unlike that of the Greenes, had never entirely recovered.

"You know Mad's in Grand Cayman," he said. "With her best friend and her best friend's brother, the goof."

"The goof!"

"A paparazzo—singular form. He takes Peeping Tom photos of celebrities."

She touched his arm. "I did know that."

"You've been talking to her."

"She's called twice, I think. Slate mostly spoke to her."

"I'm not sure what's going on or when she'll be home— or if," he added in a voice no louder than a sigh.

"Probably when you least expect it."

Being introverted herself, Julia understood his reticence, and therefore she took him to all the muckety-mucks that she and Slate had decided he should meet. "I mean who should meet you."

"The high school history teacher."

"The man who single-handedly attacked the thermostatic control valve at South Carolina House, armed only with a wrench. And thereby kept a lady from freezing to death in June. This way, now."

Under a black oak tree a short, slight man was stand-ing alone, looking at the lake. With such pensive fascina-tion sailors stare into the bubbling wake of their ship, hearing the siren call to jump. He returned to life when Julia tapped him on the shoulder.

Joc-Philip, you've met Brad Hilty, our Norfolk friend."

Joc-Philip McCracken was CEO of the Company. In the receiving line he had breezed through, looking ahead.

"Oh yes. Slate's told me about you," he said as they shook hands again. "The old man of the sea."

And Hornblower at the helm.

"I'm sure Slate was exercising his sense of humor."

"Not at all: he meant it. I don't think he *has* a sense of humor. Didn't you save someone's life in the Arctic Circle with your shiphandling?"

"He happened to fall overboard directly ahead of us."

"And the life expectancy in those waters was—what?"

"Not very long. He was nearly frozen. The credit goes to my very capable and forehanded chief boatswain's mate, who climbed down the cargo net with another man and hauled him out."

"Brad, you never told me this," said Julia.

"William Houy. I got to meet him again last month when our ship was decommissioned."

"You refer to the Taiwan sale," said McCracken. "We have a piece of that business. I don't know about your politics, sir. But as an American, can you believe that to-day, our country's independence day, China has the gall to threaten a blockade if the sale isn't cancelled?"

"Good for us, then, if it has them on the defensive."

But McCracken didn't want a reply, he had a speech to finish. "They actually accuse us of interfering with the rights of the Taiwan people to determine their own fu-ture. You've got to like the irony! One of the most repres-sive regimes in the world calling out the country whose founding documents have defined liberty and equality for all mankind."

"That's not quite true," he said, which caused the other man to blink a few times. "As I've been teaching my students, Jefferson's preamble merely summarizes—eloquently, of course—what the nineteenth century called the rights of man in a natural state, which government is called upon to protect."

"We hold these truths to be self-evident, that all men are created equal."

"Created equal by God, not governed so by the State. And not all men, only those admitted to citizenship. Never an outsider, such as someone kidnapped from a foreign shore, sold in chains, transshipped in filth, and required for the rest of his or her life to work without pay for an enslaver. White people, not Black. The Declaration was a compromise to get thirteen very different colonies—all of them slave-holding, by the way—to come together. For the South, declaring independence prevented the abolitionists in England from abolishing slavery over here. And the Constitution was written to deny the federal government the power to do it."

McCracken whipped out a booklet of the founding documents. "I always carry this with me for the ill-informed." His tone of voice anticipated his victory; to have reached his position there must have been many.

"In that case you might reread Article One, Sections 2 and 9 and Article Four, Section 2. I think that will clear up the matter." He was too excited not to walk away from both of them, though he had seen her appalled look and knew the damage he had done by putting the high and mighty one in his place.

The fireworks started at dusk. By then the picnic was essentially over, and many of the guests were gone, among them Joc-Philip McCracken. He had given Julia a kiss on both cheeks and missed Slate with a pat on the back, having been distracted by the presence of their guest.

Ordinarily Hilty disapproved of fireworks, being vulgar in themselves and possibly harmful to those veterans who might be suffering from PTSD. But in the soft Midwestern sky, still radiant, over the lake, these were well done, and he enjoyed them. They were not on the scale of fireworks in the great cities, of course. But they had many of the best effects: the shimmering fall of crackling silver...the flowers that bloomed out of other flowers...the surprising reveal after an impossible hang-time...the finale with its thunderous detonations.

When the show was over and the crowd had scattered, he found himself standing with Admiral Chen, who had just arrived.

"So soon!" Chen said, pumping his hand.

Slate grinned like the cat that swallowed the canary.

"The Indo-Pacific Command," Hilty guessed.

"We are old friends," Chen said, getting a confirming nod from Slate.

"This is an ambush," feeling a thrill at the thought.

"An intervention," Slate said. "Not for you, for us."

Julia had left them to their talk. They moved indoors, into the front drawing room, where they sat before the tall windows. The circular driveway outside was empty. The two hundred and forty-third year of checkered American independence had begun.

Slate turned to the admiral. "What can you tell us that we wouldn't have already seen in the news?"

"I have a copy of the demarche," Chen said. Within its diplomatic formality the message was clear: unless the Aegis destroyer deal was canceled, and unless the rebellious province of Taiwan renounced independence now and forever and pledged its allegiance to China, China would, under her rights, feel free to assume supervision of all trade to and from the province.

"That sounds like blockade, sure enough," Slate said.

"Your country would intervene, would it not?"

"I would guess that we would declare a sealift, like the Berlin airlift, and my old friend Robin McGill, who commands the Pacific Fleet, would run it."

"You too, who have commanded that fleet, understand the difficulties."

"And the difficulties for China in trying to blockade your very considerable nation. Those three destroyers couldn't be more timely."

But they, not the threats from China, turned out to be the reason why Chen had flown to Chicago on short notice. The crews of the Aegis destroyers were not making the progress in their training that everyone had hoped. Unless something changed they would not be ready, if they sailed for Taiwan on schedule, to fight a battle when they arrived.

Hilty felt as though someone were tugging on his arm. "Where are the weaknesses?" he asked.

"Everywhere."

"Propulsion engineering—casualty control?"

"Yes."

"Firefighting and damage control?"

"Yes."

"Combat systems and weapons?"

"Yes. I welcome these questions."

"Navigation and seamanship?"

"In that area all three ships are satisfactory. Taiwan has a long maritime tradition, Commodore."

"Have you observed them in this training yourself, sir? And you think so too?"

"We aren't ready," Chen concluded. "I regret to say it. We are supposed to sail for Taiwan in two weeks and we aren't ready. We need"—his face brightened a shade with the chance to use an American idiom—"a kick in the ass."

"That's where you come in, Brad," Slate said. "You old ass-kicker you."

"Absolutely not," he replied. "No way."

ʕʕ

"Slate, may I take your friend on a special errand?" Chen asked. "Commodore Hilty, since I have already intruded upon your plans for the evening, may I ask your indulgence for perhaps another hour? There is something I want to show you, not far from here."

Though his arm was being tugged, he could hardly refuse. Chen's rental car, a sub-compact, was parked in front of the carriage house. Intent on his task, he drove in silence down the lane, beneath the overhanging oaks; the gate slid open, and he turned left onto Sheridan Road. But where? Before Hilty could properly place himself, Chen pulled over and stopped the car.

Towering above them, radiating its own light, was the Bahá'í Temple.

"Here?"

"If you please." They walked in silence between long reflecting pools and up two flights of steps. Under the dome was an enormous auditorium facing a rostrum. The space reminded him of the U.N. General Assembly, and its purpose was similar: here let humanity bring its aspirations, its philosophies, its articles of faith: all were welcome.

They sat. Other people were present, away from them and out of earshot. In the shadows of the floodlamps, the auditorium was a dimmed version of the off-white, finely-grained concrete of the exterior. The decorations, in filagree, were mostly Islamic but with references to the other major religions. The temple had been started in 1912 and finished in 1953, spanning several generations of fidelity to an ideal. It had loomed above Hilty's mental skyline throughout his childhood.

"I was aways a little afraid of this place," he whispered.

"Oh?"

"We had a Scottish au pair with a wicked sense of humor. She told me they sacrificed children here. I refused to believe it...but I wondered. It's like classifying a sonar contact as *Non-sub*. All right, no threat, but you keep your eye on that spot, don't you?"

"I have never tracked a submarine," Chen said. "Computer simulations only. Never a real one."

"Get to datum as fast as you can," he murmured.

"You see, Commodore! None of us would know that. You have a wealth of knowledge, of experience, of *winning* experience to share with us. I don't see how our ships can be ready without you."

"Admiral, I would really like to help—what old sailor doesn't want another ship?—but my family needs me."

Chen joined the others in silent reflection. One could almost see the prayers fluttering up to the dome like doves of peace. Hilty's spine felt the chill of being a problem. His father had raised to an art-form the long pauses that preceded criticism.

"Not that I can do it," he said, "but tell me what it is you're asking. I return to Norfolk tomorrow. Is it next week you want me for, to observe the training?"

"Yes, of course. But, candidly, more than that. The navy of Taiwan—I have the authority of my superiors in this—the navy of Taiwan, viewing with concern the present readiness of these ships and the declared threat against them, requests that you, an experienced officer, take command of them and bring them safely home."

"But it's impossible."

"Yes, you have said so. Your family."

"Impossible legally, sir. As a retired officer I must never serve a foreign power."

"But that's what John Paul Jones did, in Russia."

"Before our Constitution was written."

"We are paying consultants from your armed forces now. How would this be different?"

"In the event of hostilities my position would be intolerable. How could I abandon my command, and yet how could I fight for you?"

"If there's a will there's a way. Slate can manage it."

"He's under the same constraint."

"You wouldn't have to command, officially. Mr. Lee, who is senior, could act as the unit commander for the ships. You would advise him. Knowing him and you, I am confident that he would conform to your wishes. Of course we would pay you, quite handsomely."

He had one further argument to make. "Getting approval from all the responsible agencies would take more time than we have. To comply with the law might require that I be recalled to active duty. For that I'd need a physical exam, briefings, orders, uniforms...."

More reflection from Chen. The auditorium, though symbolic of welcome and tolerance, was evidently too confining for his thoughts. Now he did take Hilty's arm. They walked outside to linger near one of the reflecting pools. The air was hot and damp, foreshadowing a thunderstorm. The pool suggested the slaking relief that would follow.

"I believe you know our history," Chen said. "An indigenous people, occupied and exploited by China, occupied and exploited by Japan, occupied, exploited, and brutally repressed by a beaten army of immigrants to whom the populace, after so much war, generously gave asylum. In the past twenty years, with great striving, we have advanced from a totalitarianism like that which our brothers and sisters endure on the mainland to a full democracy—fragile but enshrined in our own constitution and widely supported and successful! We are an Asian Tiger; our economy thrives. Our people are thriving and happy. Most of all we are free.

"It is that freedom that makes everything else possible. Over the years we have sometimes acted unwisely. We are naturally self-centered as island people are. Perhaps we like our pleasure too well. Perhaps we have not been as inclined to defend our shining achievement as we should have. Still, my fellow citizens are warm, friendly, loving human beings. I say also intelligent. They deserve to live and to live free, just as other democratic nations do—just as Americans set out to do on this anniversary! They deserve never to be occupied again.

"Ever since 1949 we have been told by the United States that it is in your country's interest to uphold our security. The terms may waver, but in the aggregate all your actions have amounted to a promise to us, which we have accepted as genuine. The real question in this new crisis—the question on everyone's lips—is whether we can continue to count on your promise. Will the Seventh Fleet come to our aid? To you, Commodore Hilty, whom I already count as a friend, I add: Will you be a friend in that effort?"

"Of course we'll come in," Slate said when Hilty returned, alone. They were drinking rare Scotch. Outside, the glimmers of distant lightning throbbed in the windows. "This administration is on record for it, and the president, as we've seen, likes to act the cowboy. We'll be there. Your old friend Ed Juventude commands Seventh Fleet now, by the way. Under Robin McGill."

"Her old XO. I gave him his oral for command."

"After which, of course, his success was inevitable."

"What do you think of this whole thing, Slate? For me. For me now. Given today's threat."

"The threat is serious. When I was a mid, the naval academy held a symposium of its so-called experts. Someone asked about China. *They row like hell* was the answer, that conceited asshole. Well, not any more. In point of fact their navy is bigger than ours, they're very good sailors, and they've been stealing our technology for so long they've got quite an armory of it."

Hilty set down his snifter. "But to take the island they'd have to land in corps-level force with a full-blown amphibious assault. A massive, low-tech challenge, dictated by logistics. Across the stormy Strait. A raid wouldn't do it. Neither would a missile barrage. The eastern half of Taiwan is mountainous. I'm sure our friends have already begun to hide their critical defenses in tunnels."

A smile. "I like it that you're having these thoughts."

"So what role for Taiwan?"

"It depends how quickly we make up our minds. It might be a week, it might be two. Taiwan will have to absorb the first blow. If you do this—and I say *if*—you'll have to find a way to keep your ships afloat until we get there."

"Can I do this, legally?"

"I suppose so. And I know you want to, you old fire horse"—his eyes twinkled—"though that's probably a minority opinion at the Hilty residence."

"You've spoken to her. Are we in trouble?"

"I doubt that. Don't you know that you two are married for life, like gibbons? To Julia and me your marriage has always been an inspiration."

"Do you really think I should do this, Slate?"

In return for his uncertainty he won a look of affection. Their history mattered. Even their differences in personality, ambition, ethics; even the rivalry between them, the ascension of one, the disappointment of the other; even their periodic fallings-out seemed invaluable now. Neither of them would know another friend like this.

"I do, Brad. I really think you should. For our ally, but mostly for you. You need it."

He needed it. Because he was lonely and grieving. The point went home unexplained.

"I'll have to mull," he said.

A growl of thunder; the storm was close. Slate cut short his pitch. Through long experience he had found that metaphor, cliché, and clever sayings, however entertaining, cheapened the message. He didn't want his last words accompanied by a bolt of lightning. In this as in many things he had grown up.

"Don't take too long," he said, tossing back the rest of the Scotch. "The ships resume their training on Monday. Chen very much wants you onboard."

.

Something Like His Old Life

Ebb Tide

In civilian clothes Hilty watched from the bridge as *Luchiang* made preparations to get underway. Everyone was speaking Chinese except the pilot, but the sequence of events was as familiar to him as an old piece of music, and from his chair on the port side he let it flow around him.

Captain Lee and the pilot were slow to agree on how to maneuver the ship. Because the tide was running out and she was moored on the downstream side, the pilot advised simply taking in the lines and backing away, without the tugs. Lee, although he wanted them to pull the ship off the pier, allowed himself to be persuaded. So much had gone into this day that only accord must prevail now.

A sailor approached Hilty with a message from the communications center, clamped in its aluminum binder as of old:

From: Chief of Naval Personnel

To: Captain Bradford Richmond Hilty, U.S. Navy

Subject: Recall to Active Duty

1. By order of the Secretary of the Navy you are hereby recalled to active service with your former date of rank and privileges. Upon acceptance of this commission you will report to the place in which ROCS *Luchiang* and other ships of Taiwan may be, embarking at your discretion, to take charge of a team of U.S. personnel assigned for training and support and to provide any and all assistance that you may deem necessary toward the safe and expeditious transit of the ships to their home port.

> 2. These orders may be supplemented by those from the U.S. commanders through whose areas of responsibility the ships travel.

Slate had done it. Here with official sanction was a blank check, a remarkable vote of confidence. And not that he cared about such crass detail but these orders would make him by years the senior captain in the service.

And yet.

It didn't give him any authority over the Taiwanese. Probably that was too hard for the diplomats to work out in the time allowed. He would have to proceed carefully and earn respect and build moral authority. Chen had told him that Lee, officially commanding the transit unit, would listen to any advice he might offer.

Which only made sense, since they had been so eager to have him along. He put the message in his pocket and gave the binder back to the radioman, who, understanding that he had received good news, waited. Waited for what: for a tip? "Thank you, carry on," he said, and with a single harsh word one of the officers sent the man away.

At the command to single up the mooring lines, he walked out to the bridge wing and took a position, which he meant to be his own from now on, several feet aft of the compass repeater. Here he could see the maneuvers without seeming to interfere.

On the head of the pier, where well-wishers had gathered, a small ensemble of the Navy band struck up "Anchors Aweigh" amid scattered cheering. Miniature flags of the U.S. and Taiwan were waved. Perhaps a hundred people had come to see the ships depart. More than a few were young Americans no doubt unhappy to be saying *zàijiàn* to a special friend. Admiral Johnson was there, in proof of his country's good faith. Admiral Chen was there too. After returning Lee's salute, he gave Hilty an American-style thumb's-up.

[46]

Someone—more than one person—was calling his name. As other commands were given and the lines were taken in and the ship's whistle sounded its throaty warn-ings, the callers understood that he couldn't find them in the crowd. They stepped into the clear and waved. Harry and Gloria Wharton. She must be home from Grand Cay-man. Mad must have told them about the sailing. She herself was nowhere in sight.

With the navigator, a Lieutenant Wú, at the conn, the ship was backing from the pier. The angle opened as her stern fell off. But the maneuver, overly cautious, was tak-ing too long. Instead of backing free, the ship was in the grip of the current, angled more and more while being carried down to the next pier. The situation had that un-easy feeling in vessels of heading one way while physi-cally moving another.

The pilot ordered the tugs in, but they were too far away to help. The ship was bearing down on a nuclear submarine, which recognized the danger by going to emergency quarters. Then Wú stopped his engines, the worst thing he could have done.

The bridge went silent as the crew waited for calamity. All the responsible authorities were frozen in place—Wú, the pilot, Lee. On the bridge of the sub her captain had an astonished face.

A voice that sounded like that of his absent wife asked if he too were not a responsible authority? Should he not say something to Lee? Or, with a little chutzpa, put the helm over and throw the throttles in reverse himself? Was he still so bound by the chain of command?

With the last of her sternway, the destroyer cleared the submarine by about three feet. The tugs, working abreast, were now able to hold up her stern while letting her bow fall off, and in a minute she had turned down-stream and was headed fair in the channel. *Hsinchu* and *Chiai* got underway without incident—*Chiai,* using too much engine power, cast about unassisted, a hot-dog maneuver, a poke-you-in-the-eye maneuver—and both ships formed an exact line on the leader.

Still shaken, the bridge resumed a semblance of order, in which routine necessity was a help. Yet Lee's eyes spoke of the international embarrassment so narrowly averted, the professional disgrace. Something for the new advisor to advise him on.

Mrs. Tsai

The half-life of seawater is brief. Memories of the near mishap slipped astern of them. Captain Hilty remained on the bridge to give countenance to the commanding officer, who, sitting on the opposite side, needed some time to recover. At the sea buoy *Luchiang* turned south-southeast to traverse the U.S. coast, and her consorts followed. To save fuel, sixteen knots was the planned speed of advance. As Admiral Johnson had expounded, fifteen would bring them to Taiwan in thirty days; sixteen was insurance. It would be a good idea to get ahead of even that pace, at eighteen or even twenty. Lee, into a light swell, ordered sixteen.

When Captain Hilty saw the RPMs rung up he stifled a comment, which however tactful might cause Lee a further loss of face. Moreover he wanted to enjoy being at sea again. Here was the gray-green Atlantic, whose waters he knew so well; continuous with those that lapped the shores of Taiwan, and China, and Grand Cayman Island, and everywhere else. At once a highway, a barrier, and a battleground. Being here felt right, a claim upon instincts ready for the challenge. Sailors belong in ships and ships belong at sea.

Lee came across the bridge to ask how he was. His brown eyes had a glimmer of amusement intended to put the incident in its proper perspective: no harm no foul but o how close! Captain Hilty told a story about a near-miss getting underway after which the skipper of the threatened ship sent a flashing light message: *If you kiss me you'll have to marry me.* Lee responded with a sickly grin, and then it was time for Captain Hilty to leave the bridge lest the crew think that he thought he needed to be there.

He walked through the ship, his ship, the former Plumpy, another dreamlike memory. He had to believe that this would turn out all right. Here were sailors. He would understand them. Good results would follow.

In CIC Kate Harcourt, the former air controller who now ran an air traffic control center, was refreshing the watch on the elements of radar navigation. On the boat deck William Houy was teaching the boatswain's mates how to rig the sea ladder. In Central Control Michael Blaylock was explaining an oil sample. Everyone was do-ing their professional best. He acknowledged them with an approving nod but didn't stop to listen.

A bugle, unheard in the U.S. Navy since the days of battleships, played mess call. He returned to his cabin to see what Mrs. Tsai had made him for lunch.

When, more than a week ago, he had first embarked in *Luchiang* for the training at sea, Mrs. Tsai had been waiting in the cabin. She welcomed him with a smile and a curtsy, ever so graceful, as nobles greet each other in the ballet. An older woman, with her hair neatly pinned up, she wore an enlisted sailor's dungarees. Her look was respectful and more than that, meant to convey kindness. Her name was embroidered above the shirt pocket: *Tsai Mei-ling*. Otherwise there were no markings.

Lee had presented her as someone of note. "Personal servant, personal chef, confidential secretary, expert in-terpreter." He lowered his voice: "Buddha of wisdom."

She laughed and shook her head and offered her hand. Her palm was warm within his, her fingers curled with just the right pressure. "You are coming with us next week?" she asked. He nodded. "You must tell me all the things you like to eat. I will shop at the Navy Commis-sary. Taiwan food too?"

"I'll trust you to bring me along gradually. You'll have to decide whether I need to know what I'm eating."

Toward that goal she had taken a cautious approach. During the training he had eaten only lunch on board, sometimes in the wardroom and sometimes on the other ships, where the officers were gleeful about the Chinese food they served him. Twice she made him American sandwiches, which were delicious, and when not feeding him she stood by with her silver pot containing the best coffee he had ever tasted.

"How do you do it?" he asked.

"It's a secret, but I will tell you because everyone should know it. Taiwan coffee is the best in the world. I have a special source for the beans, which I roast myself."

"I need to know this source," he said, remembering that Slate Greene had once bragged about *his* source in Central America.

"But you will. You are coming to Taiwan!"

Today she was waiting with a Cuban sandwich and hand-cut potato fries under the silver lid.

"And a glass of red wine?" she asked.

"I don't know. Can I drink wine onboard?"

"Certainly—in moderation. Taiwan has no Josephus Daniels to ban alcohol in ships."

"You are well informed, Mrs. Tsai."

"Buddha that I am. With my master's degree."

The wine was so good that a single sip loosened his tongue. "We had a close call getting underway this morning."

"I saw it. Lieutenant Wú was too timid with the engine power. In Norfolk the ebb current drains three rivers, so it is especially strong. Also, the placement of the tugboats wasn't optimal. Weren't the crew of the submarine surprised! Well. Better to be lucky than good."

"You know about these things."

"Of course, Commodore. I'm a sailor. By the way, I have laid out your summer white uniform on the bed, now that your posting is official."

So she had. All the decorations and insignia were correctly placed, and his white combination cap was hanging on the hook.

"And you should speak to Captain Lee," she went on, "because he wants to fly your pennant."

Night Orders

In fact a broad pennant, blue and white, was already flying from the masthead. Improperly so, for his orders had not given him command of a squadron; officially this was the Taiwan Transit Unit, and his assignment was only to provide assistance. It is a shameful offense in the armed forces to claim an honor you haven't earned; to wear a minor ribbon that isn't in your service record or to say you've crossed the Equator when you haven't. The sight of the pennant burned in his mind. He should have it hauled down at once. On the other hand, Lee and his countrymen were trying to show respect; their rules and customs might be very different than his; and any blow to national pride this early in the transit would likely doom his mission.

Lee had brought him up to the signal bridge to admire the pennant. With the near-miss miles astern of them, he was cheerful again and eager to please. He said, "All three of us captains agree: you must be our commodore. In the night orders you must assume tactical command." When he didn't respond at once, Lee added, as if the concept were new, "Officer in tactical command. OTC. You tell us how to maneuver. We will comply."

"Very good, I do think that's for the best. So let's talk about the night orders. How do you like this formation?"

"Smart, seamanlike, easy to follow the guide."

"But three ships in a line only searches the same water three times."

Lee understood. "Spread them out, miles apart. I have the formula. But our mission is to get to Taiwan. What is there to search for?"

"You never know," he said. "Destroyers must be ready for anything. And remember that's only visual search. If we want to use our full capabilities, we should calculate the optimum stationing for radar. In battle the force may be spread over hundreds of miles."

Yes, Lee understood. This was training, just as necessary for him as for the crew. But he frowned at the reference to battle. It would be good to reframe the message. "We can work up to a widespread formation gradually. Let's say *tonight* I order *Chiai* and *Hsinchu* into loose sectors five miles east and west of *Luchiang,* which will avoid the fatigue of precise station-keeping."

Lee bowed.

"And what do you think of increasing speed—say, to eighteen knots—just to have some time in our pocket? Eighteen would still allow trail shaft operations."

"What is trail shaft?"

"Something to save fuel: driving one propeller on one engine and letting the other propeller windmill in the stream. Did you not practice this economy in the *Kee Lung* destroyers?"

"The captains Zhang may have done this. I was never assigned to those ships. I come from the small fry."

"I see."

"It was thought that since I too have been a squadron commander, even of lesser ships, I would be well suited to lead this voyage as senior captain."

"Of course. That makes perfect sense."

"With an idea that I might be appointed full commodore when we get to Taiwan." His eyes fell. "But Admiral Chen saw my mistake today."

"What do you think happened back there?"

"Lieutenant Wú failed in his duty."

"But technically. The shiphandling."

He shrugged. "Not enough backing bell. A failure."

"And what did you think—I'm sorry to bring this up but it might be helpful—what did you think of your own performance?"

"I should have insisted on making up the tugs."

"As it turned out that would have helped. But I meant your performance after that."

Lee looked at him. "You have some advice for me?"

"I do. In our navy we have a tradition that the captain is the consummate shiphandler onboard. During World War II the captains of even battleships and aircraft carriers took the conn to maneuver away from bombs and torpedoes—any time the stakes were high.

"In my own experience I learned to be ready to take the conn at any moment. Once I had done this in an emergency or two—and for practice and pleasure at other times—it became easy. Easy and routine, causing no loss of confidence among the officers. In fact it built confidence, for in the moments leading up to *that* moment, while my officer was trying to make his maneuver work, I was thinking of the orders to escape from it. We used to joke *This is the captain, I have the conn, undo everything.*"

"All engines back full," Lee said, with the hint of a grin.

"That's it. That would have done it today. You're a fine leader, Captain. I've seen that already. But the excellent principle of delegating authority, which is so useful most of the time, doesn't mean allowing an unsafe condition to develop—or continue—if you can prevent it. You have more experience than anyone in the ship. You have the absolute responsibility and authority. *This is the captain, I have the conn* should be in your toolbox."

"I need to be more aggressive," Lee declared.

Which seemed among the Taiwan sailors to be a problem generally. He read his night orders to Lee to be sure they were clear. Lee nodded agreement and compliance.

After making the signal to the ships and getting their acknowledgment, he lingered on the bridge wing. It was a beautiful night at sea. The breeze felt like the tropics. He found Polaris, a straight shot from Merak and Dubhe, a handspan above the visible wake. As he watched, *Chiai* and *Hsinchu,* with only the jewels of their navigation lights showing, peeled away to take their new stations.

It was a disquieting thought, but he wondered if he should remain on the bridge to watch over the formation. These were not fleet sailors; perhaps they had never figured out a sector assignment. But the two screening ships were headed in the right direction, he couldn't stay on the bridge all night, and Lee's own orders had directed the OOD, the officer of the deck, to keep the commodore well informed. Having been told that the captains recognized his authority, he should act as if that authority were a matter of course.

One disquieting thought under the indifferent stars led to others. Did the crews know enough to operate their equipment safely? Could they control casualties? Could they fight fires and shore bulkheads and dewater flooded compartments? Could they rig emergency power? These were ordinary hazards of putting to sea. What then about battle? None of these ships had fired so much as a handgun. No one other than *Hsinchu's* captain had spoken of fighting the Chinese. Yet wars were often begun preemptively. Would these people be ready for *that* shock of recognition, that they were under attack?

And what about him? Would he be up to this, at his age, needing to sleep through his first night at sea?

Baseless fear-mongering, perhaps. Still the deck felt uncertain below his feet, with a long languid descent if disaster struck, and he hadn't felt that way in many years. He went below.

The bed had been turned down with a navy blanket neatly folded across the bottom. His clothing had been stowed in the lockers and his books on the shelf except for the one with a bookmark in it, which was waiting for him on the end table. He took off his shoes and checked that the intercom was working. If the OOD called he could be on the bridge in a minute. Without getting between the sheets he pulled the blanket up and turned out the lights and lay curled on his side. These were only the first-day blues of any departure; together with worry about the problematic mission in the incomprehensible language with a thousand strangers.

Lee would be all right, probably. Strange that he had never served in a real ship. The commodore—he could call himself that after Lee's vote of support: the OTC!—had himself commanded a patrol boat. Everything had happened more or less by tacit understanding, without any petty resistance. In a bigger command you had to assert yourself. Black Jack Cunningham, his favorite admiral of all time, had once barked at him, "Hilty, when you become the boss, don't hesitate to be a prick."

He wasn't really a prick, he thought drowsily. And he wasn't a bore, even if his wife was bored. She must have stayed on Grand Cayman alone with the goof. The transit unit was going to sail right by there. What if a boat took him ashore and he surprised them at something? But what? He couldn't imagine them having sex. He didn't want to imagine them sitting innocently over a drink and her face turned toward the goof's with that raptured interest that overcame her sometimes.

From the register above his head cold air was falling. The thermostat in this cabin had never been right. Or maybe the problem was in the fan room, he had forgotten. But no one must have fixed it during the ship's twenty years in commission, under ten captains eager to make improvements.

The tactical display was in the living room; in the bedroom there wasn't even a compass to tell what was happening. Since the lights were off, he lifted the cover of the porthole, but there was nothing to see, only the darkness. He must let the ship carry him. He wrapped the blanket more tightly around his shoulders. In the background a billion dollars' worth of machinery was making the bulkheads tremble, and beneath his head endless water, unfathomably deep, chuckled down the side of the ship.

Fishing

Before the bugle blared reveille, further unsettling him, he sat up, rubbing his eyes. Whatever had changed, he hadn't been called. Innocent morning showed in the porthole: fleecy clouds, sparkling wavetops, a float of green kelp. The lower pitch of the machinery was suspicious, however. He switched on the lights, threw off the blanket, and stood on the deck wondering what to wear.

Hanging from the locker door was a khaki uniform, on which, once again, all the insignia had been correctly placed. Also a red ballcap with the many-rayed sun of Taiwan on the crown, scrambled eggs on the visor, and the word *Commodore* in script at the back. On the deck were his black shoes, newly polished. All this had been done while he slept, while her figure moved silently about his bed.

After a quick shower he changed into the khakis, put on the shoes and ballcap, and opened the bedroom door ready with words of praise. An old mug of Plumpy and the pitcher of coffee with its delicious aroma were waiting for him on the sideboard, but she wasn't there.

He went up to the bridge while his suspicions grew.

Several Chinese conversations were interrupted by a shout, and the watchstanders snapped to attention. As in morning watches around the world, the junior enlisted were using the early light to polish the brightwork. He and the OOD, Lieutenant Wú, exchanged salutes and greetings. And had sir slept well in his old ship? He replied that he had slept very well...but his words slowed to a halt as he looked around him.

The ship was driving on both propellers, rather than trailing one, but was making only five knots. He went out to the bridge wing, below which the waves were idling down the side. At this low speed the wake was smooth and dark and edged with foam, like a chain of tidal pools.

Directly astern were *Hsinchu* and *Chiai* as they had been before he had ordered them into their sectors last night.

From the fantails of all three ships a collection of fishing poles angled out.

The ship was rolling, for the swell was greater and the thrust of course was less, much less. Against the Gulf Stream and this head sea the actual speed over ground might be nil.

A nice-sized fish, silver and blue, leapt from the surface as if summoned by the wand above its head, and a bare brown arm reached out with a net. In the silence he could hear the exclamations of the fisherman's friends.

He was eating breakfast (not fresh fish) when Lee came into the cabin. "Any orders for me, Commodore?" he asked with a face not entirely free of worry.

He finished chewing and wiped his mouth with the linen napkin. "Good morning, Captain Lee. Yes, thank you. Since the screen has rejoined us, I'd like to take this opportunity to speak to the American trainers. If the rolling of the ship doesn't concern you too much, could you arrange for the boat transfers, please?"

"Yes sir, of course." Lee opened his mouth to introduce the obvious subject then closed it again. "Yes sir, right away."

"You're displeased, I think," Mrs. Tsai observed after her captain had left them.

Anything he said now would get back to Lee. He shrugged as if the matter were unimportant. "It's the usual growing pains early in a cruise. A small question of command relationships." Then, since she probably knew it already, "Last night I thought I had ordered a different formation at a higher speed."

"I see. Tell me, please. What are growing pains?"

"I was using a metaphor. Real growing pains happen to boys and girls during adolescence. The bones ache, and

they feel clumsy. In our culture it means the awkwardness of a beginning."

"Yes sir. I thought you might mean birthing pains.
Since the Taiwan Transit Unit has just been born."

Which was true, of course. Which all of them must be
feeling. Perhaps she was telling him to be patient.

"Not *that* painful," he managed to laugh. "So my wife
says."

"The commodore has a wife, certainly."

"Yes, and two children, both adults. My daughter has
two children herself. Would you like to see?"

"Yes, please." He thumbed through an album on his
cell phone, and she admired his family.

"Have you any children, Mrs. Tsai?"

"A young man, about the age of your Adam. I will find
a picture." She meant later. "I was married for six years.
My husband was killed in the earthquake of '99."

"How terrible."

"No insurance. Only a little aid from the government.
To raise Chowa I joined the military."

"Very hard. But Chowa. I like that name."

"Handsome boy. Very kind, nice manners. Would you
care for any more of your breakfast?" Then she refilled
his mug and cleared the dishes.

He retired to the sitting area and jotted some notes
while he waited for the trainers to arrive. She brushed
and folded the linen tablecloth, wiped the surface underneath, replaced the Naugahyde cover, and carried on into
his bedroom to straighten and clean.

Unless she had married very young, she must be in
her fifties now. Certainly she didn't look it. Beneath her
soft luminous skin the vitality was everywhere. Or perhaps it was her slight quick figure, as supple as a girl's.
Or perhaps her way of presenting herself to the world.
Like cats in the wild, a young widow would want to hide
her pain. Or perhaps hers was a naturally buoyant temperament, like Lee's before the weight of responsibility—

or perhaps it was a national characteristic, as Chen had suggested. Having shared with the commodore a sad passage in her life, she set it aside. As she went about her menial tasks, she sang a song in Chinese.

He wanted to show that he admired her courage, and the change in tone gave him an opportunity.

"Your president is named Tsai Ing-wen," he said. "Any relation?"

"Yes, my sister," she replied with a guileless face.

"Truly?"

"No, no, far too grand for me." She laughed.

The Commodore and His Staff

The boat transfer was seamanlike, and the ten American trainers found seats in his cabin, where Mrs. Tsai served coffee before leaving them to their meeting. Here they confronted him, ten seasoned experts with proven leadership skills. He had recruited four of them, his old shipmates from Plumpy, and the others he had come to know during the workup. None of them spoke Chinese, but all seemed to like their charges, with reservations.

For this assignment each consultant was being paid sixteen thousand dollars a month; except Kate Harcourt, who, citing the demands of work and home, had held out for twenty. His own pay as a captain with over thirty years' service wasn't as high as hers.

However, the voice that sounded like that of his absent wife reminded him that his own assignment, as a commissioned officer, might be longer than those under contract. In fact he might be in the bloomin' Navy now till he died.

The consultants' mood was respectful but disquieted.

"A couple of admin items," he said, "before we get to the elephants in the room. First, I hope each of you will feel free to set your own schedules. By that I mean what training you conduct and when and on which ship. No one knows the readiness of these crews better than you. I'd rather we not all bunch up on one ship, but you can work that out, letting me know when you need a boat.

"If you'd like to conduct a drill affecting navigation, or a drill involving more than one ship, please coordinate with me. We have open seas today, and so I'd like to do some divtacs, but starting tomorrow we'll be in restricted waters where a lee shore might be a problem, particularly if you want to put the ship cold, dark, and silent." He looked at Michael Blaylock.

"Not to mention" William Houy put in, "the him-icane."

"The him-icane, Bill?"

"Tropical Depression Sixteen, Commodore, soon to be Hurricane Lennon. South of Hispaniola and tracking west. One moment, please, everyone: we switch you now to Bill Houy of the Houy Weather Service."

He put his hand in front of his face as if to split the screen. "'Bill, what's going on down there?'

"'Right you are, Bill, there's a lot of energy building in Sixteen, and all our forecast models show it organizing to hurricane strength overnight. And what's worse for the Taiwan destroyers, we project it turning north toward the Windward Passage. I'll be reporting from the scene, folks, so keep it right here. Back to you, Bill.'"

"It's good to have our own private hurricane center," the commodore joked, embarrassed not to have known.

"We're already seeing a falling barometer and longer swells," Houy said. "Right out of Bowditch."

"After the meeting, we should talk. It sounds like we'll have to tie everything down and maybe alter course to-morrow. This afternoon I'm going to have my divtacs. So, that's what I had. Let's get to your concerns."

"What's going on with the fishing?" This came from Donald Franzen, the gunner's mate.

"I thought we were supposed to spread out for better training," another contractor said.

"And why have we basically stopped?"

He nodded. "Yes, that's a mystery right now. Last night I ordered the ships into sectors—"

"You did, we were patrolling ours."

"At eighteen knots. I came on deck this morning to find us nearly dead in the water and the fishing poles out. Does anyone know what happened?"

No one did. All of them had awakened this morning to the same surprise.

"Then I'll have to check with the three captains. Apparently the officer in tactical command isn't. Or wasn't. It's probably something cultural. I'll fix it. What else?"

[64]

"We're hours behind," Kate said. "Can we catch up?"

"When will we get to Taiwan, sir?" said someone else.

Houy, with his meaty lips, wore on a superior grin.

"These pussies want to go home already, Commodore."

He looked surprised.

"But we've only been at sea twenty-four hours."

"It's not that," another complained.

"And now we have a storm to deal with," he went on. "Which I admit I wasn't aware of. I hear your concerns, but I don't quite understand them. If this isn't ten veteran sailors who'd rather not be at sea, which seems unlikely, then what is it?"

"Are we going to have to fight?" asked Kate.

"Is China going to attack?"

"What are you seeing on the back channel?" asked Bill.

So that was it. They hadn't signed up to dodge missiles and torpedoes; to wake up in a burning compartment.

"Okay, I hear you, but one question at a time," he said. "First, there *is* no back channel. Whatever news I get from the Navy has to be unclassified because it's coming over foreign circuits, and of course whatever I learn I will pass on to you.

"Now, is China going to attack? Your guess is as good as mine. My guess is that they won't. They've threatened a blockade. That might just be a bluff. If it isn't, then long before we get there the Seventh Fleet will have been ordered in. China, at the risk of losing all our markets and getting a bloody nose, would never interfere with us no matter how much they scream and shout. They want what they want without having to fight for it. All their threats, in my opinion, are about forcing Taiwan to accept some kind of client status, like Hong Kong's. They're in this for the long haul. They'll take what they can get now and wait for another chance to get more. In short, I don't think any of us will be putting in for hostile fire pay."

Several of them were nodding at this, which seemed to square with the news. Only Kate looked apprehensive.

She was biting her lips, as if wondering whether to speak out—a woman's dilemma in a group of men.

Out of a brief silence, Michael Blaylock spoke. "Let's not forget we're supposed to be training them to fight."

"Very true," he said, "and that has to continue to be our focus. Are any of you concerned that the ships' companies don't seem to be very aggressive?"

Of course he knew that they were, he had heard the complaint more than once. Another babble of voices rose: the sailors' undoubted intelligence and ability, but their middling response to the drills.

"Any idea what's holding them back?"

"They're afraid," said Houy. "Like wet puppies."

"All right, but of what? Of China?"

"It can't be just that," said Franzen. "They're afraid of their equipment. It's like it's too advanced for them. Whenever they run an operability test they're afraid they'll launch a missile."

"Is that particular to just one ship, Don?"

"No sir, to all of them. Less true of *Chiai,* whose captain is a real cowboy, which has filtered down to some extent. But even there."

"And I take it the rest of you are seeing this?"

They were. The Taiwanese, unlike young American sailors, who couldn't keep their hands off the equipment, preferred not to disturb anything.

"Ergo, they didn't like securing an engine and running trail shaft last night," he said. "Very well, another talking point for me. I think that's enough for now. Stick around if you want to hear from Bill the Weather Guy. I'll just run up to the bridge and get us moving again and then I'll be back."

As he did he congratulated himself on taking the right style of leadership with these professionals; more like a coach than an authoritarian. Hornblower never flogged if he could help it. But he and the old Hilty too would have predicted the hurricane.

[66]

Divtacs

He had taken the trouble to write out the maneuvers in his wheel-book and to look up the signals, the coded sequence of commands, most of which would be transmitted by flaghoist. Despite his show of modesty in the meeting, he was confident of his skill—he would hardly need to think about it even after all these years—but it was possible to paint yourself into a corner unless you looked all the way ahead. If any ship, unable to execute a command, should hoist the *Interrogative* pennant, causing the OTC to negate it, the embarrassment would be public, weakening his already challenged authority.

He began with the ships in a column, illicit though it was. The order was *Luchiang, Hsinchu, Chiai.* To facilitate maneuvering and also comfort levels, he slowed the formation from twenty knots to twelve. Then the script, which had everything: turning all together and then one after another in the wake of the ship ahead; exchanging stations and back again; and his particular favorite, the search turn from a line abreast, by which the ship away from the turn turns first, like a shuttle weaving a weft through the wakes; then the middle ship, then the near ship. By the magic of this maneuver a great deal of water is searched (for example, in case of a man overboard), and the order of ships is inverted as well. On *Luchiang's* bridge all the watchstanders were grinning.

It was a fine day for feeling like sailors. The swell, from the southeast, was unusually long, as Bill Houy had pointed out, and without significant wind waves. The ships were about the latitude of the Georgia/Florida line, where summer still reigned, and the day was warmer still in the beryl-blue Gulf Stream. A few diaphanous clouds floated high above them. The mild sun was a blessing on the skin, with just a hint of breeze to ruffle the collar. When the ships passed each other in the maneuvers, sometimes close aboard, their topsides were crowded with gleeful crews waving to each other. Truly it was a fine day for being at sea, for learning the skills to defend your country, for gaining confidence in yourself.

By now a great many officers were on the bridge and eager to have a chance. It was fun to conn the ship but almost as much fun to work out the signal and call the result to the conning officer. A few more exercises like this and they would be a band of brothers and sisters.

Having completed his list of signals, he ordered *Hsin-chu* and *Chiai* into sectors on either beam of the flagship. Here again would be the night steaming formation, at twenty knots to regain their track and give them time in their pockets before the hurricane picked it. As they gained confidence he would move them farther apart each day until they ruled the ocean like predator birds on the wing.

Chiai was flying a new flag: *Interrogative.* He hurried to the chart, knowing the problem before he got there. Her sector would run over a small but clearly marked scab of shoal water. There was room for her to go around it, and in any event she should never obey a command that would hazard her safety. Perhaps her captain was trying to embarrass him. In a calm voice over the radio, the commodore put out a signal to change the course of the formation and avoid the shoal.

Solace

When he came off the bridge for dinner, Mrs. Tsai was waiting with a *bifteck au poivre, pommes de terre dauphinoise,* and a Taiwan sunburst of *haricots verts* radiating from a small round cheese. Also another carafe of red wine.

"I'm humbled by such a meal," he said. "The only way you can keep me from wallowing in shame is to join me."

"Oh no, thank you, that's *your* dinner. Well, all right, maybe just a small dish." She laid another place, served a sample onto her bread plate, took a bite, and smiled at him. "Yes, not bad, says the cook."

"Where was the cook trained, in Paris?"

"Spiritually. Gastronomically. My husband and I used to cook for each other. After he died, in the early days of the navy I wasn't making a lot of money, not enough for Chowa and me to live together, so I worked in a French restaurant in Kaohsiung. The chef was kind to teach me. I worked for him until I began my master's degree."

"But when did you get your bachelor's degree?"

"Not long before."

"So, for at least a few years you served in the navy, worked in a restaurant, went to college, and raised a son, whom you also put through college?"

"Apparently I kept busy. Life went very fast, meeting the needs of each hour. I never got sick. Just putting one foot ahead of the other."

"And only one pair of feet."

"One pair of adult feet, one pair of a child's."

"I will never complain again about being too busy."

"But you never would." She said this with her eyes looking into his, reading him.

"I made a mistake on the bridge today, Mrs. Tsai."

"Surely not serious."

"It might have been."

"Perhaps that captain exaggerated it."

"Perhaps. But this morning I learned what I should have known earlier."

"We're going to have a hurricane," she said brightly.

"Well, we're going to avoid one, but the seas will be rough. I understand the geometry, like two ships on a collision course. After all these years away from it, I still have good instincts, but they come more slowly now. I have to dredge up old knowledge. Nor do I see as much— I used to see every detail. I'm sixty. I wonder if I'm too old to be doing this."

She thought about it. He had left on his plate a single ray of *haricots verts* with a morsel of the sun-cheese, and she scraped it up and ate it with a private smile at her effrontery. Then more thoughtfulness.

"Admiral Chen doesn't think you're too old. Captain Lee wishes he had your instincts."

"You know these things."

"Hmm. I keep my eyes and ears open. Sometimes the important people confide in me. Admiral Chen told me that your friend Admiral Greene told him that you were the most capable officer he had ever served with. Believe me, we need your help."

"Why?" he asked on impulse. "What's holding you back?"

"Everyone is afraid."

"Afraid of what?"

"Afraid of this sale. Of China. Afraid to bring these ships into the balance of power."

"I can understand that. But it seems also that many of the sailors are afraid to operate their own equipment."

"Fear is contagious, isn't it. Not wrong but not reasonable either. Maybe, the sailor thinks, if I push this button a war will start."

"Who are you, Mrs. Tsai?"

"I'm your personal servant, personal chef, personal assistant, and Buddha of wisdom. Ask me anything. But if we're going to have a hurricane tomorrow, you should ask me now to clear the table so you can go to bed."

"Why did the ships change formation and slow down this morning?"

She made a secret smile, which he might interpret as either knowledge pretending ignorance or the other way around. Or some many-layered indirection that not even she could disentangle.

The Commodore and His Captains

The bridge watch called the commodore three times that night, once, at two a.m., to discuss with the captain of *Chiai* a trivial point of station-keeping. Perhaps, since the radio net was public, he was keeping the needle in.

Returning to bed after this call, he was awake but tired and disheartened. It was an effort to roll up in his blanket, despite which the icy cold air tumbled down on him. A change in the vibration of the bulkheads raised his suspicions, but he was too tired to look into it. He was too tired even to turn off the lights, though the blanket was no security blanket.

It was a bad mistake. On the chart the shoal was obvious; he had noted it before he started the maneuvers. What a picture if *Chiai* had run aground: a billion-dollar ship high and dry while beginning a transit under such scrutiny. In benign conditions. In broad daylight. Under the tactical command of an officer in his home waters.

The contrast between the ease with which, as a new teacher, he had penetrated the culture of the high school and the near impossibility of doing so with these Taiwanese was itself disheartening. All languages have their secrets, but Chinese...! Much of it was just a series of intonations: yes or no, life or death could be hidden in a word that sounded like a grunt. And that was one speaker. A roomful of Chinese speakers was impenetrable. And the writing—he doubted that he would ever recognize a single character, and even the Pinyin transliteration wouldn't save him, he just couldn't remember these foreign words. How would he ever build a rapport with these officers let alone persuade them of something unwelcome?

The voice that sounded like that of his absent wife reminded him that it didn't require any language skills to notice a shoal.

Well, he was sixty. Going to sea was a young person's calling. Too old, Hilty!

But Mrs. Tsai, to whom he had whined about these things, had only said *So what?* She, some junior enlisted person, carrying more than one burden in her life and no advantages, had showed real courage. He should suck it up. Here he was on active duty again, sailing toward the horizon as he had always loved to do. He'd been given a clear mission and the resources to carry it out. Tired or not, he had better do his job, starting with no more care-less mistakes.

At first light, suspicious and sleepless, he jumped to the bridge and gazed around the horizon. Once again the ships had slowed, once again they were in the old line of column, and once again the fishing poles were out.

"You would think," he said to her over breakfast, "who-ever's doing this, I should at least get some nice fish out of it."

(She enjoyed the joke, then and later: for dinner that night she served him a filet of flounder with a coconut, lime, and cashew crust and mango aioli for a relish.)

"Would you do me a favor?" he asked over coffee.

"Of course."

"Would you give Captain Lee my compliments and ask him to hang out the signal for *All Captains?* We'll need to talk about this hurricane of ours."

She left the cabin at once.

By custom the captain is often called by the name of his ship. This was useful in the case of *Hsinchu* and *Chiai,* both of whose captains had the last name of Zhang. Soon, however, the commodore had different names for them.

The captain of *Chiai,* who spoke the best English, was tall, dark, and vain—he must have taken lessons from General MacArthur. His style of listening was to hear just enough to respond even as he heard the rest: occa-sionally he would veer in mid-sentence as the true

[74]

meaning went home. The best way to speak to him was to begin with topic sentences. The commodore thought of him as *Zhang Lite, Zhang (L)*, or just plain *(L)*.

The other Zhang, the captain of *Hsinchu,* was a slight figure who swam in his clothes. His English was good, but his accent was so thick that sometimes the commodore had to ask him to repeat himself, and other times he didn't understand him until he thought about it later. His heavy brow dominated his face, under which his dark eyes watched what was going on. He was the smartest of the three captains in analytical intelligence, common sense, and imagination; the best read and most worth listening to despite his accent. The commodore knew him as *Zhang Heavy, Zhang (H),* or *(H).*

From the cabin he heard the two hails, which must have meant "Boat ahoy" in Chinese, and then the replies from the coxswains: first "Chiai" because (L) would always strive to be first, and next "Hsinchu." The ship's bell rang and the bugle blew. Lee brought them in.

"Good morning, gentlemen," he said without inviting them to sit, though he was sitting. "We have a great deal on our agenda, but I must begin with a more fundamental matter—"

"More fundamental than a hurricane?" (L) interrupted.

"Yes, indeed: fundamental to the overall mission. The subject itself is distasteful to me"—at this they glanced at each other—"but I have a duty to bring it to your attention."

He rose and approached them, standing too close. "Captain Lee has been good enough to advise me that all three of you have agreed to my acting as officer in tactical command." He looked at each of them in turn, receiving nods from Lee and (H) and at least no protest from (L).

"Having accepted that responsibility, which ten thousand years of history tells us cannot be divided, let me say that I mean to be OTC in fact. Drawing on my experience, I will make decisions for the greater good of our mission. No doubt you won't agree with all of them. But you will please *comply* with all of them unless they would put your ship in immediate danger, as *Chiai* properly did yesterday.

"Now to the matter at hand. The past two nights, gentlemen, I issued specific orders as to course, speed, and formation. These were acknowledged and, I had thought, executed by each of you. In the morning, however, it was clear that these orders had been countermanded to place the squadron in an ineffective formation at hardly more than bare steerageway. I wonder if you could enlighten me on this."

Consternation before him. (H) looked phlegmatic, like a mobster who would never squeal. (L) consulted Lee, who then spoke for all. The mysterious discrepancy was much to be regretted. Each of them was well aware of his own lack of experience and their need for him as OTC. He could count on their loyalty and that of their superiors at the fleet command in Tsoying.

"I appreciate that, Kuan-lin. Perhaps the non-compliance will cease now. Otherwise, of course, I could not fulfill my duties as your commodore, and with the international situation as it is, I would be unable to accept the responsibility for leading you—possibly into harm's way—in the Taiwan Strait. Moreover, I assume that our consultants would feel the same and insist on disembarking with me in Colon. Very well. Let us all obey orders as we are required to do, and let these unfortunate occurrences be forgotten now. We have a more immediate problem, as Zhang Yu-hsuan reminds us, and that's what we should talk about next."

After yesterday's embarrassment, the commodore had delved into the storm. Besides the evidence of his own eyes, he had available to him satellite images and computer models on the internet; a message from the Fleet Weather Center in Norfolk with forecasts and alternate routing suggestions; a text from *Hsinchu* pointing out the falling barometer; a cable from Admiral Chen assuring him of Taiwan's confidence in the commodore's seamanship; and a single line from Slate: *Don't break the ships.*

Well, he would try not to break them, as long as they followed his orders.

He invited the captains to join him at the table, and Mrs. Tsai brought in the coffee service and three different pots of tea, according to each man's preference. Then she sat in the chair at his desk and swiveled toward them. He glanced at her. She was holding a steno pad and a pen.

"I know shorthand, Commodore. Expert level."

"Of course you do," he replied, which only she seemed to understand as an American form of compliment.

On the bulkhead above the couch was a large monitor connected to the Aegis system. With a minimum of fumbling he put up a weather map of Tropical Storm Lennon, now south of Haiti and moving west by north. The computers couldn't make up their minds about its future course. The majority thought it would brush by the western end of Cuba and land in Texas. However, there was a nearly equal chance that it would turn directly north, as Houy had predicted, toward the Windward Passage, where the ships themselves were headed.

"No problemo," (L) said before the others could speak. "Put the metal down and cross ahead of it."

The commodore refrained from pointing out that they would have crossed its path already, or nearly so, if they had not slowed to a crawl every morning.

Lee, shaking his head, offered, "We must go to shelter. Turn around and go to Jacksonville."

(L) didn't like the shake of the head. "May I quote you on that to fleet command?" he asked. "The biggest arms deal in our history, and we, sailors all, hide in port?"

"Shelter, not hide."

"We'd look pretty stupid whatever you call it."

"It would be wrong to risk lives. And these valuable ships. How stupid would we look if there was a disaster?"

"It's just nature. Step on the gas."

Silence fell as they pondered. Or else they were reluctant to air their differences in front of a foreigner.

"What do you think?" he asked (H).

His sad smile had the startling effect of lighting up his face: "O Lord, your sea is so great and my boat is so small." He sounded like Demosthenes with the marbles still in his mouth. "It cannot be wise to race a hurricane, even if we could be certain of its course. On the other hand, if it turns north, Jacksonville won't be safe either. The entire East Coast would evacuate as the storm approached, and we'd be chased back to where we started. Truly, we must regret not going faster before."

More silence, with an awkward constraint: the secret behind the regret.

"Commodore, you have faced many hurricanes in your career," Lee said more calmly. "Safety first, yes?"

He sipped his coffee. "Gentlemen, what is your fuel status?"

Only (H) knew. Being forehanded he might have read a fuel report before coming to a meeting about hurricane evasion, but just as likely, he was the kind of officer who would always know such things. *Hsinchu* was at fifty-eight percent.

Lee had to phone down to Central Control; *Luchiang* was at fifty-three percent.

(L), unembarrassed, replied that he left all that to the engineers.

It was time to give his decision; his decision for the greater good, which they had promised to obey. "A lot will depend on the storm's movement over the next few hours. We'll reach the Turks and Caicos this evening. If the storm continues west at its present pace, we'll take a slow speed—something that apparently we've been practicing—and transit the Windward Passage after the eye has cleared. Sailing across the back of a tropical cyclone, at a safe distance, is surprisingly smooth.

"If, on the other hand, the storm turns north, we'll turn east, putting Hispaniola, with its mountains, between us and the danger. That will bring us to the Mona Passage, being confident that we may then take a direct line to Panama."

None of them objected. Lee looked apprehensive of any change in the status quo. (L) looked bored. (H) looked satisfied by the plan, with its creative use of an island barrier.

"Three major actions will keep us safe, gentlemen," he went on, not liking his pedantic tone but needing to sound like the Buddha. "The first is our own track, which we've discussed. The second is our fuel status. If we have to go via Mona we may reach Panama at less than twenty percent. Accordingly, beginning at noon today please report your fuel status to me *every four hours.*"

Again, no objections.

"The final action is to prepare our ships for heavy weather. I assume each of you has a bill for this; if not I brought one with me in my dunnage, and Mrs. Tsai will furnish you with a copy. Beginning now, have your people tie down every possible missile hazard in all your compartments, double the frapping around the boat falls, and rig your heavy weather stanchions. Your engineering configuration should be as redundant as possible. Two shafts, four gas turbines, all three generators running— you see what I say about fuel consumption. I will want a written report from each of you as soon as your ships are ready for heavy weather. Shall I tell you how Admiral Halsey, in 1944, lost three destroyers in a Pacific typhoon?"

That had been someone else's failure. He should.

"First, he drove Third Fleet directly into the eye of the storm—perhaps he thought he could cross it," with a look at (L). "Next, he didn't refuel soon enough, before the weather made that impossible, and his ships were sucking fumes. Third, they had omitted to ballast down. Fourth, they hadn't kept up with their maintenance, and many of their watertight fittings weren't watertight. Fifth, they didn't pay enough attention to protecting their electrical systems, so when the green water rolled across their decks—waves you cannot imagine, gentlemen—it

[79]

leaked through the faulty hatches onto their switch-boards, which of course caught fire. Powerless, the ships drifted broadside to the waves, where they rolled and rolled and rolled beyond the point of no return. Eight hundred sailors lost their lives in what could have been, should have been—"

"All right, enough!" shouted (L). "Enough. We get it. Dismissed. Don't tell us how to do our jobs."

As they left the cabin, (L) muttered something more. It took a good deal of back and forth, with him citing the moral position and promising his discretion, for Mrs. Tsai to translate:

"A tempest in a pot of tea."

The Hurricane

There was not a moment to lose, and onboard *Luchiang,* the crew lost not a moment. After Lee spoke over the general announcing system, his XO held quarters. Soon the passageways were filled with voices, and the overheads resonated with equipment being dragged into place and secured. All over the ship, teams with blue chalk were testing how watertight doors and hatches sealed. The really vital compartments were pressurized and metered, on the theory that if they kept air in, they must keep water out, waves they could not even imagine, gentlemen.

The commodore went to the bridge. It was no slight on their captain that the OTC should observe the conditions for himself. He studied the barograph, an instrument he had bought for Plumpy when he'd commanded her, replacing the standard barometer, which recorded no history. The pressure had fallen steadily since yesterday as if the stylus were descending a long slope on cross-country skis: they were certainly heading into a storm.

Lee arrived, rubbing his hands with satisfaction. The look of worry was gone. So it happens when we are responsible for work performed by others: that joy when their dedication matches our own.

"It's coming on to blow," Lee said, a piece of sailor talk that could hardly have an equivalent in Chinese.

"If you'd like to spare a couple of junior officers," he replied, "I'd be happy to show them the signs."

Within a few minutes the bridge was packed with officers. None of them was worried either. This was pure excitement. The possibility that the storm might be dangerous was far from their thoughts, held off by the more powerful idea that with blue chalk and doubled frapping they controlled their own fate.

"First, of course, is atmospheric pressure," he said, tearing off the strip of graph paper. "At sea level 1013 millibars is roughly normal. That's where the barograph has been, plus or minus, since leaving Norfolk. Right now it's 997. The eye of a Category 1 hurricane has a pressure of 980. So you see, by pressure alone, we're halfway to hurricane strength."

They did. They were excited to see it. Next he pointed out the long swell coming at them; its origin would be just to the left of the center. Then the clouds, snow white and fibrous and beginning to concentrate. "By dusk they'll be low and dense, a dark bar on the horizon pointing toward the storm. The question is whether the center will keep going west, so that we may pass under it, or whether it turns toward us, in which case we will haul out to port."

But they weren't worried.

As if to provide a teaching aid, the ship put her forefoot into a swell, with a lurch from which some of the officers were saved from falling only because they were so tightly massed.

On the bridge and all through the ship were the de-lighted cries of people riding a rollercoaster.

"Who gets seasick?" he asked above the din. "Come on now: confess." He held up his own hand, though in thirty years this had never been true. The officers grinned at one of their company. "You sir, Lieutenant Wú? I'll bet you have plenty of company tomorrow. May I offer some advice? Stay hydrated. Distract your thoughts. Ask yourself if you really need to be on deck. If you do, sit in a chair. If you don't, go to bed: rig the heavy weather bar and slip one leg under your mattress for extra security."

Someone in the back made ralphing noises.

He nodded. "Good point. If you have to heave, heave to leeward. Which way is leeward, young sirs?" They all knew.

The wind and seas mounted through the morning. By noon *Luchiang* was taking long plunges into the swell then shaking free of them like a dog shedding water. On the fo'c'sle the wind sang a low keening note, and sheets of spray tossed up from the bow blew obliquely across the wet nonskid, one after another. All the decks were silver with spray. Even with the extra stanchions rigged, the prudent thing was to keep the crew indoors. To his credit Lee made this decision without consulting him. By four p.m. all the captains reported that their ships were ready for heavy weather.

At six he put the formation in a loose column at ten knots, for the waters approaching Turks and Caicos were full of hazard. The ships were keeping good station, rising and falling in different combinations like the valves of a trumpet. He went below long enough to gulp down the flounder from the morning's catch; at his haste, rather than from the working of the ship, Mrs. Tsai grew thoughtful. He returned to the bridge.

In just that time they had encroached upon the storm.

The wind was raking the sea, and some new invisible force was shoving it from underneath. The ordinary waves were level with the bridge while from time to time some monster rose too high to be seen from the trough. The barometer had fallen to 989. One port after another along the Windward Passage—Kingston, Port-au-Prince, Guantanamo—had closed. But all such news reinforced his decision.

Southwest of Great Inagua Island, the transit unit came upon a container ship wallowing in the seas; hardly making way. Wrapped around her mast was a scrap of red with a couple of yellow stars showing. The name on her transom, nearly submerged, was *PLUTO / Shanghai.*

On Channel 16 a guttural voice asked, "Do you know my position?"

In normal times this would have been a routine request, fulfilled at once. The OOD looked at his captain, who looked at the commodore. All the destroyers were flying the underway ensign of Taiwan; not to be missed by the *Pluto.*

With an open hand he passed the decision back to Lee, who nodded to his officer, who, applying the offset from *Luchiang,* provided the coordinates.

"Many thanks. Is the storm coming *here?*"

In the background a shrill voice was speaking Chinese.

He left his chair, and the OOD handed him the mic. As he pressed the button, the *Pluto* sat down in a trough, shooting water in all directions. If he wasn't mistaken, she was listing a few degrees to starboard; some flaw in her load, exacerbated by the heaving.

He said, "From the hurricane's position at 1800 hours local time, it has turned northward, heading for a landfall at Punta del Quemada, Cuba."

"Thank you."

"It has been upgraded to Category 3."

"Category 3, understood." The voice said something in Chinese to the background.

He said, "The Windward Passage will be blocked soon. We are preparing to turn east toward the Mona Passage and increase speed as the seas permit."

"That is my intention also" was the reply, which warmed his heart. But the other voice, high and insistent, could be heard objecting until the master unkeyed his mic.

He asked, "Do you need any assistance?"

The shrill voice answered: "No. No assistance."

According to the law of the sea, the proper actions had been taken, and given the state of tension between their nations, any further exchange would be undesirable. If the *Pluto* turned east as announced, she'd be fine. By midnight she'd be out of the reach of the most dangerous conditions and continuing to open the distance. As would the transit unit.

The bugle announced sunset. There was no color in the sky, and soon the night became so dark that the waves breaking over the bow, sending water as far aft as the boat deck, were mere shadows. The ship was pounding: it was time to turn.

[84]

He put the signal in the air, giving his listeners time to think about it. The maneuver was simple enough in concept: *Turn in the wake of the guide ninety degrees to port. Increase speed to twelve knots.* He would not offer advice.

Lee didn't ask. All watertight fittings had been tested and secured, and the weather decks were closed. The four engines provided more than enough power. There was plenty of sea room. While in command of Plumpy he must have made a turn like this a dozen times: full rudder and add turns on the outboard propeller. If necessary back the inboard. He would not say this. Taiwan had a long maritime tradition.

Standby, he signaled. *Execute.*

"Left thirty degrees rudder," said Lee, standing by the commodore's chair so he could look in the direction of the turn. "Starboard engine ahead full."

Exactly.

The ship's head, on a short lever, fought to come upsea as the water crashed over the fo'c'sle, ton after ton. Her stern moved a few degrees and stalled, with waves rolling down either side. She was in irons. Something more was needed.

"Starboard engine ahead flank," Lee said.

This was so much power that the turbine intakes could be heard above the wind. The seas yielded grudgingly in jags. Still the struggle continued. The ship pounded and rolled too; pounded and rolled and shook.

"Back your port engine," he said to Lee quietly.

That was enough to haul the bow across. The compass repeater began to turn.

"All ahead standard," he said to Lee. "Meet her with opposite rudder early, before you want to. She has a lot of inertia to overcome, and the seas are on the other side now."

Lee gave the commands. The heading overshot but not by much, for the rudders, to starboard, were enough with

[85]

both propellers driving ahead. The ship settled out on the ordered course and speed.

"Well done, *Luchiang!*" he said to the bridge watch.

Having made himself conspicuous to them, he felt that everyone must be looking at his wet armpits, always so visible in khakis. Lee seemed embarrassed for his own reasons, but that couldn't be helped either. In war soldiers threw away their underpants.

Now for the other ships. The masthead and after range lights on *Hsinchu,* which looked like a driver and a backseat driver, began to foreshorten. Closer and closer they approached, and then they aligned, with both running lights visible, which meant that she was bow on in the flagship's wake. *Chiai* was lost in the storm clouds, but on the surface tracking display her course leader came around nicely, and soon all three ships were in loose column at approximately their correct distances.

With the seas to starboard, just abaft the beam, *Luchiang* was rolling, sometimes thirty degrees to each side, but the rolling was easier than the pounding had been, and soon the Haitian coast would give them a lee. The barometer ticked up. The emergency was over. They could go faster. He increased the formation speed to fifteen.

In the chartroom he put his arm around Lee's shoulder; probably by an act of self-control, Lee didn't shrink from the touch. "You made a good turn back there."

"Not entirely. *This is the commodore, I have the conn.*"

"You got it started. You recognized the problem. I reacted because I know the ship." And when none of these worked: "Kuan-lin, you'll just have to forgive an old man for his impatience."

Lee pulled back and came gently to attention. "No forgiveness is necessary, sir. If I did not see that you were right, I would have given contrary orders since I am responsible for safety. As it was, I would have been wrong not to take advantage of your greater experience."

꒰꒱

"Well, I luffed Captain Lee," he said to Mrs. Tsai as she gave him a midnight snack. The cabin was rolling so much she had wet down the linen tablecloth to prevent the dishes from sliding and had moved his chair athwartships so that he might brace with his feet. Occasionally the bow would drop into a trough with a crash that set the bulkheads shaking. She herself was standing to serve him but tired from the strain; the strain of fighting the constant motion and the worry about what lay ahead. Gone was all her excitement of the morning.

"What does this mean, please?"

"We were bringing the ship about, and I helped him more than he wanted. Took the wind from his sails."

"Necessary?"

"I thought so."

"Then he knows this. Are we in such trouble?" Her delicate face, so ready to be pleased, was dull with worry.

"Not any more. We turned east. That was the point, you remember from the meeting. We've crossed ahead safely, with Hispaniola to shield us. We should find calmer conditions soon and then always improving. The other ships seem to be doing fine."

"Thank you, Bradford. You reassure me."

"Heaven help sailors on a night like this."

"I have read about typhoons, of course. But I never imagined being in one. O Lord, your sea is so great, and by the way I cannot swim."

The Rescue and the Near-Rescue

At first light the commodore and Lee were still on the bridge. The ship was riding comfortably upon abating seas, running free as it were. The barometer had risen to 992. Both the captains Zhang reported all secure; (L) said he could take a higher speed.

Over the intercom Kate Harcourt, the air controller, called from CIC. A merchant ship had sent an SOS from the Windward Passage, and Coast Guard Air Station Borinquen, on the northwest coast of Puerto Rico, had ordered out a search-and-rescue helo.

"Have they passed us a datum, Kate?"

"Yes, sir. You'll see it in the system. The helo's almost there. Reporting winds marginal for hovering, seas too high for their rescue swimmer."

But perhaps they could drop a life raft.

"Let me know, please, if they find anything."

Could it be the *Pluto?*

Lee came over. "One of our ships could be detached, Commodore."

"Possibly. Who would you recommend?"

He grinned. "Me."

"It's too rough now, though, don't you think?"

"We could start back that way...." He shrugged.

"If this unfortunate ship has gone down and the helo can't hover, I don't see what we could do. A search will be mounted after the storm passes—a recovery operation, I'm afraid. Even if the helo finds survivors and manages somehow to get them onboard, they'll take them back to Borinquen. Either way we should continue our transit, especially since we're so late."

"Get to datum as fast as you can." He had said that to Admiral Chen about the last-known position of enemy submarines.

"Quite true. When it's safe."

"These are tough ships, built to take punishment."

This from the man who had wanted to shelter in port.

"Yes they are. You'll understand, however, that I'm reluctant to endanger another country's ships."

"But it's the law of the sea, Commodore. Any vessel in distress. I believe *my* country, even though we may soon be needed in Taiwan, would want us to honor that. And if the ship is P.R.C...." He ended with another shrug.

Well, why not? The storm would forgive a lot of sins. They weren't going to make Panama on time unless they sprinted, and their fuel might not allow that. And if she *was* that ship, besides the glory of the thing, the controversial destroyers of Taiwan might be responsible for a diplomatic coup. He thumbed the intercom.

"Kate, I'm going to come about and close the scene, as much as the storm allows. Please advise our Coast Guard friends. Have someone patch the SAR radio channel to the bridge. I'll speak to all the captains now and then put the signal out."

At six-thirty the formation reversed course. When they were steady, he put them in a line abreast with two miles between ships, to comb a wider expanse yet not miss in heavy seas something the size of a human head.

Heading toward the Windward Passage again was like reversing the tape. They breasted the swells, riding dizzying heights for a long moment then falling into the troughs on random headings as the helmsmen fought to regain control. The wind, in their faces, was strong and getting stronger, with violent gusts: a rough ride for the helo.

Kate came up to show him a photo. The ship dove into tons of water, and she had to hold onto the grab bar.

"Oh, how I missed this!" she said with a laugh.

"Air traffic control centers don't tend to roll and pitch."

"So deadly dull, which is what we like. The HH-65 Dolphin, Commodore. Four souls onboard: pilot, co-pilot, EMT, and swimmer. Three hours on-station time. We have good comms. Call sign Red Owl 154."

[90]

"I've been listening. I remember your radio voice, Kate."

"I don't get to use it much anymore. By the way, sir, this aircraft, unlike its predecessor the H-52, cannot land on the water, even smooth water. And you remember that none of these ships has a certified helo facility."

He nodded. "Nor have they drilled at flight quarters."

"Exactly."

Overcoming the temptation to enjoy the view once her errand was complete, with a toodleoo wave of her fingers Kate went below again. It was nice to see someone so cheerful in such miserable weather.

On the bridge, however, spirits seemed to be waning. The ship was constantly in motion; the endless swoop and plunge had lost its novelty. Seasick or not, everyone was tired, and perhaps there was an element of worry in it, the realization that ships can sink. Certainly their present mission should remind them of that. He missed the happy exclamations in Chinese.

Conscientious Lee took a party of officers around to inspect the ship. He must talk to him about not selling himself short, for dedication to duty was a talent too, which not all leaders possessed. Though it was questionable whether he would have crossed those seas without help. As in the near-miss leaving port, he had left too much to chance (and to body English). At least in both cases he had seen the need; the rest could be taught.

Hsinchu and *Chiai* were keeping good station. Occasionally one of them, crashing into a trough, would raise a giant ball of water, iridescent in the fleeting sun, a spectacular sight far more entertaining when it didn't happen to you. The seas were high and rolling, shaped like the back of a hand, their surfaces checkered by crosswinds. Their tropical blue had dredged up swirls of gray and brown. Even with extra lookouts posted nothing had been reported. No lifeboats, no figures in international orange, no arms raised above heads. No debris. *Chiai,* wasting airtime, reported periodically "Nothing sighted." He had to smile when Lieutenant Wú, with the hubris of those

[91]

close to the throne, started to order (L) not to submit negative reports but stopped in mid-transmission, not wishing to offend. Wú probably figured that at some point he might work for (L), who would remember him.

Over the speaker of the SAR circuit, a young voice said, with a strange sort of calm, like a TV announcer under tight control while announcing a disaster, "Red Owl 154 has a chip light."

Kate replied, "Roger. Are you declaring an emergency?"

"Wait: yes. Yes: affirmative. Mayday, Mayday: Red Owl 154, with six souls on board and one in the water, is reporting a possible rotor casualty. I am aborting search, steering for home plate."

Kate's voice was flat, infallible, irresistible: "Red Owl 154, your vector to home plate is one-one-zero magnetic, distance two hundred thirty."

"Roger, concur. That's too far."

"Nearest bingo field is Fort Liberté: steer one-eight-zero for forty-five. I will contact approach control."

After a short silence, a new voice with a slight French accent came on to ask the caller's identity.

"This is Red Owl 154," said the pilot. "I am showing rotor coupling vibration. Moderate and increasing. Request emergency clearance to land."

"Red Owl 154, conditions are unsafe for landing. Airport is closed and evacuated. No personnel or equipment available. Do you have alternate?"

A longer silence, enough to make him fear the worst. Then: "Fort Liberté, I am diverting to my control ship. *Luchiang, Luchiang,* Red Owl 154 requests immediate green deck, ETA five minutes. I have a man in the water at the position indicated."

"Roger, Red Owl, steer zero eight five. We are the center ship of three. This is an uncertified facility. Winds are thirty degrees left at forty knots. Pitch is five degrees and rolls are ten. I will advise green deck. Sir," she called to the bridge. "I know we haven't practiced it, but there isn't time: please set flight quarters. Keep all personnel,

[92]

hoses, and stretchers in the hangar. Don't worry about the safety nets."

"Chocks and chains, Kate?"

"They'll have them onboard."

"A man in the water?"

"Send one of the other ships to look."

"Captain to the bridge," he said, but Wú had already passed that word. If Lee were deep in the engineering compartments, he wouldn't make it in time.

Going to the captain's chair, he switched on the plat TV, which gave a rainy-day view of the helo deck. He brought Wú to the centerline compass repeater and turned him partway around to look at the helmsman.

"Gentlemen, your job is to keep the ship on a reasona-bly steady course—let's say plus or minus five degrees. The ship will pitch and roll. Don't worry about that: the pilot will allow for it. What he needs is the steady course. In general not too much rudder. Work to the average." Both of them nodded, and Wú turned to the repeater.

The helo was in sight, a tiny white tadpole just below the dark clouds. It would pass ahead of *Chiai* as it ap-proached. A quick descent and a hard turn into the wind should do it. The ship's course was steady enough.

It grew larger; it was turning down *Chiai's* side, prob-ably to take a wider turn, putting less strain on the rotor. Lee was still off the bridge.

"Kate, green deck."

"Aye-aye, sir."

"Green deck," he said to the bosun's mate, who re-peated it over the announcing system in English.

But instead of turning toward them, the helo banked the other way and dropped onto *Chiai;* dropped fast but accurately, surrounded by the still-vertical safety nets; there to stay as the flight deck crew rushed from the hangar to chock and chain it in place. During the confu-sion and despite not being designated as the landing ship,

(L) had hoisted the *Hotel* flag, which meant, "I am operating helicopters." Perhaps he flew it as bait.

"What about the man?" he asked Kate as soon as she returned to the bridge.

"They picked up four survivors, Commodore. The rescue swimmer...." Her eyes had gone bright.

"He jumped despite the swells?"

"Yes sir—and was caught in one of them."

"No sign?"

"Only for a moment. Then the chip light. They couldn't
afford to remain in the hover, and when they transitioned
to forward flight they lost sight of him."

"We're searching, of course. Is the helo secure?"

"Yes sir, but one of the ship's crew is badly burned. I'd
recommend—"

"Yes, tell me."

"Sending *Chiai* to Gitmo."

"I thought Gitmo had been evacuated."

But this was thoughtless. Surrounded by Communist
China, where would they go? "Only Leeward Point, sir.
The base is on the less destructive side of the storm—
most of the tidal surge will have been away from the
shoreline. The naval hospital can treat the victims, and a
crane can take off the helo. Also she can get fuel there.
Also it's U.S. territory."

"Was it the container ship?"

"Yes, sir. The *Pluto,* a P.R.C. flag."

With a bone in her teeth, *Chiai* left them. (L) would be
thrilled to arrive in an American port as the hero of the
hour, the savior of an adversary. Also to be independent
of *him* and what seemed the disapproval and dislike of
his fellow captains.

The two remaining ships continued to search.

This was exciting at first, doing something important; and then it was tedious, when nothing was found or likely to be found.

The seas were moderating. Extra lookouts had been posted, and other shipmates had come topside to help.

Lee said, "I wish to rig cargo nets on each bow, Commodore, and the pilot rescue davit."

"If you're comfortable with that, Lee: of course."

"I am comfortable." He looked through the open bridge wing door at his consort. "Captain Zhang is rigging out the boat boom."

So he was. Two teams of linehandlers, one to haul, the other to ease, were pulling it into place. When made fast it looked like an arrow impaling the ship.

"I don't know what good that will do," he said.

"A recovery from the bow might endanger personnel. It would be difficult to keep the hull from striking the victim. Captain Zhang is an excellent seaman. If you wish it I will do the same."

"I have no experience with that. I've always rigged to recover from the bow." The voice of his absent wife agreed with him, recalling that he had actually saved a man this way in the freezing waters of the Arctic Circle. "You're an excellent seaman too, Lee," he went on. "You were quite right to double-check the compartments."

"Though the captain's place is on the bridge."

He let it drop for now.

They were conducting search turns, that satisfying and useful weave; less satisfying, however, with only two ships involved and no swimmer sighted.

Lunch was passed. Mrs. Tsai brought an egg sandwich to the bridge. Although the ride was nearly as rough as last night, she was relaxed again but worried for the swimmer she didn't know. Like Kate she didn't linger.

They searched. Searching wasn't easy. The scored surface, veiled by wind drift, could easily hide a single head, and so could the dark green depths as the swells rolled underneath.

Hsinchu turned the wrong way, which brought her astern of the flagship. Almost at once she called over Channel 16, "Man in the water!"

She spurted a few hundred yards then stopped. She had the swimmer in sight, however. Slowly she came ahead, stepping left and right to find her way, like someone walking in a swamp.

The captain and he went out to the bridge wing. Something round and shiny appeared for an instant then vanished in the waves. Another glimpse—true or false? He pointed; Lee was pointing too; from the deck below them a hundred arms were pointing.

Hsinchu was taking an offset approach to that spot, or where Zhang imagined it to be. Too far for a bow recovery, the destroyer passed her boat boom over it and backed her engines briefly, riding up and down in tune with the elements.

A snatch-block had been fixed to the end of the boom with a line roved through it to another block at the gooseneck. This line, tending aft, was handled by a third team. At its business end was a rescue collar, which they lowered to the water's edge.

The seas were unpredictably high, but the Coast Guard swimmer, afloat, alive, knew how to slip victims into the collar. Weak as he was, he got one arm through and then the other and then his head, and with a thumb's-up he crossed his arms and waited. The third team hauled—in their excitement too fast—just as a swell lifted him improbably high: he crashed into the boom then dropped with a jerk. They raised him again, limp in the collar, and the first two teams eased the boom back to the ship's side, where, rushing to avoid the next swell, they lifted him onto the deck.

"Amazing! Remarkable!" he cried, thinking only of the recovery. From the deck came cheers and whistles. The bridge was in a bedlam. But Lee was still frightened.

Over the radio Zhang himself reported. He keyed and unkeyed the mic, and his mouth was full of marbles, but the gist of the report was intelligible enough:

"Dead."

The Isthmus

A Man, a Plan, a Canal

The Aegis destroyers, in formation, their sailors at the rail, entered the harbor of Colon and anchored at short stay, expecting to be called at once to transit the canal. Half a dozen merchant ships waited too; presumably the warships, though delayed by the storm, would be given priority since they represented a nation.

The commodore, having transited twice in his time, went to the quarterdeck to receive the expected visitors. He was gratified by the fine appearance of his ships, despite their thick coating of salt, which itself told a story.

The boat that took off the pilot brought four visitors: a doctor to receive the certificate of pratique that there was no infectious disease in the squadron; a representative from the U.S. Embassy in Panama City to discuss the political situation in the country; a consular agent of Taiwan to address the ships' needs; and an official from the Panama Canal Authority to provide details of the transit.

The latter three visitors, two men and a woman, came onboard arguing, and the argument continued in the cabin to the point that the woman, from the embassy, shouted in Spanish at the man from the canal authority.

Captain Lee and Mrs. Tsai were sitting on the couch, under the video monitor which showed a chart of the canal. Lee was pleased by the smart performance of his crew this morning. Mrs. Tsai was amused by the argument, as she often was by eccentricity.

"Sit down, won't you?" the commodore said to the three remaining visitors, the doctor having gone to sick bay. "Perhaps you can tell me the problem," he said to the embassy officer, whose name was Emily Villaseñor.

"I am not in a fit condition to speak of it."

She was a slender young woman with an aesthetic face behind outsized glasses. One hand was flat on the table, and the other made a spider on her chest. She sipped from a glass of ice tea. When she could continue, she said, "It appears that, according to Mr. Aparicio, some irregularity exists with the safety certificate of your three ships. Despite assurances received by the embassy five days ago and reservations made personally by me to transit this afternoon." Then she burst into a Spanish harangue, to which her adversary, a bald middle-aged man in a white suit, listened impassively.

When she had finished, Mr. Aparacio said, "I am the counsel general of the Panama Canal Authority. My office has been researching this question ever since the American embassy informed us—informed us—of the ships' arrival. Despite the imperious manner in which it was presented, this is simply a question of law. The certificate may be invalid because Taiwan is not a state as defined by the United Nations, and therefore—"

"Yet it *is* a state under the Montevideo Convention, ratified by your country on November 13, 1933, and which became a fundamental tenet of international law per Article 2, Paragraph 4 of the Charter of the United Nations."

Aparicio smiled patiently, though not without a hint of condescension. "Yet the United Nations does not recognize Taiwan as a state. This is the rub: which norm takes precedence? We must have clarification from our Cabinet Council, and my office is striving to obtain this."

"Utter bullshit, Tomás" she said. "Bullshit, horseshit, rabbitshit. It isn't as hard as you're making out, and it certainly shouldn't be taking this long. The council meets daily. Something else is going on, and you know what it is as well as I do."

"For such an important question the council must seek guidance from our National Assembly."

"Que está en sesión!" she shouted.

With this outburst, the U.S.-Panamanian dialogue fell silent. The commodore looked at the representative of Taiwan, a Mr. Correa.

"My client's hands are tied," Correa said. "Though this matter is indeed of vital importance to Taiwan. We depend on our ally to look after our interests. I will meet separately with Captain Lee and the Captains Zhang to determine any logistical needs that may be met here in Colon while we wait."

"Those will all be provided in Balboa," insisted Villaseñor. "Once this charade is over and the transit has been completed."

Leaving her the last word, Aparicio left the ship. Corea finished his tea, complimented everyone in the room, and also left.

Villaseñor turned to the commodore. "I'm sorry I lost my temper," she said. "The operation of the canal falls within my portfolio. Tomás has become an expert at pushing my buttons."

"You said something else was going on."

"Of course it's the Chinese."

"What influence could they possibly have here?"

She rubbed her thumb and fingers together.

"Truly?"

"Truly."

"But why?"

"That's above my paygrade. You might speak to Jim Johnson, our political guy. There might have been something in the cables that didn't come to me. Well. You must have had some excitement with that hurricane. Sorry you lost a crewman."

"Do you know how the P.R.C. reacted to the rescue?"

"Jim Johnson."

"So what do we do now, Emily?"

"Unfortunately, we wait. Tomás will punish me by doing nothing today, and then it's the weekend. I don't see you getting through until Monday at the earliest."

"How times have changed," he said.

"Enjoy the respite," she said. "There are some decent places to eat here. But keep your people under control, won't you? A barroom fight would ruin everything."

Then she left.

"A man, a plan, a canal: Panama," said Lee with a boy's conceit in knowing something.

The Respite

The ship was washing the salt away. Fore and aft, sailors were playing hoses on the superstructure, and streams of water mixed with gray flakes of salt were gushing overboard through the scuppers. Wherever he tried to use his cell phone he had trouble hearing over the work, like rain on metal. He gave it up and stayed out of the way until only dripping could be heard, and then he went to the bridge to get the best reception, encouraged by the sun on the gleaming windows.

"It's the hero of the hour," Slate Greene exclaimed. "How nice of you to notice us little people."

"Are we at war?"

"Not yet. But just you wait."

"The half-life of charitable feelings is three days."

"Not even that long. *One day* after politely thanking the U.S. for rescuing part of the merchant crew, the Chinese government suggested that we had deliberately left the rest to their fate. Yesterday they repeated their threat of the blockade. Don't ask me for details over a cell phone connection, but we have given certain orders."

"I don't understand what they gain by this."

"They gain time. As Sun Tzu must have written somewhere, delay an evil thing as long as possible. Or was it Confucius? Anyway, they aren't ready to fight, and their upbringing is cautious: they'll wait. Meanwhile, if their adversary stumbles, so much the better. Speaking of which, are you through?"

"We're stuck in Colon. Maybe Monday."

"Or maybe, depending on the market for graft, you'll travel the scenic route, via Cape Horn."

"That suggestion has been made here."

"If you were the Chinese, how much would you pay to delay an evil thing?"

"That's my problem. I can't imagine being Chinese."

"I can see that. How's your wife?"

"I'm going to try her next."

This was received with a low chuckle. "If she answers. Didn't a hurricane just hit Grand Cayman?"

"It was going to, but it turned."

"Near enough. Don't you think she's been expecting, these several days, a call from you?"

"Why," he said, "have *you* spoken to her?"

"Not since you chided me for it. But still."

"She's probably been having the time of her life. If there had been a real threat, she and the goof would have evacuated."

"Actually, when it looked like Lennon was going to hit, the Caymans evacuated all non-essentials."

"Oh. Well, then maybe she's home now."

"Maybe so. When you get to Pearl, give Robin McGill my love."

"What do you think she's planning for us?"

"Open line," Slate replied and rang off.

To his surprise Mad picked up on the first ring. "Where are you?" she said.

"Done with the first leg."

Before he could ask where she was, she said, "Nice PR about the rescue. It was all over the news. The captain who brought the survivors into Gitmo was impressive."

"Yes, he's quite telegenic, although actually he didn't have much to do with saving their lives. But he's also good at taking the credit."

"You've commanded his kind before."

"I have. A sad thing, though: we lost the Coast Guard swimmer."

"I saw that. It is sad."

"I never lost anyone before."

"It couldn't have been your fault."

"But it was my responsibility."

[106]

"I never understood that logic. Not in all those years."

But she had once embraced it, the illogical irrefutable logic that made you responsible for *everything* under your command, waking or sleeping. And by extension, for everything in your life.

"Were you hit?" he asked.

"No, we missed it. We had pulled out a couple of days earlier, first to Miami so Dustin could get some things straight with his editor, and then to the British Virgins."

"You're there now?"

"Yes."

"Which one?"

"Well, the main island is Tortola. We have a cabin on another island."

Apparently she wasn't going to be more specific. Perhaps she was worried that he would come to their island and surprise them *en flagrante.*

"Still flying drones?"

"Depending. Are you far enough along to say when you're coming home?"

"I'll have to send it to you more securely. We were late arriving here, and there are some uncertainties about the future."

"Well, let me know. It's pretty hot down here, so I'm not sure about us either. This time of year all the beautiful people go to Nova Scotia to see the total eclipse of the sun."

When he didn't respond to her opening with something like *They're so vain, aren't they, aren't they?* she added, "You know, Bradford, I don't worry about you. I wasn't thrilled that you took it, but you can do that job with your eyes closed."

"And Ginger Rogers danced all the same steps, only backwards and in high heels."

ᏒᏒ

As he and Captain Lee looked on, a railroad mule pulled an enormous grain carrier through Gatun Locks. Lee shook his head in wonder at the existence of such a thing.

"Impressive," he agreed, moved by pride in this largely American achievement despite the bigotry, cruelty, and greed that had driven it. "At the time this was the largest concrete structure in the world—beaten only by the locks at the Pacific end. Feeling hungry?"

Taking advantage of the respite, he had invited each captain to dine alone with him. In any military service such an invitation, coming from a superior officer, must essentially be a command performance. Zhang (H) had accepted for tomorrow, when they were to meet anyway. Zhang (L), however, had declined for Sunday, citing a prior commitment.

Emily Villaseñor had recommended a Middle Eastern restaurant, a cuisine that Lee had never tried before. So he ordered for both of them a sampling of dishes, breads, and desserts, which, along with the local beer, seemed to set the right tone.

"This feels normal," Lee said.

"By the time you get home, being at sea will feel normal. You'll be telling your family what a blue-water sailor you are."

"That's the question, isn't it. That's what you want to know about me. Brown-water sailor that I am."

His face was serious, expectant, sad.

"I have no doubts on that score, Kuan-lin. I wonder about myself sometimes. It's a challenge to find the right relationship with a flag captain, let alone to get past the cultural barriers. What are your impressions so far? Have I given you too much direction?"

"Maybe not enough direction. After all the training I still get lost. You know my ship better than I ever will."

"After two years and two long deployments. And many years of sailing in other ships of the class."

"And you know how to handle her."

"So do you."

"And you don't freeze."

Here it was: the close call with the submarine pier, his hesitation when coming about in the storm. The healthy thing would be for Lee to forget it and move on, the way a good defensive back forgets a touchdown pass, but he himself still remembered—often involuntarily—all the mistakes he had ever made in a thirty-year career.

"I knew the commands to give," Lee said, "but the emergency was in charge, not me. *You* could do it, I could only watch. Even though I was responsible. You ask me my impressions, Commodore. My strongest impression is that I don't like responsibility. It's too heavy for me."

"It's something we all learn to accept. We work into it, just as Atlas takes the weight of the world. Very few are born to lead."

"I keep thinking I'm not capable. A voice keeps saying I will fail in this job and maybe get people hurt and damage this valuable ship that my country needs."

"More, gentlemen?" asked the waiter.

"Another pitcher of your excellent beer," he ordered. "We're going to be here a while longer."

In fact quite a while longer, through two more pitchers of beer. Lee was depressed. The commodore had dealt with this before in his captains. One man named Bishop had been so frustrated by his inability to sustain perfection—his own idea of himself—that on the eve of a deployment he threatened suicide. What all of them needed, when they didn't need a kick in the pants, was to be heard and encouraged from a place of greater experience.

He gave that to Lee now. Lee should be realistic. All this would come. He was still reaching his full potential as a commanding officer. Constantly improving—it was obvious. If he was worried about taking charge, just wait until his people let him down. When he was really angry he wouldn't think twice about asserting himself.

It was all true. It was his experience. Nothing he said, however, erased Lee's doubts.

"May I confide in you?" he asked Mrs. Tsai after they had returned to the ship. It was late, but she was waiting in the cabin. She looked much happier to be standing on a stable deck.

"Of course."

"Am I missing something in the difference between our cultures? Does Captain Lee need a style of leadership that I haven't given him?"

Her smile encouraged him from her own experience. "In Taiwan his superiors would only want to know which party he supports," she replied.

When a member of the U.S. Armed Forces dies, an investigation must be held to determine whether that death occurred in the line of duty and whether it resulted from the member's misconduct (in which case, by a logic charming in its innocence, it couldn't be in the line of duty). The commodore assumed that the Coast Guard had the same policy. It would be appropriate, then, for him to investigate the death of the rescue swimmer.

The problem was that the death had occurred during the operations of three ships belonging to a foreign power, among which he was the only U.S. officer and technically in a consultative role. The navy of Taiwan might handle the death of a service member differently, and even if its rules called for an investigation, those with knowledge of the facts might not wish to confide in him. To carry out his responsibilities in this matter, then, he must draw upon his unofficial standing with the transit unit.

As he went to work, he was pleased to learn that such a standing existed; that the parties concerned were happy to help with what was, after all, when a life had been lost, a sensible, human requirement.

Though not everyone saw the event as he did.

On Saturday morning he reviewed the weather, the navigation, and the relevant logs and reports. Onboard *Luchiang* he took statements from Lee, Lieutenant Wú,

Kate Harcourt, and others. He sent a message to the commanding officer of the air station, who, from his own investigation, provided details about the helo and its crew and requested in turn the commodore's report from the ships' perspective.

That afternoon he went onboard *Hsinchu.*

He and Zhang (H) met in the inport cabin, which looked much different than *Luchiang's.* Taped to the bulkheads were photos of weapons systems, computer printouts of numbers and capabilities, and navigational charts of every relevant waterway, harbor, and approach. Here in effect was a war room, typical of an admiral's flagship. Some of this information was certainly classified, but (H) seemed pleased to take him around and show him everything and see his reaction.

When the commodore asked about his logistics needs, he recited them off the top of his head, fuel being foremost. "I could also use a few more missiles and a helo," he said with his grave smile.

Their rapport was advancing nicely. As with the labial speech of a young child, he was beginning to understand the captain's English.

But when he brought up the subject of the investigation, (H) frowned—a look of intimidating power from under that dominant forehead, that seat of judgment.

"I will certainly give you a statement, sir, and my people will comply with any request you wish to make. But I can save you time. Of course Petty Officer Davis died in the line of duty and not through his own misconduct. I killed him."

"But of course you *didn't* kill him."

"I killed him as surely as if I had used my own hands. I broke his neck." He gestured at this.

"I have to disagree. He died because the sea threw his body against the boat boom. It was nothing *you* did. Your shiphandling was brilliant. I've never seen such skill."

"A rising tide lifts all boats. The sea rose, but the ship was rising too. What killed him was that my people

pulled the line too fast. *My* people. *My* training. *My* supervision. I am responsible. Your report must blame me,
or it dishonors me. I have already written fleet command
to request appropriate punishment."

"Even the Coast Guard thinks it was an accident."

"They weren't there."

"His death was inevitable from the moment he jumped
into those waves. The act was astonishingly brave but
doomed and therefore mistaken. Your ingenious attempt
to recover him faced impossible odds."

"But I *wanted* it to work, Commodore. For me, not for
him. To show what a clever seaman I am, superior to
Zhang Yu-hsuan. Davis would have had a better chance—
in fact, a good chance—if I had just launched a lifeboat
for him to crawl into until the seas went down. My ego
killed him."

"No, Zhang. Not guilty."

Zhang composed himself. The emotion—did he really
feel dishonor, a loss of face?—had run through him like a
boxer's anger, cut off by the bell. "Very well. What other
topics do you have for me?"

"I was hoping to take you to dinner."

Zhang countered with an invitation to dine in *Hsinchu,* in this "map room," as he called it, where they could
talk about the strategic situation; a special interest, he
surmised, to both of them. Here at least was a handhold,
however tenuous: the commodore grabbed it.

A few minutes later a chief and two sailors entered the
cabin. Tonight's dinner from the mess decks, *chu dofu,* or
stinky tofu, with three types of wine, was served them on
linen by candlelight. The dish did stink; he didn't like to
think of its taste. But he had a duty to the food as well as
the mission and, truth be told, a desire to be admired by
this admirable man. Actually it was very good, and the
dinner passed off well. The chief and his people were
pleased. The scuttlebutt on the ship would approve of him,
and he had renewed hopes with her captain.

In the kindly shadows he got him to talk about himself.

[112]

The Respite

Zhang had a military background, army not navy. His great-grandfather had fought under Chiang Kai-shek and died in the early years of the civil war. His grandfather had escaped to Taiwan with Chiang and two million refugees, mostly from the shattered K.M.T. army, which nevertheless had organization and cruelty enough to subjugate the island. Zhang's father was a general under Chiang's son, serving in the Military Intelligence Bureau, eventually becoming its director. During these years the K.M.T. imprisoned or executed anyone denounced as Communist, including members of inchoate political parties as well as personal enemies.

"Stalin in the Terror, Mao in the Great Leap Forward," Zhang said. "We were no different. Absolute power corrupts absolutely. More than twenty thousand of our fellow citizens were slaughtered *in one week* in 1947. My grandfather never spoke of the lives on his conscience, but I felt them even so many years later, to my shame."

He was expected to follow the family tradition. Growing up, he lived by the regimen of bugles and drums. Of course he would enter the Military Academy. He knew it wasn't for him. When he resisted, his father threatened to cut him off from every blessing of the family, including the worship of ancestors. But that was his father. His mother, tough as nails, army all her married life, brokered a compromise: he attended the Naval School.

"I found I had a gift for strategy and tactics. And a vanity that I was a sailor. I sailed every class of boat at school. I won races in them. I made perfect sightings of the celestial bodies and did the reductions in my head."

"I was the same way, Chia-hao. I went to a civilian college instead of the naval academy, but I had that same love of the sea. That vanity, you call it. Though I think once again you're being too hard on yourself."

Zhang bowed: they would not recur to the swimmer's death. "Why don't we talk about the problem of invasion? I understand you believe it is like 1940."

"1940 and 1944. The English Channel is impassable unless you have command of the sea, which of course means command of the air too. I think the Taiwan Strait poses the same challenge, only wider."

"But the target is softer."

"Softer?"

"Will Taiwan fight? You wonder that yourself. Something has been lacking from our training, from our drills: the killer instinct, you might say. I think it's something else, perhaps temporary and more manageable."

"I'd like to hear it."

Zhang rose and went to a map of the island, marked with military positions. "This is our navy. Small ships here, here, and here. A few World War II amphibious ships, which we hang on to as a deterrent, a reminder to the P.R.C. that we have a stinger. The four *Kee Lung* destroyers, our main line of battle. But who are we fooling? We have no main line of battle, only annoyances to an invasion and short-lived ones at that. Those ships cannot survive a full-scale attack by China. We would have to hide them and sneak them out, like your PT boats in the Solomons. As the inferior navy, we would be better with submarines.

"Now imagine the added power of these three Aegis destroyers. Here is a real line of battle—not enough but capable. These ships have the defenses to survive, at least much longer than the *Kee Lungs,* and the offensive weapons to poke holes in a lot of Chinese troop ships. So China, fearing them, makes dire threats about the sale. If we'll buy three, why not thirty? But then China would need to build more aircraft carriers, and that's terribly expensive.

"That, I think, was your government's calculation when you offered them to us, much to our surprise. It goes back to Reagan: build Star Wars and the Soviets will quit.

"But will China quit? They can spend a lot more money than the Soviets. Commodore, you are troubled by our lack of enthusiasm. You aren't wrong, but you mistake the cause. Many in our country view this sale as a needless provocation by Taiwan and the U.S. They don't see, as I do, that we are unprepared. They want to believe that the president of China is a decent, peace-loving man. They go through the motions here because their hearts aren't in it; on the contrary. Put your Vietnam war protesters in Taiwan uniform: that's this squadron."

"Was that a protest, then, Zhang? Abandoning their nighttime patrol sectors and slowing down the formation every morning to fish?"

"No, that was the decision of the PWOs."

"The...?"

"The political warfare officers. Each ship has two or three, Commodore. They are responsible for morale. A holdover from the K.M.T.—also from China and Russia. They share authority with the captain: he fights, they motivate. The PWOs decided that it would be good for morale to allow fishing every morning and not to challenge the watchstanders with difficult station-keeping at night. That's what we get when civilians in uniform make decisions about ships."

One Leader Calls on Another

On Monday morning, having heard only silence, he telephoned the U.S. Embassy and spoke to Emily Villaseñor. She had no news for him, and more than this, she seemed irritated by his line of questioning, especially about the possibility that the Chinese had bribed the Panamanians to delay the transit, an idea she herself had introduced. Patience, she counselled; we're working on it.

"We're working on it." In his experience that had always meant *If you ever get this, it will be blind luck, later than you want, and no thanks to our efforts.* When he was a boy, the Tribune Company had bought the Chicago Cubs with the promise of making them World Series contenders. "We're working on it" had been their slogan through years of futility.

He forced himself to be patient during that long day, chained to that harbor floor only fifty-one miles from freedom. As countless merchant ships proceeded into the locks, the destroyers carried on a leisurely routine. Mrs. Tsai used the opportunity to dust the heroic sea prints on the bulkhead and vacuum the furniture.

He turned toward her from his desk, and she, sensing the gesture, shut off the machine.

"What are you doing tomorrow?" he asked.

"Nothing special. What should I do?"

"Come with me. I'm going to see the president."

"Such an important man. Yes, of course." She smiled, thought, smiled again. She had a charming smile, outwardly respectful, inwardly amused. "But why me, sir?"

"There's something rotten in Denmark."

"Yes, certainly. But we're in Panama."

"I'm going to see the president to straighten it out. These ships will help deter a bully. He'll understand—Panama knows about bullies. You're the living reality."

"O such pressure! You should pick someone else."

But of course she wanted to go. What a treat for her, somewhere new to visit, perhaps they could shop, she had seen pictures of the president, such a handsome man and about her age too. She made him feel that his perfor- mance of a duty was also an excuse to be kind.

Keeping to the duty, he said that he would wear his dress uniform with ribbons and without sword and was there something in her locker that might be appropriate?

"I will see, there must be something," she replied.

The next morning a ship's boat took them to a landing by the railway station. The respectful faces of the crew hid any thoughts about their countrywoman and the American commodore traveling together. In a louder voice than usual he talked about the call on the president, and she listened as if he were instructing her.

The train was part of the local color, red and yellow, sleek and cheerful, meant to go both ways, like a palin- drome. One of the cars was reserved for employees, but when the commodore in his whites and Mrs. Tsai in a blue business suit walked down the platform, an execu- tive insisted that they join him, and during the trip he entertained them with stories about the canal and the railroad, which actually predated the canal.

"There are miles of track under that water," he said as they crossed Gatun Lake on a long verdant causeway. "Millions of dollars in abandoned digging equipment."

"Not saved?" she asked in the role of the ingenue.

"Colonel Goethals wouldn't wait. Or maybe the world wouldn't wait. The track was forever shifted to dump the dirt. Guess how much for the project?"

"A million cubic yards," she said.

The executive shook his head with a broad smile.

"Ten million cubic yards," Hilty said.

The executive laughed. Both his listeners were playing up to him. "Forty-seven million cubic yards," he said with great satisfaction. "Thirty million from the French—let us not forget their contribution—and seventeen million from the *Nortes.* This railroad had to dump it all, in the rain forest, in the ocean, in backwaters, wherever space could be found. Many machines were invented. Sadly, many lives were lost."

Besides showing them the marvelous canal—"eighty-five feet above sea level!"—the executive pointed out sights in the rain forest, which pressed close upon them. If they were quick to follow his arm—Mrs. Tsai was quicker than he—they saw monkeys, opossums, tapirs, twice an armadillo, once the brilliant smear of a parrot, and the most dramatic sight of all, a family of madder-brown alligators, long and short, sliding down a riverbank.

The pretty train clicked amiably over the rails. The trip lasted an hour. Through the rain forest and past Lake Miraflores, they approached a modern skyline rising from the wilderness. At Corozal, the passenger station, they left the executive with their thanks and took a taxi to the Herons' Palace, the White House of Panama, one of the oldest houses in Old Town.

"So pretty," she said. "Such history." Indeed it looked like some of the patrician houses, with their welcoming personalities, that he had seen in Seville. Though called a palace, it wasn't meant to overawe. How could such a place fail to admit them to the president's office?

"Do you have an appointment?" the secretary asked.

"No, ma'am. I'm sorry but there wasn't time. I am here to help resolve a problem between our two countries and yours." Representing hers, his companion supported him with a wholesome nod.

"Will President Varela or his staff have heard from the American embassy about this?"

"I would hope so. Perhaps from Jim Johnson. There appears to be an unfortunate impediment to the passage of the canal by three ships of Taiwan under my command. I am here on my own initiative but in accord with our embassy's position. I need only fifteen minutes with him. Perhaps you could send in my card?"

[119]

This she was happy to do, even after he borrowed her pen and lined out *Teacher of American History* from his only business card and wrote in *Captain, U.S Navy, Commander Taiwan Transit Unit.*

They had to wait half an hour, during which the smile never left Mrs. Tsai's face, which asserted that even to wait in such an important office was a privilege, delightful.

The secretary's phone buzzed. She listened, looked at her computer, and replied, *"Ciertamente. Con gusto."*

"Thank you for waiting," she said to them across the reception area. "The president apologizes for the delay, he is grateful for the opportunity to meet Captain Hilty and the lady, and if it is entirely convenient to you, he suggests a meeting at two-thirty."

"Perfect," he said, though already he could feel his indignation ebbing, the emotion he had counted upon for eloquence. But a cooler approach might be a good thing. They went down to the street. "What would you like to do for three hours?" he asked her.

"Shop. Eat. Talk. Not nearly enough time."

They started with shop. Here was a side of her he hadn't seen before: the materialist. She took pleasure from shopping as his mother had used to do in the heyday of department stores. She looked, she tried on, she lingered. She asked his opinion. She reveled in indecision. Always she enjoyed herself. Indeed, there was not nearly enough time, but she dropped a hint about returning after the office visit.

For his part he enjoyed the role, false though it was, of the grand señor in the easy chair, waiting for each appearance by the slender lady in the beautiful clothes.

They had lunch, tasty empanadas from a street vendor, and talked about their families. Her parents, like his, were gone. She had a sister in Taipei. Her son, Chowa, had been a late-bloomer, just like his Adam. After trying several fields and enjoying life between them, he was now a barista in a superior coffee house in Tainan City—her source for the transit. But making delicious coffee beautifully decorated with crema a hundred times a day hardly built a future.

"I tell him money, yes, but self-respect is the important thing."

"*Ciertamente.*"

"What is your wife like?"

She asked this in a tone of polite interest, as if his marriage must be as blameless and happy as hers, so briefly, had been. He was tempted to tell the truth, that his wife and he had grown apart after thirty-six years; that he bored her and she disregarded him; that she had left their home to gad about the tropics with a younger man; and that he feared a sordid ending like so many other service marriages.

But he wasn't ready with her to confess these things. What he wanted in sober daylight was just this tone of spontaneous friendship, if mysterious in motive then ultimately innocent, without entanglement.

"It's two, we should go," she said. "You will succeed, I think. Lion that you are."

Through the beguilingly gentle air, they returned to the palace, where the other lions had been brought up in the realpolitik of the Serengeti.

The doors to the great office opened and President Varela himself, handsome as advertised, permanently bronzed and coiffed with postmaturely jet black hair, came out to greet them.

"So pleased to meet you, Commodore. Mrs. Tsai, charming, charming. Please, won't you follow me? We'll sit here and be comfortable. Will you have a cold drink? Coffee? I understand you visit me today from Colon—on the train! Beautiful, no? How may I help you?"

Choosing his words carefully, which required longer periods than usual, of which he was increasingly self-conscious as he brought out clause after clause, he replied that the ships under his command had been waiting to transit since Friday, about which it now seemed that some other impediment had arisen.

"I understand the scheduling problem, Mr. President. We were supposed to have arrived last Wednesday. As you may have heard, we were held up by the hurricane."

The president scoffed. "As the *world* heard, Commodore. Such a feat of, of—what would you call it?"

"Luck, sir."

"Seamanship, sir. I was thrilled to follow your adventure, and I assure you that we have moved heaven and earth to arrange for your passage."

His listeners waited.

"As it so happens, I have learned just this hour from the administrator of the Canal Authority that every impediment, as you call it, has now been removed, and barring only the difficulty of returning you and the charming señora to Colon in time to pull up the anchor, the ships of Taiwan will enter the Gatun Locks at eight p.m. tonight."

"Well, that's marvelous," he said, reeling a little as if he had put his shoulder to a door just as it opened. "On behalf of two governments, sir, I thank you."

"Yes, of course, it's my pleasure. Now, while I would like nothing more than to hear of your exploits, I do fear we are short of time. I'm informed that if you miss the window tonight, there must again be a delay due to scheduling conflicts. Therefore, I have taken the liberty of calling for my car, which will make the trip across the Isthmus expeditiously as well as safely. Is there anything else I can do for you, Commodore? Señora?"

Just one thing, he was tempted to ask: *Get me out of trouble with my embassy.* But the idea of trouble, if there should be any, felt good now. He was a high serving officer in the U.S. Navy, appointed by the president. The American virtue of taking initiative would protect him.

Getting into the car their mood was lighthearted. Each of them offered the president's seat to the other. He insisted. In acquiescing she did the gracious thing, as she always would, and then again his leonine powers today were not to be denied.

While still in Old Town she touched him on the arm to have the car stopped. He was slow to understand—something she wanted in a store? The tugging turned into a yank with a muttered curse. She opened the door while the car was still rolling and leapt out, landing lightly on the sidewalk, and ran like an athlete despite the encumbrance of her business suit.

Across a plaza, under the shining black statue of a Panamanian hero on a horse, a young couple was locked in an embrace. *Swapping spit,* Adam would have said. *Speaking in tongues,* Sarah would have countered. Mrs. Tsai shouted a peremptory word. At once the young man leapt to attention. It was Lieutenant Wú from the flagship, looking ridiculous braced up in a flowered guayabera shirt. With a pointed finger she scolded him—it was certainly a scolding, witnessed by passersby. Meanwhile his girlfriend waited. When she looked at the car, he knew her. It was Kate Harcourt, his air control expert, wife and mother back home.

The Grand Order of the Ditch

By law all ships transiting the Panama Canal, including ships of war, are under the command of the local pilot. Therefore the captains of the Taiwan destroyers, though they would remain on the bridge, had nothing much to do, and the commodore, a two-time member of the Grand Order of the Ditch, had nothing to do at all. A chair was brought to him on the fo'c'sle so that he might enjoy the transit as a passenger.

This would be his last time through the canal, just as this active duty was for the last time. Whatever it held. Possibly a war with China, at his age. But more likely a peaceful arrival in home port, after which both the U.S. and Taiwan governments would say *Thank you for your service: now go home.*

The darkness abroad was absolute, but the lock was so brilliantly lighted that it seemed like a world unto itself. The water rose and the ship rose with it to the level of Gatun Lake, which was next. He had to keep moving out of the way of the linehandlers as they surged the mooring lines. The gate swung open; the ship glided ahead as if leaving the known world behind them. The dark lake was surrounded by the jungle, which breathed upon the humid air a rich odor of decay. Aloft was a black dome full of stars. Close to his seat a fish broke the black water.

At the Trinidad Turn he could feel the rudders bite. The new course, though an abstraction, was as definite as the highway over which his assistant and he had returned to Colon this afternoon in their awkward silence. Behind the bridge windows a controlling intelligence was at work. It had nothing to do with him. He went below.

It had not been a complete surprise that Mrs. Tsai lived in Officers' Country. He knocked. Someone stirred within, and the door was opened. It was she, wearing a khaki uniform in the rank of a lieutenant commander.

She invited him in and turned the two desk chairs to face each other. They sat, knees almost touching. Her small home was spotless. You could bounce a quarter off her bed. On both desks were piles of books and papers, whose contents he would rather not know. Her locker door was open; inside hung khaki and white uniforms and civilian clothing, including today's blue suit.

The light overhead was the light of the third-degree.

"Not staying up to watch?" she asked hopefully.

He shook his head, pretending to fuss with the chair.

"Of course we saw it all today, so close. So beautiful."

"We did."

"I apologize if my actions embarrassed you."

He looked at her, trying to read her eyes, trying to find the right words, which would set the right tone, which would dictate the right decision. Those eyes had simulated much and concealed much else. He wasn't sure he saw her even now.

"I suppose there's no point in pretending that you're not a political warfare officer."

"I am, yes. My specialty."

"The senior PWO on the ship."

She nodded.

"In the squadron."

"Yes."

"It was you who countermanded my night orders."

"A mistake, regrettable but sincere. The people are afraid—I did tell you that. The officers have always sailed in columns. They promised to learn your methods, only not as fast as you wanted. The fishing is a Taiwan custom, good for morale."

"So what was the mistake?"

"Not telling you, of course. Not trusting you."

"And spying on me?"

"I am sorry to spy on you. Sorry from the beginning. Someone above me suggested it. I accepted—you are important to our success—and I foresaw no harm. I didn't know that you cared only about our progress and that there would be such nice chemistry between us."

"You've been reporting on me all this while."

Her voice was near to breaking. "I have served you with a good spirit. I have tried to make you comfortable. Often I refused to tell. More and more. And never personal things that you confided in me. They know I have this impediment now."

This impediment.

He was aware of hugging himself, a defensive reaction that his absent wife had often used to interpret his feelings. Well, what *were* his feelings and what was the right thing to do? A coward would let this go, pretend that nothing had happened. An opportunist would get an apology from that "someone above me" and written authority as officer in command. The impactful act, which appealed to him for its dramatic value, would be to take his consultants and go home. At the very least he must come to an understanding with her. From now on their relationship must be strictly professional. She should call him *sir*.

Beyond doubt she was sorry. Her lovely eyes, brown and fluid, pleaded with him to let it go, even though the exposure of the deceit would be known throughout the ship with a loss of face for her and others.

"I'm uneasy that you should still wait on me."

"It is something I wish to do. No work is too humble if it serves the nation."

"Then at least delegate the really humble parts."

"I will."

"I'm not unselfish enough to give up your cooking."

She smiled.

"But no more intelligence gathering." Which hardly mattered since he would be careful around her.

"No sir."

"Then give me the phone number of this stateroom in case I need to contact you here."

"Day or night," she agreed.

Preparing for the Worst Case

Saving Every Barrel

Leaving Balboa at night, they sailed through the Gulf of Panama with its twinkling of fishing trawlers, then around the Azuero Peninsula, then west by north toward Pearl Harbor. This was a long leg, almost five thousand miles, more than twelve days, and they must be sparing of fuel.

He ordered seventeen knots at one engine, trail shaft with no discretion left to the captains except for safety. He put them into sectors and advised them, with regret, that there would be no further divtacs—they simply hadn't the fuel for it. Each ship would report to him in writing her fuel status twice a day. If any ship burned just one barrel more than the minimum, she would enter Pearl Harbor under tow. Nor would the transit unit stop to fish. Good morale came from being ready to fight and winning the fight and being ready to fight again. That's what they would learn on this leg of the voyage.

The next morning, somewhat to his surprise, the ships were in their assigned sectors at seventeen knots. Neither he nor Commander Tsai mentioned it.

Among his resolutions following the disclosure of the spying, he resolved to stop assuming that *Luchiang* and the other ships were the same as he remembered from Plumpy. To know who they really were he needed to get off the bridge and walk about more. He began in the engineering spaces, the foundation of battle readiness.

In the forward engine room, which was mostly silent with the starboard shaft trailing, Michael Blaylock was talking the watch through a casualty control procedure.

"What happens when you emergency stop the engine?" Blaylock asked, speaking slowly.

One young man with too much hair for his ballcap shouted, "Fuel valve shuts. Igniters off. Brakes on." He clapped his hands to show how fast.

"Very good. And then?"

No one was sure of the answer, and all were reluctant to guess. Blaylock took another tack. "What was the temperature in the engine when you stopped it?"

Several shouted the number.

"That's a lot of heat, isn't it," Blaylock said. "What does that do to the turbine rotor?"

"Turbine rotor bow if not rotated."

"Exactly. Do you have to memorize this?"

"Yes. Always memorize."

"No, *not* always. You memorize your *immediate* actions to put the plant in a stable condition. Then you always, always, always break out the casualty control manual, check that your immediate actions were correct, and follow the written procedures for then on. What are your immediate actions for a high vibrations alarm?"

He was a natural teacher. Like his former captain he had much to tell and he wanted to tell it.

"How are they doing?" he asked after Blaylock had dismissed them.

"Which version would you like, Commodore?"

"You know me better than that, Senior Chief."

"They have the knowledge, with a few holes. If they could really put the plant through its paces, they would fill those holes and learn better hands-on skills."

"But we would run out of fuel in mid-ocean. Drift for days. Drink our urine. Eat the smallest sailors."

If Blaylock had a sense of humor, it never came to work with him. "I had an idea last night when I read your orders. Why don't you let one ship burn as much fuel as she wants, bringing the other crews over to train on her equipment, then go ahead and tow her—tow every night. The deck hands will get experience towing, and you never know with this China thing when they might need it."

"The same ship or rotate them?"

"Doesn't matter, really. Just make it realistic."

"That's creative," he said. As he had always admired in Blaylock (whatever Blaylock thought of him), he approached each problem on its merits. "I like it. It will be good for the skippers to try something new."

"It's all new to them, Commodore."

"It is. But Lee understands what these ships need as well as you and I do. I'll start with him."

Start with him right away, for even if (L) opposed the idea, as was likely, if the other two outvoted him the training could start this afternoon. By then his own team would be ready. He smiled to imagine the surprises they might pull.

He was told that Lee was in his sea cabin, just behind the bridge. Before knocking on the door he reflected that he had never been in this cabin since the day he had left Plumpy, after two years of mostly living here.

The voice barked at him in Chinese. He opened the door to a blare of sound and light. Lee was reclining on the daybed enjoying a Chinese sitcom on one of two bulkhead monitors. The other showed tactical feeds from CIC, which rotated every minute. Also on the bulkhead was a radio speaker patched to the coordination channel between the three ships, over which a conference was being held in a mixture of Chinese and English, one of the speakers being Kate Harcourt, who had shifted to *Chiai* in Balboa.

Lee greeted him coolly, remained at leisure, and left the sitcom on. It was Thursday, a working day.

Making himself heard above the din, which felt like speaking through a hose, he explained Michael Blaylock's idea for training harder while saving fuel. To sweeten the deal, he suggested that *Luchiang* could go first as the training ship.

Lee's eyes kept drifting to the sitcom, whose canned laughter seemed to govern the expressions of his face.

"Being towed, the training ship might actually save fuel. When I had Plumpy I used to figure—"

"Yes, yes, I'll send a message about it."

"Send a message?"

"Yes, this will need approval by Tsoying."

Tsoying was the site of the naval headquarters.

"I don't understand."

"For so much towing. To use so much equipment."

"But isn't that decision within my authority as OTC? Perhaps we should consult the other captains about it."

Before Lee could respond, Kate Harcourt over the radio began a lecture about the rules of engagement, which might outweigh the natural desire to shoot first.

He raised his voice. "Could you turn all that off, please, so we might discuss this?"

In the relative silence Lee said, "OTC is tactical command. This is a strategic decision. My hands are tied."

"I don't see that. This is our responsibility, at the scene."

"You don't see it. You don't see it. Let me show you something you can see." Lee picked up a tablet, thumbed away the dross, and held it up.

"Of course I can't read that," he said quietly.

"Here, here: Mr. Correa, Taiwan's agent in Panama, rebukes us for arranging to transit the canal without consulting him. Your embassy amplifies the rebuke, up here, because they too were left out of the loop, despite sensitive negotiations going on with, quote, every expectation of success. Here, the top of the cable, is an apology from my government to both senders. And here next, this cable, is a personal rebuke from my admiral—to *me,* no one else, not you—for exceeding my authority. Exceeding my authority in a decision I didn't make! You have proposed an idea for training, Commodore. Very well: I will forward it to my superiors to be considered, although personally I don't like so much towing."

"Apparently I've offended you," he said. "I'm sorry."

"No sir, Commodore. I hold you personally in high regard. Your *actions* have offended me, embarrassing me in front of my crew, the junior captains, and my superiors."

"My actions—they were mine, not Commander Tsai's—resolved an impasse that was delaying the arrival of these ships in your country."

"Not according to Mr. Johnson."

"That's just petty hindsight. The embassy was getting nowhere. You heard Emily Villaseñor: China was paying bribes to keep us in Colon."

"A young woman of no experience and a bad temper. Hardly a proper diplomat."

"It was the right thing to do, Kuan-lin."

"I am Captain Lee."

"Yes, you are Captain Lee, who commands three of the most advanced warships in the world, and who is once again at sea, able to exercise his independent judgment."

"Never independent. Everyone works for someone."

"As you had led me to believe, you work for me."

"Apparently a mistake. I will review it."

He took a breath. "Captain, what is your mission?"

"I know my mission."

"Is it not to sail your ships to Taiwan in the highest degree of readiness to defend themselves? And to support your country's defense? You and I, over dinner last week, both agreed that the ships are not ready now, not even close. Therefore, in the limited time remaining, we need to train as realistically as possible. It's a vital matter. All my experience teaches me that as you train, so you fight. The more you sweat in peace, the less you bleed in war."

"Our disagreement will not be resolved by easy proverbs, Commodore. Your orders last night, which I approved, struck a balance between training, transit speed, and fuel economy. I see no reason to change them."

"But the most limited resource of all—and the most difficult to achieve—is training. Except for actually firing weapons, Senior Chief Blaylock's idea gives us the best chance to maximize realistic, robust, *live* training."

"So it's his idea not yours?"

"It's his idea, but I strongly endorse it. I have come to you from your forward engine room. Your outstanding, intelligent sailors are just walking through procedures that they will need to *sprint through,* possibly in chaotic conditions, to save their plant and provide you with the maneuvering ability to defend your ship. It's all theoretical for them. We need to make it real for every sailor in the squadron."

"But safety first. I told you the other night: I fear only to get someone hurt and damage this valuable ship."

Such was the result of his taking Lee out to dinner. In the light of day the sharer of secrets, regretting his candor, resents his confidant. And it may be—the evidence certainly suggested this—that Lee's temperament was that of the petty bureaucrat; that Jim Johnson's whining had resonated with him.

"I wish you'd approve this—you yourself," he said.

"I will forward it to headquarters," Lee repeated and unmuted the sitcom.

He needed to see Commander Tsai, but it was Thursday, the day when Taiwan's PWOs met to talk about—whatever it was. She and her two colleagues were in the wardroom. He thought about interrupting them but reminded himself of the bigger picture.

"Tsai Mei-ling, I need help," he said when she had come into the cabin. Her servant/replacement, Seaman Wang, was vacuuming the carpet, so they went onto the port quarterdeck to talk.

The ship was cutting through the waves—even at seventeen knots, the impression of speed was thrilling. The deep blue surface of the Pacific was roughed up by a north wind, and the ship raced past the whitened crests as if they had been painted on a field. Her motions, easy on the legs, yet made them feel like veteran sailors. *Hsinchu* was abaft the beam a few thousand yards away. Her own speed, the way she leaned into the seas with a tremendous curl about her cutwater, was thrilling too.

The wind gusted between the deck houses, and he and Commander Tsai, at the same time, pulled their red ball-caps down on their heads. They laughed at this, the common need. She waited to hear what he wanted.

He explained Blaylock's idea and described Lee's objections after the rebuke from Tsoying.

"I read that cable," she said. "It was no rebuke, not from our side: just asking how the squadron had managed it."

"Where is Third Fleet the world wonders," he said.

"I'm sorry."

"Captain Lee is *very* cautious."

"Yes, incorrectly so. The training needs to be much more challenging. This morning at the PWO meeting we spoke of how to convey such a message."

"I don't think we'll actually have to fight the Chinese."

"Yes, but if we do...! We can barely load our weapons, let alone fire them, let alone fire them fast and accurately when being fired upon ourselves."

She had come a long way from that officer who had let the sailors have their fishing.

"I tried to make the same points," he said. "Would you mind talking to him?"

"Better if I talk to all of them. As you have learned, I'm very important." She smiled. "But it may take time, so that no one loses face."

"Is that really such a concern?"

"Very much so. Later I will teach you all the ways of face and how they survive in our modern life. But now I will get to work."

She had something to do at least. For him it was a day of waiting. He waited through the morning, he waited over a congealed lunch from the mess decks that Wang

[137]

put on his table, and afterwards he waited lying in his bed with a tape of regrets running through his mind.

Late that afternoon she found him in the barbershop. "It's approved," she said after thumbing out the barber. "Too late for today, but starting tomorrow. We had a video conference, actually several conferences. Zhang Chia-hao convinced him."

"Zhang Heavy, I call him."

"Yes, very good. Heavy in a nice way. Zhang Yu-hsuan, of course, opposes everything that is not his idea."

"Zhang Lite."

"Zhang Lite and Captain Lee wanted to forbid you, but we did some smoky talk—is this right?"

"You made a decision in a smoke-filled back room."

"Yes, that's it. *Hsinchu* will be the first training ship, but all will participate. Captain Lee agreed."

"And Zhang Lite?"

"Will participate."

"I can't thank you enough, Mei-ling. This will make a tremendous difference."

"It was not spying, but I talked about you: right about the fishing, right about the hurricane, right to call on the president of Panama—and brave too, helping foreigners. I do trust you. This is not guilt—or fondness—talking. This is earned. You should know: among the captains you have one enemy, one who wishes he could be more like you, and one true brother."

"In my experience I've seen that success has many brothers. Or maybe it's parents. If I fail I'm an orphan."

She took a step back and studied his head.

"I would have done your hair, Bradford."

"You would. But now I know your secret identity."

What is War?

A crowd had gathered in the wardroom. The three captains were sitting at the foot of the table, by the projector, with their chairs facing the screen. Everyone else was sitting wherever they found room and standing otherwise.

An order was rasped as he entered, and all came to attention. *"Yuán di dàimìng,"* he said, as best he could, and they relaxed. "Such a turnout: is anyone on watch now?" They grinned, and a jokester called, "Only Mickey Mouse." There was a place for him just a few feet in front of the captains, two of whom were stony-faced.

"Thank you all for coming. And thank you to *Lu-chiang"*—he looked at Lee—"for welcoming our shipmates. I want to begin by saying something you should never say in a speech, in case your audience believes you: I don't have all the answers." Laughs and grins. "That's all right because you don't either." More of both. "I hope the topics I'm introducing will move you to ask the most important question of your lives, in or out of the service. The question is *Why?* Just that: *Why?"*

"Why are we here?" the jokester said.

"Good question, Lieutenant Cài, missiles officer in *Chiai,* soon to be transferred to the American base in Antarctica. Congratulations and enjoy the penguin soup." Ribald laughter. "Now, sir. I have singled you out to give us a light moment, but I hope you will never be afraid in the future to ask your seniors why."

"Only of you, Commodore."

"Fair enough. To get back to your question, you're here so I can tell you the stories of two American ships, destroyers that fought in World War II not far from Taiwan. The first story is about active courage, sacrificing yourself for a greater cause. The second story is about passive courage, the ability to take hard hits from the enemy and keep fighting."

He brought up the first slide. "This is USS *Norman Scott,* a Fletcher-class destroyer, named after an admiral killed on his bridge in the Naval Battle of Guadalcanal. Killed by shellfire—remember that. Japan's gunnery was extremely accurate, and the crew of *Norman Scott* was only too aware of it.

"The ship was assigned to support the invasion of Tinian in 1944. Why was Tinian important to us?"

After a moment, when they understood that he had asked a real question, a voice responded, "Atom bomb."

"Just right. We needed an airfield in the Marianas to bomb the Japanese homeland, including, finally, Hiroshima and Nagasaki. Now, you see from this picture that *Norman Scott* had five five-inch guns, none as capable as yours, but five of them. So along with other, mostly bigger ships, she used her five guns to bombard the enemy's positions that threatened the landing.

"On the morning of July twenty-fourth, a bright calm morning like this one, she was not far offshore when her captain, Seymour Owens, saw that the battleship *Colorado* had come under heavy fire and was taking multiple hits. In an instant he weighed the greater good and gave orders to shield *Colorado* from further damage. Think about that: he put his 'tin can,' as she was called, in the line of deadly artillery fire to protect the more valuable ship."

"Suicide," said a voice.

"Yes, or self-sacrifice. He knew it and his crew knew it. The act was intrepid. It's one thing to expose your own life to the enemy's fire. But what moral as well as physical courage to make that decision for the more than three hundred people you lead and love."

As he said this he looked at *Luchiang's* captain, whose stern expression was unchanged.

"At sea it takes time to go anywhere, doesn't it. There must have been a few minutes while *Norman Scott* moved into position, even at her best speed. Meanwhile, the shells would have been falling all around her. Shellfire! Deadly accurate! The very thing that had killed the ship's name-sake. What was the crew thinking? How did they stand the strain of it, even for those few minutes? It's a wonder to me."

He waited.

"What happened to them, sir?"

"Six rounds hit *Norman Scott* within a matter of seconds. Captain Owens was killed, along with twenty-two of his crew and fifty-seven wounded. The ship survived."

"And the *Colorado?*"

"Stayed in the fight. Helped the landing succeed."

He said, "This is the other destroyer, USS *Laffey,* of the Allen Sumner class. She had *six* five-inch guns, but that's not what made her so valuable. Look here: a bedspring air-search radar, the most advanced of its day. Who has the most advanced radar of this day? That's right, *you* do. *Luchiang* here, and also *Hsinchu* and *Chiai* where no one's on watch now.

"By April 1945 the offensive against Japan had progressed to her very shores. The allies decided to invade the homeland by a frontal assault. So, target: Okinawa.

"But Japan had developed the *kamikaze.* Thousands of aircraft—nearly everything that was left in the country—were committed, and pilots and pseudo-pilots were trained for a one-way trip. To protect the armada, *Laffey* and other tin cans were stationed as radar pickets between Okinawa and the threat.

"War is unpredictable: the landings themselves were unopposed. But Japan was just getting ready. The *kamikaze* struck, and the radar pickets received the first of the deadly attacks. On April fifteenth it was *Laffey's* turn.

"Follow me on the screen as I read the main events from the ship's log that day:

[141]

8:32. Two Val dive bombers shot down ahead.

8:35. Two Vals shot down astern.

8:36. Suisei dive bomber shot down to port during strafing run. Bomb from second Suisei bursts close aboard, causing multiple shrapnel wounds.

8:42. Val strikes main deck and starts fire.

8:45. Val strikes small-caliber gun tub on port side, killing three, destroying guns, and setting fire to ammo magazine.

8:46. Val on strafing run strikes after 5-inch gun mount, destroying gun, detonating powder magazine, and starting major fire below decks.

8:48. Val strikes already-burning after mount.

8:49. Bomb from Val detonates close aboard fantail, jamming rudder to port and killing several men.

8:50. Suisei strikes port side as bomb detonates.

8:51. Val strikes port side as bomb detonates.

8:55. Oscar fighter strikes mast. Pursuing friendly Corsair, unable to pull out, strikes mast and falls into water; pilot rescued.

8:58. Bomb from Suisei detonates close aboard transom, opening deck plates to sea.

8:59. Suisei shot down but bomb detonates in gun tub, killing crew.

"If you've been keeping count, by this time *Laffey* has been hit by seven kamikazes, one friendly fighter, and four bombs, and has been strafed at least twice. She has lost thirty-two killed and seventy-one wounded. Besides the large fire aft, she is listing heavily to port and turning in circles with a jammed rudder. Here's a photo of her in extremis.

"Note the caption: *The Ship That Would Not Die.* At the worst of it, one of her officers asked the captain,

Frederick Becton, if he intended to abandon her. He replied, 'Not as long as a single gun will fire—if there's a man left to fire it.'"

"Lieutenant Cào may ask—I hope by now all of you would too—why I chose these stories. Mostly it's to give you a sense of war at sea. War at sea is chaos because war is chaos. The display screens in our command and control centers make the tactical picture look so neat and clean, so well ordered. I assure you it isn't, it won't be. The enemy will surprise you. No matter how good your weapons are, some part of his attack will *always* get through. Your fabulous technology will fail in some way.

"Picture it. Your ship is struck. You are blown from your bed and you come to to find the compartment in flames, men and women screaming in agony, horrific injuries all around you, the decks slippery with blood, the sea rushing in...and even if you are not paralyzed by the shock you might well be overwhelmed by the thought *How can I ever deal with this?*"

He was careful not to look at Lee now.

"Or why, sir?" someone asked.

"I'll get to *why* in a moment," he replied. "The answer to *How can I deal with this?* is simple to state but hard to do: train for it. With superior training you can learn to cope with any situation, no matter how desperate or gruesome. You can learn to fight well. When you take a hit, you'll treat the wounded, control fires and flooding, restore electrical, propulsion, and steering. You, you yourself, may be the one to get the ship underway again. And as Captain Becton tells us, if you have a single gun still capable of firing, you will fight on.

"You ask me *why* make such an effort? I'll tell you, you wonderful sailors of Taiwan: besides the obvious thing, defending your homeland, it's because you have something to prove. To your fellow citizens, to your shipmates, but most of all to yourselves.

[143]

"I've heard that some of your senior officers—not these fine men who lead you but the higher-ups—some of them wonder if Taiwan has the will to fight.

Our people are too easy-going, they say. *After years of peace they are soft, they like their comfortable lives. They don't know the world. They think that China will not attack us, but if she does, would it be so bad? We have been their subjects before. And Japan's. We've had dictators. Would it be so bad to lose our independence?*

"That's what they worry about. Some of you have said the same thing: not that you're afraid but you worry about your shipmates. So you have that to prove. To each other. To yourselves. And I am certain that you *will* prove it with the right training. Now: any questions?"

One of the PWOs from *Hsinchu* raised his hand. "Besides training, proper orders must be given."

"You would think so. Myself, I've received too many stupid orders to believe it." This caused a stir: he was winning them. "But it doesn't matter, or at least it shouldn't matter. You may have heard this saying, Lieutenant:

It is better to beg forgiveness than to ask permission.

He drew it out for effect, with merely a glance at Lee. "Starting as a junior officer, I have lived by those words, and since I was never court-martialed and the Navy kept promoting me, I must have been forgiven. Forgiven for taking initiative if I made the right decision. And even when I didn't—forgiven for trying." Another glance.

"But, sir, higher authority may have information not possessed by those who engage the enemy."

He gave them his brightest smile, all around the room. "You're quite right: they may, they probably do. But from that distance they can't see the gritty details of the battle, in the same way that your computer screen, so neat and clean, can't see the mess underneath. The first way for leaders to empower subordinates in battle is to *share information with them ahead of time.* Ahead of time which, because war is uncertain, means *all the time.* And the second way is for every leader to make sure that his or her people keep asking that one most important question. And what is it?"

"Why," said a smattering.

"I can't hear you," he said, as men with bullhorns do.

"Why," they shouted.

"That's right: *Why!* Not just *what* to do but *why* we do it. The *what* can change, and if it does, we may not have the time or the means to consult with higher authority. If we know *why,* however, we can figure it out for ourselves. We can gain that crucial split-second that often spells the difference between victory and defeat. When we know *why—why* anything, friends—we won't be afraid to take an action for which we may have to beg forgiveness afterwards. So if ever you don't know why you've been ordered to do something, ask. Even if the answer is *Because I tell you to do it.* Ask why and take initiative. I assure you you'll be forgiven."

Everyone came to attention. In English Lee ordered them to remain in place for an address after the commodore had left them. He went into the passageway, wondering what the address was about, but Lee followed him.

"You want me to ask why, Commodore? I saw you look at me. Now I look at you. Why have you seriously damaged my authority and that of the captains Zhang and *all* the leaders in our ships? Why have you compromised our mission? Why have you given aid and comfort to the enemy? That was unforgiveable and I will not forgive you, sir."

"I think you should calm down, Lee."

"Captain Lee. I am your peer across nations, so you will speak to me with respect. A mutineer could not have done more damage than you did."

[145]

"Speaking from real-world experience, I say you're mistaken."

Lee jabbed his thumb in to the palm of his other hand. "So many things. You say our equipment won't work. You say question orders because orders are stupid. You say it is better to beg forgiveness than ask permission. You say there will be war!

"Do you not think all the sailors saw you looking at me? Do you not think they know that you arranged the canal transit and I was blamed for it? Do you not think they are afraid of war? What are you trying to do? Is this some last hurrah for you, old man? Is it you who will have to face the Chinese missiles, who will have to show the two types of courage in chaos?"

"Obviously, we cannot talk about this now."

"No, no more talk. I will go in there now and try to undo the damage without blaming you as you blamed me. We will continue to carry out your training program, which Zhang Chia-hao insists on. But perhaps you should shift your pennant now, Commodore, so you can bring your enlightenment to all ships equally. *Luchiang* has been enlightened enough, I assure you."

"If so, that will be my decision, Captain, not yours" was all he could think to reply.

He yanked his ballcap from the rack and hurled it across the cabin. He couldn't remember being so angry. Unfair, unreasonable, inaccurate, *wrong!* If nothing else Lee in "undoing the damage" would weaken his own authority. He was no seaman, he was no warrior, he was no leader. That's the thing that his sailors knew about him.

He would be God-damned if he would shift his pennant. Tsai Mei-ling would probably agree with him, but even if she didn't he had been directed to help these ships as he saw fit, and he would carry out that direction. If he embarked in *Hsinchu* it would be a pleasure, but then in fairness he would have to shift his pennant at some point to *Chiai* as well, where (L) would drive him to despair. No, Plumpy was his flagship, and here he would stay. To leave would be to admit the rift between captain and commodore. There might be a day or two of awkwardness, but Lee would get over it. The half-life of seawater, etcetera.

Someone tapped on the cabin door. He wrenched it open. It was Kate Harcourt.

"I'm sorry," she said, looking at his face. "It can wait."

"No, come in, Kate. Sit. The petty pace of international relations. Coffee?"

"No, thank you. And I'll stand if you don't mind. Sir, I feel bad that you had to see what happened in Panama City. Lieutenant Wú and me."

There was only one way to play this: "I'm sorry? What happened?"

"When Commander Tsai jumped out of the car."

"Yes, I wondered. The driver was telling me a story."

"You're kind to say that."

"I really don't know what you're talking about."

"Well, in case she told you, I just wanted to say that, for both personal and professional reasons, I have transferred to *Chiai* until we get to Pearl, and then probably *Hsinchu* for the final leg."

"No one needs to know the reasons, Kate."

"No sir. But I'd like to say—to you, since it's come up before—that I've thought of what my family means to me."

"You can't go wrong there."

"Thank you, sir. I guess that's all. Except, and not to brown-nose, I thought that was a really good presentation. And it moved them, even after whatever it was that Captain Lee said. With these battle exercises I'm going to light a fire under *Chiai*. You've made that a lot easier."

"Thank you, Kate."

He retrieved the ballcap and took a turn about the deck among the teeming officers waiting for their boats.

As You Train So You Fight

He stood on the bridge wing with her captain while *Chiai,* close and massive, glided by. *Luchiang* was lying to as a disabled ship would, subject to the elements. Her rescuer stopped engines to windward with a narrowing margin of water between them. If either ship fumbled the next exchange *Chiai* would have to back out against the seas, and only the angle of her approach, no more than a sliver, would prevent the rough embrace.

A burly sailor at her quarterdeck swung the bolo over his head and with a fluid snap of his spine released it in a high thrilling arc. It just reached *Luchiang's* fo'c'sle. Her people shrank from its whistling leaded end, but it fell across a lifeline and someone retrieved it. Hand over hand they hauled in the cord until it grew into the manila messenger, which led aft on the towing ship, stopped to the lifeline stanchions. As she came ahead again, a man walked her deck cutting the stops, and the messenger peeled away to stretch across the water.

The margin closed, and the envisioned margin was too close to call: on *Luchiang* Lee resorted to body English. On *Chiai* Zhang (L) watched his ship's stern, which told him all he needed to know. He looked relaxed to the point of apathy. Yet twice he glanced over to see who was watching him. The two bridge wings were as close as conversational groups across a room.

Chiai slid just clear of *Luchiang* and stopped on the same course, like one foot in front of the other. The two ships drifted across the surface gently rising and falling. This alongside approach was faster but riskier than crossing the T. If (L) had misjudged his last bell, it would have been nearly impossible to work the stern into place, and Lee would have had to drop the messenger so he could try again—a lubber's humiliation. But he was a drunkard for both attention and risks. The key to (L) might be to watch him perform.

By now both ships' towing hawsers were deployed with a wire pendant connecting them. Bill Houy, in a voice as loud as a heckler's at the ball park, reported that the lay-out looked good at each end.

Chiai inched ahead. As soon as the towline showed in the water she stopped again. Her momentum lifted the line clear, dripping throughout its length. When it settled, her screws took a tentative bite, then a bigger one; *Lu-chiang* began to move without feeling a pull; and in fifteen minutes the ships had worked up to seven knots, with *Hsinchu* screening them.

The sun was setting off the port bow. The tips of the waves were flecked with gold. The murmur of the swell sounded like sleep. He had an appointment, but there was one thing first.

Lee stood with both hands on the bulwark and his shoulders tensed to receive the commodore's feedback, while he pretended to study the waves.

"Very well done, Captain Lee. Especially for the first time. Your people did a nice job paying out the hawser. And now you can start saving fuel!"

"Easy at our end," he said to the ocean. "All we had to do was lie back and think of England."

They would not stop to fish, but now that they were being towed only a tyrant would forbid them. Among the fishers one of the leeward bitts was vacated so Tsai Mei-ling and he could sit together. In sailing ship days this would have been on the windward side, where the sailors would smell the officers but not vice versa.

Even as the sun set he could feel its warmth, and she stretched her legs to it, balancing the soles of her shoes on the deck combing. They were being pulled along with merely the tracings of a wake. In his time in the service he couldn't remember such an hour of idleness.

"For my education," she said. "Your comments?"

"It went very well. Both ships did well. Zhang Lite's approach was one for the ages."

"Never was a talented man so insecure."

"That's not a bad motive to accomplish great things. The captain of this ship, I will tell you, refuses to look at me. For *my* education, did I weaken his authority?"

She turned to him with a sympathetic smile in which a correction lay. "I said I would teach you about face."

"Please do."

"In America your reality is what you see and the judgments you form about it. In our culture we think more about what others see and how they judge *us:* our position and wealth in society, to be sure, but also that we demonstrate good qualities, like kindness, integrity, and honor. We call that face. There are several words in Chinese for it, so you know it's important to us.

"Captain Lee has earned a great deal of face. He has a high position, and his political ties are strong, but also he is honorable and kind, humble and sincere. When you criticize his leadership style, which it seemed to me you did in your lecture, Bradford, he feels it as anyone would, as a personal sting, but also as a judgment of how others see him.

"That's the thing to remember. The gain or loss or gift or revoking of face may be objective, so that anyone would agree. But it may also be subjective—the self, imagining that judgment of others.

"Lee Kuan-lin is the most sensitive of the captains. He feels everything, which would be okay if he didn't also care so much. He *wants* his ship to be ready. He *accepts* this is not true yet and that your criticism of him must be helpful. But he cannot bear it—both the actual words you speak and the words he imagines you imply; both the looks his sailors give him and the thoughts he imagines they must be thinking.

"So: did you weaken his authority? In observing the crew and those of the other ships, I see no sign of that.

[151]

Your speech thrilled them, made them feel important. Made me feel important." She pressed his hand. "I assure you none of them will question their superiors' orders. But in Captain Lee's imagined society, so important to him because he is so sensitive, he has lost face, and it would be good to give him room while he gets over that."

"I'm not one to put my foot on someone's neck, Mei-ling."

"Of course you're not. He knows that you too are kind. Tell me"—and the returning humor in her face showed that the lesson was over—"were you such a bad-ass for fighting the last time you served?"

"That was the party line, and in public I repeated it—loudly, like Bill Houy. Privately I was after something else. I had a theory that the way to be a sailor—to live your life—was to constantly fight entropy."

"What is this?"

"The tendency of things to fall apart. I wanted a place for everything and everything in its place."

"But someone told me that war is chaos."

"Of course it is. My attitude was obsessive, and it took over my judgment. The gods of the Navy must have decided that when I was passed over for admiral."

"Yes, sad. But maybe good for you as a man."

"I'm not sure of that myself. In the past six years I've lost a lot of face. Objectively lost it. Now that I'm not important, my wife thinks I'm boring. I've been reluctant to tell you this. She gets impatient with me if I take too long to make a decision, and then when I do decide, she doesn't seem to care."

"Maybe her way of accepting what she doesn't like?"

"Maybe."

"Or a phase of life? A passage?"

"It could be that too. She has left our home to go celebrity-watching with a younger man."

"Ah." She didn't dwell on her sympathy. In its place—he could be mistaken—there seemed a glow of self-interest.

卬 卬

"Watch this, now," he said.

Ahead of them the horizon was clear, brimming with the sea, offering a lip where it was touched by the sun. The pairing went on and on, the sun elongate like a cell reproducing. Then it disappeared in a splash of crimson, which spread across the sky. With every breath the colors shifted through the palette until the entire sky was green as if the world were an emerald.

"Oh!" holding up her green arm. "So beautiful."

"That was a green flash, Mei-ling. Extremely rare, almost mythological. Sailors pretend to have seen one, and most of us never have. But *you* have, now."

"An omen."

"Why not? Maybe a thousand years of good luck."

The general alarm sounded: *bong bong bong bong....* The bugle played. In repetitive sing-song a drill was announced.

To their credit the sailors raced from the fantail with their poles. He and Mei-ling got up, and she would like to run too. Her battle station was the wardroom, where she performed first aid and triage and encouraged hope.

"What is it?" she asked.

"A tactical problem for all the ships. Kate Harcourt is running it from *Chiai.* An enemy cruiser has just been detected twenty-five miles ahead of the formation."

"While towing?"

"Cutting the towline will be simulated. Houy won't let them actually cut it—Jesus Christ!"

For there was a roar from ahead and *Chiai* erupted in smoke and flames. A missile streaked from her port side, tipped over, and turned toward the sunset, its light reflected in the water.

"Cease fire!" he shouted. "Abort!"—forgetting it was a Harpoon missile, which could not be aborted.

He ran up to the bridge, outrunning several sailors, not hesitating to order them out of his way. When he arrived his heart was pounding and he had to catch his breath. "What is...downrange?" he managed finally.

The bridge was a bedlam; he had to outshout them to get their attention.

"How was it fired? What mode?"

Lee looked at him as if he were crazy.

"*Chiai* fired it, Commodore," Lieutenant Wú replied.

"I know that. Ask them. Get Kate Harcourt on the line. Ask what mode the missile was fired in."

She could hardly get the words out. Gone was the unflappable air controller. As the scenario had unfolded she would have been half a second too late staying the hand of Lieutenant Cào, the firing officer. For who would have thought that when he heard the order to fire, he would have forgotten it was a training exercise?

Lee was without ideas.

"In that mode," Hilty said to him, speaking loudly so the watchstanders would hear, "the missile will fly out to the designated point, look for the target—the first target in its annulus—then continue until it runs out of fuel. We have to know if any vessels, large or small, were downrange. Check the database. And order *Hsinchu* to search down the firing bearing."

Then an even more awful idea struck him: "We have to report it. Our satellites will have picked up the launch, which might look like a nuclear missile fired at Hawaii." He scribbled a message with familiar prowords. "Add our position to this and send it to these U.S. commands, emergency precedence. Say amplifying info to follow."

The Pigpen

That was a question: what amplifying info? After the message had gone out he conferred with the three captains and Tsai Mei-ling. He was running on adrenaline, like battle itself. His voice was clipped, decisive. The badass. No asking *why* now. But he used a handset in a corner of CIC, hiding his sweaty face.

The first reports were encouraging. No ships in vicinity; indeed, the firing had been outside the usual shipping routes and fishing areas. No calls had been heard on the distress frequencies. *Hsinchu,* as she passed through the target area, found nothing but open water; no oil, no debris, no sign of human presence. It might be that this was just one of those empty expanses of the wide Pacific.

"So tell them no problems, final report," (L) said.

"They will want more," Lee said.

"An independent naval unit, being careful of safety, can we not shoot in the middle of the ocean?"

"Not when it's picked up by satellites," growled (H).

This was getting nowhere. "For a firing exercise," he said, "clearance is obtained ahead of time, and ships and aircraft are warned."

"Well, they know now!"

"It's a question whether we should remain in the target area and—"

"No way, keep going," said (L).

"And conduct a coordinated search by daylight."

The other captains agreed with (L). In his breezy manner he didn't leave it at that. "And search for nothing. What's the big deal, after all? Our own missile, bought and paid for. I tell you it was a mistake to send that first report. Without that this would have been a spreadsheet error. Lost by inventory, easy to explain. But you were right about one thing, Commodore: it is better to beg forgiveness than to report mishap."

"Captain Zhang is more unhappy than he pretends," said Lee when, after the radio conference, the three of them gathered in the great cabin to review the situation. "It is not acceptable to fire a missile and make light of it. In the Taiwan Strait this could start a war."

"Do you think China will treat it as a provocation?"

"It gives them an excuse, at least." Lee turned to Mei-ling. "What do you think?"

"Possibly. And it has unfortunate intelligence value. It tells them our crews must be untrained to make such a mistake. Uh-oh."

She was holding her cell phone. "Hawaii has been put on alert for imminent missile attack," she said. "People have been told to seek shelter, causing panic."

Lee slumped over the table with his head in his hands. "What is that boy in the American comics by Schulz? *Zhūjuàn?* The Pigpen? We trail disaster like a cloud of dirt."

Moments passed.

"Okay," she said, "the alert is cancelled. No attack."

"I have to write a message about this," he said. "May I ask both of you to remain here while I compose it?"

He went into the bedroom and shut the door. For the next few minutes he was happy, as he always was when writing—something he could do through his own effort. His thoughts came quickly and in good order. He ignored the talk in the next room. Not even the silence of the ship while under tow distracted him. The tone of the message was clear, as was the effect that he wanted to have on the reader. A little polishing made it just right.

He brought it out to the living room for them to read. Lee, slouched in his chair now, straightened up. His expression as he read was serious, perhaps satisfied by the justice of it. Mei-ling's was sad, perhaps for the author.

After a brief discussion they both agreed that he might send it. Lee left. She reached out and squeezed his hand.

This is what he wrote:

During a training exercise that I supervised, the operator of the Harpoon control console onboard ROCS *Chiai* mistakenly initiated an actual firing sequence at a computer-generated target. The selected missile flew a nominal profile to the designated coordinates, where, finding no target and continuing until fuel exhaustion, it must have fallen harmlessly into the sea. Search of the area continues. However, I am confident from all available data that no vessel or aircraft was endangered.

Preliminary investigation has revealed that the operator, the missile officer of the ship, properly trained in the system, was apparently excited by the realistic tone of the scenario and acted before anyone could stop him. This although the scenario had been briefed as an exercise and the participants advised that all engagements were to be simulated.

After full investigation, a written report will follow.

In view of the mission that these ships will be required to perform, and the state of tension between Taiwan and the P.R.C., realistic training has been, and continues to be, absolutely vital to the success of this transit. Despite the seriousness of the mistake made tonight, and after conducting a thorough review with all ships' companies of the lessons learned and the precautions to be taken, I intend to continue the training regime.

All of us here are deeply sorry for any distress caused to the people of Hawaii by our actions, and no one more than I. Whatever procedural errors may have been made by others, the responsibility for this mistake is entirely mine.

B. R. Hilty, Captain, U.S. Navy, Commander Taiwan Transit Unit.

৮ ৮

After an uneasy night, he read this at breakfast:

It was late afternoon on a blissful Saturday in Paradise. The surf was up, and at Waikiki Beach music-lovers had gathered for a free concert by the up-and-coming singer/songwriter Melody Lyme. Suddenly thousands of cell phones, on the beach and in all the islands, were sounding an alert from the Hawaii Emergency Management Agency: "Ballistic missile threat inbound to Hawaii. Seek immediate shelter. This is not a drill."

God, the panic, he thought, and that was the point of the story. There had been a scramble to find shelter in the volcanic rock, but what shelter could there be from a nuclear strike? The alert was all too clear: here was Death, the destroyer of worlds. The stress must have been intolerable. Think of the heart attacks.

"Thank you, no more," he said to Wang, though the meal was good and better served; the result of training, he thought ironically. "No cleaning this morning, please: I don't feel well, and I'm returning to bed."

He, who thrived at sea, was sick of sailing. He lay on the bed without taking off his shoes and pulled up the blanket. Someone—he could guess who—had fixed the air conditioning. He had no reason to wrap himself in a cocoon, but he did.

Sending that message was the correct thing to do, but why on earth had he sent it? Just imagine the panic: you're not going to survive *this* nuclear missile, but even if you do, you and everyone and everything you know and love will never survive the resulting catastrophe, the breakdown in order, the nuclear winter.

By now he should have received an acknowledgement from the Pacific Fleet, from Robin McGill or her people.

Silence in naval communications was the silent treat-
ment of prep school, often leading to suicidal ideations.

He was sixty—past the life expectancy of half the
world. How could he possibly have thought he could do
this? The Pigpen.

Among all the other dirt following him was the likely
end of his teaching career. At the present rate he would
miss the beginning of the school year. When he had accepted this assignment, he had emailed the principal
about it, assuring her that he would return without missing any time. She had replied with something equivalent
to *Thank you for your service*—the kind of courtesy
meant to stand up under review after she had fired a
teacher she had never liked but who had never given her
cause before. Now he would have to tell her that he might
be away until October and to suggest that his Civil War
Roundtable, which was popular with the students if not
with her, should be postponed until the spring semester.
Her eyes would gleam over this unexpected gift.

A life wasted. Utterly wasted.

He was rolling about. He tried to calm himself.

It was possible, no matter how hard a couple tried,
that marriages did run dry. One stopped liking the other.
One found the other a bore. Veiled criticisms of appearance or behavior were unveiled, until even fond teasing
was received as ridicule. Irritating habits, given up out of
kindness, were resumed and received in wounded silence
The idea of loving became indistinguishable from the idea
of loyalty, of hanging on. All things were subject to entropy.

He had believed that that would never happen to his
own marriage—the idea was horrifying to them both. But
as he looked back it was clear that Mad and he had been
hollowing out for years. Now the crisis: he had answered
the call to serve his country once again, and she had gone
off to have fun she couldn't talk about.

It wasn't so much the horror of infidelity: it was the
accumulated weariness of thirty-six years of living

together, set aside in the fantasy of escape. When both of them returned to Norfolk, the weariness would catch up to them. She would remember his foibles. He would feel anew all the little darts she flung at him. At some point they would have a conversation whose sad outcome both would be ready by then to accept.

He said aloud, "A tale told by an idiot, full of sound and fury, signifying nothing."

But enough wallowing. He had duties to perform, the first of which was to conduct the investigation that he had promised, in keeping with the sense of responsibility that he had bragged about. He threw off the blanket.

Escalation

He did conduct the investigation, in the course of which he visited *Hsinchu* and *Chiai* and took statements from witnesses. Lieutenant Cào had known it was a drill, even at the order to fire, but had become so nervous when (L), approaching his console, had followed it up in English with a "Shoot, shoot, shoot!" that he had turned the key.

The investigation was completed, reviewed, endorsed, and printed, awaiting only their arrival in Pearl to be delivered to both national authorities. (The endorsement of *Chiai's* captain was one line: *I disagree with this report.)*

Meanwhile, the destroyers beat on steadily toward the west: one bright windy day after another, the endless traversal of the jutted surface, the endless working of the ship's head, the endless sluicing of water down the side out of which it wasn't difficult to imagine voices of the deep calling enticements and reproaches.

The rigorous training continued, itself a kind of routine. There were no more accidents, and the trainers were generally pleased by the progress. The towing at sunset became a kind of ritual for the community, like a council fire, bringing shipmates together. Each ship took her turn, to be judged by the many onlookers for her seamanship. Whenever he had the signalmen hoist *Bravo Zulu*—meaning *Well done!*—the satisfaction was general. Whenever he withheld it there was grousing at the umpire's call, and he might be accosted for it afterwards.

It was fun to engage with them. Nevertheless, the days and nights were dull. However much he cared about the result, he found it hard to be excited about the training itself, which he had seen by now hundreds or thousands of times. The Oxygen Breathing Apparatus, or OBA, vital for entering compartments on fire, could be donned correctly only one way. He had seen all the mistakes. As the ships worked west, he spent a great deal of time on the bridge, not paying attention, simply staring at the water.

It was on the bridge one afternoon, as the ship lay to during yet another boat transfer, that a sailor approached him. The captain sent his respects and would the commodore join him in the sea cabin? He was there in a dozen steps. Inside was a crowd. The Zhangs sat on the sofa bed, Lee and Mei-ling at the table. All rose when he came in and made a show of according him the desk chair, which was turned toward the room.

He looked at them. Their faces were grave. The radio speakers and TV monitors had been turned off, and the silence was pregnant. He understood. They were going to relieve him of his command. Too much dirt had followed him. Probably the orders had come from Tsoying. He was endangering the "very quiet, very circumspect, very stealthy" arrival that Admiral Chen had devised.

Well, so what? He had tried his best, and it hadn't worked out. They weren't ready to be ready; they didn't want it enough. Leaving them in Pearl would be a relief, for the most part. He could do without the drama. Back in Norfolk he could get on with his life: resume his teaching, address his marriage. He had been passed over for admiral despite outstanding performance (and Mad had been a great comfort then). Compared to that, this disappointment would soon feel like nothing.

Lee spoke for them: "There has been a new incident in the Taiwan Strait, and we would like your advice on what it means and how the transit unit should respond."

"An incident with China, Captain?"

"Commander Tsai has gathered the reports and translated them into English. She will present them, which of course you may read if you wish."

She had them in a three-ring binder, neatly tabbed.

[162]

It appeared that a Chinese cruiser had rammed the destroyer *Tso Ying,* formerly USS *Kidd,* and nearly sunk her.

Tso Ying had been operating in the Strait, well to the Taiwan side of the median line, which both nations had tacitly observed until now. On her side of the line and in international waters, where she had every right to be. She had left the shipyard at Magong Island and was conducting sea trials to verify the work.

"Was she armed?" he asked.

"Yes," Mei-ling replied.

"Always, in the Strait," Lee said. "Enough to defend herself. But the trials were only for engineering—full-power run, steering tests—not for weapons."

"What does China say?"

Mei-ling read from the binder: "China claims that *Tso Ying* crossed the line to collect intelligence on a training exercise and pointed weapons at various ships."

"Not true, of course."

"Not true, Commodore. Both sides always take photos, but China has no photos of this. They say *Tso Ying's* behavior was even more dangerous because other ships, illegally sold to Taiwan, the so-called 'American Aegis destroyers,' were rehearsing nuclear strikes on the Chinese mainland, including live firings. Strictly as a defensive measure, the Chinese say their cruiser gently shouldered *Tso Ying* away with minimal damage, a practice for dealing with intruders since ancient times."

He could attest to that: in the Black Sea Plumpy had been shouldered by a Soviet destroyer. Other than the surprise of it, it was hardly a bump. He found himself tapping his knee. Something like spring fever was surging in his blood. Relief? Yes, and something more, approaching delight. He composed his expression to appear unmoved.

"I take it the shouldering must also be a lie."

"Sir, in fact, the Chinese cruiser rammed *Tso Ying* head-on. *Tso Ying* followed the rules of the road until, at

[163]

the last moment, her captain had to decide whether to turn away and be cut in two or stay on course and trust to his bow."

"That's more than shouldering, certainly."

"Unfortunately, the impact was very great. *Tso Ying's* forward bulkhead collapsed, and for more than an hour it looked as if she must sink, during which time no Chinese ship offered assistance. Somehow a temporary bulkhead was put in place. After these emergency repairs *Tso Ying* returned to Magong, sailing stern-first."

He thought of his lecture: waking up to the shock of an attack. "And what's the reaction around the world?"

"News commentary is divided. Some say China means war. Others say China was justified. In Taiwan the active forces have been put on alert. The reserves have been advised to settle their personal affairs and wait to be called. However, they are not well trained or organized because the period of compulsory service is so short."

"Ships and aircraft will be dispersed," (H) said. "Moved to shelters. Hidden. The great thing is to survive the first strike, to hold out."

He and (H) had discussed this.

"Until we come in," he said. "As we will. Have you seen any traffic about that, Commander?"

As if on cue there was a knock on the door and the same radioman who had brought the orders restoring him to active duty entered with his aluminum binder.

The commodore lifted the lid and glanced at the message then read it to them:

From: Commander Pacific Fleet

To: Commander Taiwan Transit Unit

Subject: Expedited Arrival

1. Increasing tensions between the Republic of China and the P.R.C. (see reference reports) necessitate the presence of the Aegis destroyers in Taiwan as soon as

possible. While the attainment of a high state of combat readiness by the ships remains desirable, this objective is secondary to rapid completion of the transit.

2. Accordingly, make every effort to expedite the ships'
arrival in Pearl Harbor. In view of the higher fuel consumption, an oiler will join you to provide dedicated
refueling support. The identity of the ship and rendezvous position will be signaled separately.

3. Advise intentions.

"That seems clear enough," he said, pulling the message out and returning the binder to the radioman. "Now
help me with paragraph three: what are our intentions?"

All of them looked at him for guidance. If a survey
were to ask, *How much confidence do you have in your
leader?* Mei-ling and (H) would answer, *A great deal,* Lee
would answer, *Some confidence,* and (L) would answer,
Prefer not to answer.

The confidence of two and a half was enough. He felt
happy and awake again. Apparently no one in the transit
unit thought he was Pigpen after all. There was every
chance that he might lead these ships into battle. In his
renewed optimism battle was just an abstraction, easy,
harmless, sure to be victorious—the same fallacy he had
been warning them against.

The Secret Fire

The rendezvous position was sent; a ship he had actually been alongside, *Henry J. Kaiser,* was enroute to refuel them. It looked good on paper, but he knew better. Nothing had been said about the fortunes of the sea. If for any reason the oiler failed to appear or a storm blew up or the refueling itself, which these crews had only walked through, proved too difficult, the ships would be running on fumes. Against that contingency he worked out a plan to reduce speed again and tow continuously, no matter how it looked at Pearl. This, however, he held close.

The afternoon before the rendezvous he was on the bridge. *Hsinchu* and *Chiai* were in their patrol sectors on either beam, barreling along. Down a little by the bow, *Hsinchu* sent up sparkling sheets of spray as her forefoot pressed the waves. Drops of spray collected on *Luchiang's* windows too. From time to time the watch would turn the wipers on.

The seas were six feet high, mostly in rolling swells. If they were no worse than this tomorrow, the refueling would go all right. Bill Houy had visited all three ships to rehearse the linehandlers (with so much wind across the deck they had looked like extras in his hurricane podcast), and Michael Blaylock had ensured that the engineers knew the refueling sequence. He himself had looked up the name of *Henry J. Kaiser's* captain: over the phone-and-distance line a friendly conversation while alongside might provide news of the fleet.

A mat of kelp flashed by at twenty-five knots. But they were sailing in something else as well, something widespread and unnatural. He went out to the bridge wing to get a better look. One of the watchstanders had to help him open the door against the wind. Holding the visor of his Taiwan ballcap, he looked over the side.

The water, bluer than it should be, was filled with a myriad of points of light. Microplastics: the ships were passing through a garbage patch, perhaps one of those that extended hundreds of miles. Fifty trillion pieces of plastic had found their way into the oceans, and they would still be around when the next asteroid hit the Earth. Over the years ships he had served in had contributed their share, never questioning the practice. Here was another comfortless memory and a comment on his service. But he wouldn't dwell on it, not today.

Above his head he heard a pleasant anticipatory *whoosh,* like a barbecue igniting after a heavy squirt of starter fluid. He looked up. The forward stack sent up two black puffs of smoke followed by billows of it. He struggled to pull the door open. The watchstanders thought there was no hurry. He waved his arms. "What just happened?" he asked the OOD. "Has Central Control reported a fire?"

The young man's eyes went wide. Just then a voice shouted in Chinese over the intercom. As they had been well drilled to do, all the watchstanders made some sort of noise. The ship's bell was rung, the bugle was blown, the emergency was called away, the general alarm was sounded, *Hsinchu* and *Chiai* were told, and the whistle blew five short blasts.

In a moment, people. A phone talker drew the letter *B* on a diagram of the ship and reported to Lee: the forward engine room had an uncontrolled oil fire.

Mei-ling was at this side to interpret for him.

Time passed, relentless time. Small fires unconfronted become big fires. The right things were happening but too slowly:

☞ All doors were closed and fire boundaries set.
☞ The starboard propeller shaft was locked.
☞ The equipment in the space was shut down.

[168]

☞ The engine room was evacuated.
☞ A muster of the crew accounted for everyone.
☞ The firefighting team was ready and waiting.

"Waiting for what?" he couldn't help asking.

"They're being briefed," was the answer.

"Has the Halon system activated?" he asked.

"Lights say *Activated.*"

But if that were true the fire would have been snuffed out already. Lee and he went to the bridge wing to check. The ship was adrift. The other ships were approaching. They looked up and then at each other: black smoke continued to billow from the forward stack.

"Central, Bridge: the fire is still burning."

"Central asks how do you know, sir?"

Lee told them. They were unconvinced.

"Some vent must still be open," the commodore said to the phone talker, "and the Halon has leaked out."

"All vent lights say *Shut.*"

"We'll have to fight it with water," he said to Lee.

Apparently the briefing was going on and on.

"When will the hose teams enter the compartment?"

"Chief engineer says soon."

"*Hsinchu* asks what assistance," said the OOD. "*Chiai* has rigged hoses and is preparing to tow."

"How long has it been now?" he asked.

"Twenty minutes," replied the phone talker.

"That's too long," he said to Lee.

Lee pointed below decks and bolted from the bridge. Mei-ling and he followed.

The two younger ones jumped down the ladders by vaulting from the handrails as gymnasts and young sailors did. He himself went down as fast as he could find the next rung.

On the second deck the heat was there, and on the third deck it was stifling, the kind of heat children and the elderly are warned against. A skeleton watch in Central Control was monitoring status panels and relaying reports. The chief engineer and his damage control assistant had gone to the scene, as they should. Lee took them there.

The heat attacked them, as if they couldn't possibly endure it. The bulkhead of the forward engine room was cherry red. On the other side the fire roared. The passageway was crowded with the squatting fire team, of whom many seemed unable to move. The air was polluted by smoke. The three senior officers made their way along the line, sweating and coughing, the heat increasing with each step. The door to the engine room, of heavier steel, was deceptively its usual color, but when, per doctrine, the commodore touched the back of his hand to it, the hairs sizzled.

Two hoses had been rigged. Attached to number one hose was the all-purpose nozzle, which could send either high-velocity fog or a powerful stream—usually that. Attached to number two was the low-velocity fog applicator, used to protect the team on the number one hose.

Both hoses were lying on the deck. Squatting over them were the hosemen, each in his OBA, which looked like a gas mask over flak jacket. The on-scene investigator, who also wore an OBA, was filthy with soot. He at least must have gone inside. The chief engineer and the DCA, unprotected, were suffering from the air and the dearth of facts.

Even now there was a hierarchy. He should let Lee command his ship. On the bridge he had asked too many questions. Lee spoke with the chief engineer.

He reported, "Cheng says Halon should have worked."

"Yes, but the fact is, it didn't. We have to enter the compartment and fight the fire with water. Both teams."

"Maybe it's working."

"No, Yu-hsuan. We know it's not. Your ship's on fire."

"You right." In halting speech he issued the commands to the chief engineer, who nodded eventually and relayed them to his people. After countless simulations the teams knew what to do, if only they could be moved to do it under these conditions.

The investigator, in fire-retardant mitts, pushed up the quick-acting handle. The door sprung open, and all of them ducked as the heat and smoke rolled out. The investigator and both team leaders went inside. The rest of the team followed, frog-walking the hoses.

Seven minutes later by his watch, they backed out and dropped to the deck, so there was no one to shut the door. The DCA, pulling his shirt sleeves over his palms, shut it, an act of mere seconds, but both of his sleeves were smoldering.

Lee said, "Very hot and dark, Commodore. Dangerous. They don't know where the fire is. Better to shut everything and let it burn up the air."

"But that won't work," he said. "One of the vents is open—maybe more than one—or the Halon would have put it out by now. The fire is sucking air from the rest of the ship. We have to go in with water everywhere."

A pause. Both Lee and Mei-ling agreed with him, but the team leaders hesitated, raising again, if anyone cared at this point, the larger question of whether Taiwan would defend herself.

"I'll go," Lee said, and he meant it; he wasn't trying to shame them. He motioned for the number two leader to give him his OBA and silver mitts.

Here was the fleeting moment upon which destinies turn. "And I'll go," he said. "I know this compartment as well as anyone." He motioned likewise to the number one leader. The left side of his brain told the right side they were going to die. He told them both the water would be lifesaving.

Mei-ling began to put on the investigator's OBA.

He shook his head.

She nodded and made a muscle of her biceps.

"I know you're strong," he said into her ear, over the industrial roar. "I'd be so worried about you I wouldn't be able to think."

"I'd be so worried about you I'd go inside without the gas mask. Let's control entropy together."

"It's called an oxygen breathing apparatus," he corrected her, which drew the desired laugh, and a moment later her face looked like a frog's.

The three of them crouched at the door. He would blast away, Lee would protect him, and Mei-ling would find and break up the fire. The DCA, now with mitts on, lifted the handle. The door crashed back against the bulkhead, and they were crouching at the entrance to a crematorium. His forehead and ears hurt already. The rest of his skin was covered, but the cloth was already hot.

Leading with the hose, he pulled back the bail. The nozzle recoiled as the stream shot out, so that he nearly dropped it. He pointed the water along the beam of his helmet light and followed it to the upper catwalk. When he was first learning to drive a car, he had not understood his power over the controls.

Above his head, a soaking relief from the heat, Lee's umbrella of fog followed him.

He turned to go down the ladder. The hose refused to follow. It was caught on a stanchion, so that even with the fog to protect him he would be roasted by the heat. He pointed at the stanchion, his number two pointed, and a hoseman kicked it free. As seamen they knew about rendering lines around obstacles. Now they would know about this.

He went down to the turbine flat. Despite the smoke and dark, his mind was clear and working quickly like the Hilty of old. Something had started the fire, and it couldn't have been the gas turbines, enclosed in their fireproof boxes. He gave the boxes a good dousing anyway. Crossing over he avoided spraying the control panel in case it still had power. The time was getting on, and the fire was still at work. He had to put it out *now,* to give the shipyard at Pearl a chance to repair the damage. In the poky light of the headlamps he couldn't see how bad it was.

What mattered most was he saw no flames to put out.

He kept the stream ahead of him as he went down to the generator flat. The hose, although it had traveled a long way and around several corners, now followed him obediently. Plumpy had never had a fire except once, when a corroded section of pipe had leaked seawater onto a transformer. The flames had been five feet high. Being the first at the scene, he, the captain, had put them out himself. Trained well, he had acted automatically, hardly thinking about what he did. He had not been aware of any heat, just a glow on his face. This heat would stop the heart.

The generator was shut down, and the switchboard was de-energized. He swept the stream over everything then switched the bail to high-velocity fog to soak the in-sulation. Mei-ling, seeing what he was after, jabbed at the fabric with her investigator's tool. Steam rose, as if fire were inside, but no flames awakened. He switched back to the stream to scatter the debris.

He was getting tired.

With an effort he climbed the short ladder to the boiler flat, spraying from the hip as he went. There was more lagging here than anywhere else. He swung the hose left and right as Mei-ling hacked at it with both hands. Again steam everywhere but no flames: he soaked, power-washed, and soaked again. His hand struggled with the bail. All the atmosphere was steam, like the Earth before living things.

He told himself to breathe normally, but he was gulp-ing air and his chest was heaving. The OBA canisters were good for forty-five minutes sitting around, thirty minutes when laboring. It was possible he was running out. But it had only been ten minutes, plus seven from the previous user. But the compartment was still so hot and dark, and the fire was now in all his muscles, and what he needed was even deeper breaths than he was taking; than he could take; than the canister held.

The hose was too heavy. He couldn't hold it up, and his legs had no bones. The second hoseman, seeing that he was in trouble, took over the nozzle, and the rest of the team moved up. He sat on the wet deck, put his head down, and tried to breathe. At firefighting school so many years ago, they had taught him that there was always air around the hose. He struggled out of the mask and lay on the deck with his face against the hot smelly canvas. Perhaps this was folly. In the wilderness people suffering from advanced hypothermia shed their clothes.

He tried to help his mates by pointing out the corners to soak. But his headlamp battery was running low too, and the light was failing. He could see the scant criss-crossing of the other lights as if miners were seeking a way out from a cave-in. From a subterranean fire. He seemed to be watching them on TV. The heat had been too much for him. He had done better in firefighting school, though that fire was designed to be an inferno. He couldn't breathe. O Lord, your fire is so great and my lungs hold so little. The light contracted within a closing periphery; the darkness expanded until that's all there was.

He was lying on his bed in the commodore's cabin. But something wasn't right. Perhaps this wasn't Earth, the Pacific, Plumpy, his life as he had lived it. The mattress was different; there were more pillows. The bulkhead was hung with charts and graphs and photos of weapons systems. Now he knew: he was onboard *Hsinchu*.

Zhang Heavy, sympathetic, mindful, was sitting in a chair beside the bed. The porthole cover was up; it was daytime. But what day? How far from Pearl? Beyond this room were the usual sounds of engineering and displaced sea. The ship was making way at a decent speed.

"What about the others?" he said. His voice sounded like a cold.

"Fire is out, but there is much damage. Captain Lee has his hands full. We thought it better if you came here."

"Is *Luchiang* still in company?"

"Yes. Sixteen knots, starboard shaft locked. Fueling rendezvous is delayed until tomorrow."

"And Commander Tsai?"

Under that brow a grave smile lighted his face. "Fine. All are fine. Minor burns only. One sailor broke his arm falling down a ladder."

"What happened to me?"

"Heat exhaustion. Smoke inhalation. Corpsman says you may have strained your heart. Probably not serious."

"Stupid," he said. "I'm not as young as I used to be."

Zhang shook his head against such foolish talk. "You put out the fire and saved the ship. You yourself."

"Not by myself," he said, thinking of Lee and Mei-ling and the firefighters, their courage roused at last.

"Saved the ship, and your shipmates saved you. Tsai Mei-ling shared her oxygen. Lee carried you out on his shoulders. You awakened on the boat deck and we talked, remember? You asked a great many questions."

He shook his head. "Is she...?" *Here,* he meant to say. But just then Mei-ling came into the room. Setting down a tray, she gave him a few sips of a sweet electrolyte. With her finger she spread petroleum jelly on his lips. She used a warm wet cloth to wipe his eyes. The joy of serving him never left her face.

"Number One nurse," Zhang said.

His stricken heart turned a somersault.

The Grave of the *Arizona*

Admiral Robin McGill

As *Hsinchu* was doubling her lines, a black Navy sedan pulled onto the pier, flying the flag of a four-star admiral. Zhang hissed at the quarterdeck to be ready. Eight side-boys with the bosun's mate to pipe for them assembled inboard of the brow. The OOD tugged imaginary wrinkles out of the awning then stood beside his captain, both of them at attention. Commodore Hilty took a place in the back, under the overhang of the boat deck.

The driver came around to open the door, and Admiral Robin McGill, Commander Pacific Fleet, stepped out like someone famous stepping from a poster of herself. There was that familiar face, of beauty called to service. There, always and never feigned, was that irresistible interest in those she commanded. The smile that played about her lips like scattered sunlight—was it there? was it not?—told of her absolutely real, unwavering confidence in their abilities and dedication to duty and in the inevitable victory. A few leaders had such charisma. He had admired it in her years before, when he had wanted to prosecute her for adultery, fraternization, and conduct unbecoming an officer.

Eight bells rang, in their groups of two, as she came up the brow and turned toward the fantail to salute the national ensign of Taiwan. On the quarterdeck she shook hands with Zhang. Then she came to *him* with open arms, so that the salute each owed the other was lost in a warm embrace.

"Oh, my dear friend," she said.

"Admiral, how good," was all he could say before choking on his voice.

Quickly and with a laugh they wiped away the tears.

"We must go to a photo op," she said.

Onboard *Chiai* cameras from a local news affiliate had been set up. Pausing only to be briefed by a reporter and to pin a mic to her collar, she brought the three captains into the frame and welcomed them to Pearl Harbor and the Pacific Fleet. She assured them of the unflinching support of the president and the American people. Lee returned compliments for the transit unit.

Afterwards, (L) pulled her away from the others so that he might remind her that *Chiai* had brought into Gitmo the survivors of the Chinese shipwreck. She acknowledged that he certainly had done this, though she didn't know all the details because that had been in another ocean. He began to describe for her the dangers he had overcome with his seamanship. *Hsinchu* had regrettably lost an American swimmer, but all his survivors had survived.

"Let's be sure, when we have a moment, to finish this story, Captain," she said. "I mustn't keep the admiral waiting."

(L) thought that right now was even better than when they had a moment, but (H) set a pick and she escaped with Lee and the commodore. He remembered that other escape, when Slate had set the pick.

By the admiral she meant Rear Admiral Cromarty, commander of the naval shipyard, who was waiting on *Luchiang's* quarterdeck with some technical people. Lee led them below to the forward engine room, where, putting on hazmat suits, the party fanned out to inspect the damage.

Within the compartment the soot was everywhere—the air, certified fresh now, smelled of it. Portable lamps had been rigged at all levels and in the corners, but they seemed hardly to cut the dark. Certainly the damage was serious. The control console, the generator, and the boiler were destroyed, the boiler flat warped like the sculpture of a wave. The crew had had to recut some of the deck gratings to fit them into the catwalks.

The place both awed and depressed; silence seemed the best response. Also it seemed a curious fact that he might have died here.

"Two thousand degrees easy," Cromarty said. "Lagging fires are notoriously hard to put out. They're like white phosphorous. All you can do is hose them down and keep hosing. Someone used their head."

"This man," said Lee, pointing at him, which drew a smile from Robin.

"New equipment is on its way," she said to Cromarty. "How long to restore full functionality? I don't care if it looks pretty."

"Six to seven days at three shifts, Admiral. Depending how much of that deck I can save."

She approached him just close enough to touch his chest while she smiled at the humor of their respective roles. "David, the president has decided to send a message. *T.R.* and company are coming down from San Diego to escort the ships to Taiwan. I'll give you *three days.*"

"Aye-aye, ma'am," Cromarty replied with a slow grin. All sailors liked to be part of history. "Three days." He scratched the back of his head.

After they had stripped off their sooty outerwear, she led them up to the quarterdeck. This one engine room, of course, was a mess, but the rest of *Luchiang* was immaculate. The crew must have worked around the clock to make her smart. That was pride. From pride in self and ship a good leader could build the devotion willing to sacrifice both for a greater cause.

On the pier (L) wanted to give it another try.

Robin went right up to him. "So good to see you again, Captain. I would love to continue our talk, but *Luchiang* needs my attention. By the way, there's been a lot of interest here in the missile alert. Would you like to go on TV and explain how it happened?"

From habitual self-regard, (L)'s face suddenly became young and startled, like a fawn sensing an intruder. With a muttered excuse he darted away.

"Priceless," the commodore said. As if in agreement his cell phone, deep in the pocket of his whites, shook itself with laughter.

"He had that coming" she said. "I wonder if knows why."

"And was there a deadly panic?"

"The whole thing was a foobar. The state emergency folks panicked when they saw the first warning from StratCom. The missile had already splashed before the state sent the alert. Yes, for a few minutes there was fear in the streets, but no one died."

"I suppose the White House wants my head."

At this her eyes gleamed.

"Actually, they look at it as fortuitous. China's over-reaction has given us this excuse to protect the ships." She paused. "Some of the folks at DoD would like your head, but they aren't willing to pay the price for it."

"What's that?"

"My head. I cried when I read your message, Brad. Others have told me they did too, including my very macho deputy."

She was ready to cry again. But thirty years of serving with men had taught her to make light of emotion.

"How's that for theatrics? Still, you have to admit, my best line was *I'll give you three days*—the very same words Nimitz used to the commander of this very same shipyard when they had to patch together *Yorktown* for the Battle of Midway. I could retire now and live on the story. There's my faithful car. Come, let's talk about you. I really don't want to go back to the office today.

"Well, you heard me," she said as they stood beneath *Hsinchu's* bow. "These ships will sail on Sunday or, allowing a fudge factor, on Monday. Say Monday to be safe. The question is whether you should go with them."

"I'm up to it, ma'am," he said stiffly.

As she had done with Cromarty she put her hand on his chest. At some point the woman who had once told him she didn't like to be touched (i.e., by a paramour) had learned this gesture. "Brad, you don't think *that's* a concern, do you? In a pig's eye! I would never have had the courage to go into that engine room. Also, and you don't care about such things, but their navy wants to decorate you for heroism."

"That's nice to hear. Actually, I was just pissed off because the fire team was taking too long."

Her contralto laugh. "As good a reason as any, I suppose. And just like you. Now, I know you'll answer me truly, as an old friend. Would I be doing you and dear Mad a favor if I detached you to return home now?"

Well, there it was. Obviously she knew about his marriage. Of course she did, she and Slate talked all the time. The favor might be if she took the decision out of his hands.

He took a moment to admire the frapping of *Hsinchu's* mooring lines.

"Before you answer I should tell you, Brad, that Leo isn't here."

"Oh?"

She managed to look resigned and hopeful together. "He didn't come with me on this assignment. I think he's in South Carolina, playing a lot of golf. Nothing official. Both of us need to think about it. We'll see what happens."

He nodded. It was easy to be sympathetic. In the worst moments of his prosecution of Commander McGill, he had thought Leo unworthy of her.

"My own marriage has always been a mystery," he said. "Even without the sea duty. But I want to take the ships home. I care about them. Though maybe it's a problem for you, ma'am. The command relationships might be a little fraught...." He shrugged.

Her smile reminded him of Mei-ling's: amused by the situation, fond of him. "As you know, you are the senior captain in the whole bloomin' Navy. If you're sure— you're *sure,* yes?—then we can iron out any wrinkles at the pre-sail tomorrow. Give me some advice about that before I go. Tell me who should represent the ships."

"Lee is senior," he said, "but he'll have his hands full in dry dock. It will have to be Zhang."

"Good God, not him!" Her face showed horror.

"No, ma'am. Zhang of *Hsinchu.* An excellent officer."
"Zhang Chia-hao," she remembered.
"That's him. You won't be disappointed."
"You got that right: I'm thrilled already," she replied.

Three Views of Responsibility

Mad had been the caller. She had rung twice but left no message. When he dialed her number she picked up on the first ring.

"Where are you?" she asked.

"Hawaii. Looking across the water at the grave of the *Arizona,* which I ought to visit."

But disclosing even this much information made him uneasy. Probably in some warren of cubes in Shanghai, a young person with attentive eyes had the two voice prints up on her screen.

"When do you get to your destination?"

"I don't know," he replied.

"Will you be home for the children's birthday?"

This was September first, a nice number anyway but particularly important because both children had been born on that date (Sarah supposedly at seven months, but she never asked about it).

The young person would certainly know his family's birthdays. He replied, "Impossible to say."

"What about in time to teach your Civil War course?"

"Since that's in the spring semester now, I'm sure I will." He could feel the cords in his neck; he strove to keep the censor out of his voice: "Let's change the subject, shall we? Are you still in the British Virgins with Dustin?"

"No, I'm home. He's a nitwit."

"Other than that, did you enjoy yourself?"

"Listen, did you tell Adam you would visit him and then not do it?"

"Well, that's right."

"Why not?"

"We had a disagreement about modern art."

"That's not what he says. He didn't know why you canceled, and it hurt his feelings."

"The disagreement was in my mind. After seeing Sarah I wasn't in a fit condition to spend time with him."

"So you're at odds with both your children?"

And my wife, he wanted to say, but he was hardly in a fit condition to talk about that either. He rang off, without telling her about the fire on *Luchiang* that might earn him a medal or his fears of being caught in a war with untrained ships. Nor did he tell her, because she wouldn't understand it any more than he did, about his feelings for Tsai Mei-ling.

There was a *thump thump thump* as someone came down the brow pulling a suitcase: Kate Harcourt, in pain.

"I need to go home," she said before he could ask her.

"All right."

"It's a family emergency."

"Then you must go home."

"I have to save my marriage. My husband knows. Wú 'accidentally' replied to our joint email account."

"Not a good basis for a trusting relationship."

"Also, I'm not wild about being in a war."

"You were concerned about that in our meeting."

"*Chiai* will get you all killed. You need to shift your pennant there and keep Zhang under your thumb."

"Thank you, Kate. Although I have to say that's not great news to hear."

"No, but it's true. He'd fire the first shot just for fun."

"We're going to discuss it tomorrow at Makalapa."

"Where's that?"

"Fleet headquarters. Admiral McGill is chairing a pre-sail conference." She couldn't care less, which challenged him to change her mind. "It's where Nimitz directed the war in the Pacific. You're standing on historic ground, Kate. You should take the day to sightsee. Makalapa, Ford Island, the famous Royal Hawaiian hotel, where the submariners had R&R before so many of them were lost

[186]

on patrol. The *Arizona* Memorial's just there. Leave your bag with the quarterdeck, and we'll see it together."

"It sounds like fun, but I have to go. Sorry to end like this, sir. It's been a pleasure. You've done well for them. Good-bye."

Dread is a one-track mind, he thought.

She pulled her bag down the pier a few yards then stopped and turned. "I'm not sure how to get paid," she called.

"I imagine someone will take care of it."

She frowned. Perhaps she expected him to reach into his wallet for twenty thousand dollars.

Even without looking he felt the pull of the battleship; in death so visible, so present. The *Arizona* memorial, the pyramids, the Eiffel Tower, the Statue of Liberty, the Taj Mahal: there was something to a bucket list.

The Park Service ran a shuttle from the old Fleet landing, where the bodies had come ashore on the Day of Infamy; in his whites he was shown to a privileged seat at the stern. They arrived at the Memorial and gathered around the guide to begin the tour.

Not that there was much to see. Across the sunken remains a hogbacked white shell had been built with cutouts that suggested both loss and peace. At one end of the platform was a roll call of names; at the other an area for viewing.

When the tour moved on, he stayed. At one time he had read every book about the Pearl Harbor attack. By now he had forgotten many details, including the toll of the dead: 1,177 in the ship, 2,403 in all.

And then the vengeance: how much killing, maiming, suffering, xenophobia, racism, and injustice had followed, not to mention the atomic bomb. Millions of lights, each so vital to itself, snuffed out or dimmed. And this was the Good War, fought by the Greatest Generation—the legacy of values he himself had served. Some day the last humans

[187]

would ask whether their kind had done more damage to the planet or to themselves.

And yet how much hard work, courage, self-sacrifice, resilience, teamwork, and genius. Perhaps calling major programs "The War on -------" came from nostalgia.

His tour group moved on. Another came and went, leaving a solitary tourist at the viewing area: Tsai Mei-ling. She was leaning over the rail, looking into the limpid water at the silent gray shape at the bottom. When he came up beside her, she glanced over and smiled through her grief.

"It's all so theoretical," she said.

"Don't you mean it's all so real?"

"I mean the calculus of war: here are the X and Y of the target coordinates; with Weapon A you have Probability B of a kill. For these men, in one instant that they probably never knew, their ship blew up. What was that like?—not the instant of obliteration but the moments of fear leading up to it. A peaceful Sunday morning with war very far away, being fought by people of another race. Then seeing these impossible planes with the strange markings flying over your ship, your own home? Then this explosion."

"I was wondering the same thing."

"Sometimes when I'm sad I think we will never understand each other. The world is dangerous enough, as I know: my husband's body was never recovered. Yet we have to add to the danger from some arbitrary idea of what belongs to us."

"Or some arbitrary idea of what *us* means."

But in her need to say what she was feeling she hadn't heard. "Let me show you." She reached into her handbag. Balancing her steno pad on the railing and holding the end of her pen in three fingertips, she sketched a line of Chinese characters:

让爱而不是战争

"Do you see? No? Perhaps if I simplify it." Moving her hand down on the barrel, she wrote a transliteration:

Ràngài érbúshì zhànzhēng

"Yes? Still no? This is what it means in your language." With a grip like a claw she wrote again:

Make love not war

"Just a language problem, you say? Three things that mean the same? Well, not quite. And remember that the P.R.C., the U.S., and Taiwan represent a lot of people but only a fraction of the world, where more than seven thousand languages are spoken. Just three things? Three completely different things! In the P.R.C., this would be propaganda. In the U.S., the painful lesson of Vietnam. In Taiwan...." Here that charming smile spread over her face as if she were seeing both the present moment and a memory.

"Yes, Mei-ling? What in Taiwan?"

"Life, Bradford," she replied. "Loving your life."

Allies and Adversaries

Vice Admiral Edward Juventude had once been Lieutenant Commander Juventude, XO of Robin McGill's destroyer. He had quaked in his boots to be examined by Commodore Hilty and two other senior officers on his qualifications to command a ship. Now he commanded the Seventh Fleet, and Robin, always his mentor, was once again his boss.

He was a tall, lanky man with a long face and a fuzzy complexion who radiated self-effacing charm. He liked everybody and everything, and if any unsavory matter crossed his hawse he ignored it. Underneath, to have gotten so far, he must have been able to make hard decisions, however softly he imparted them.

Just now Robin and he were sitting on opposite sides of an oval conference table at the Makalapa headquarters. They were as comfortable with each other as wife and husband, beyond any need to pose.

On Robin's right was Rear Admiral Chen of the Taiwan navy, in his country's uniform. On her left was Hilty, Chen's recruit.

He sat opposite Rear Admiral Charles "Cheat" Taylor, commander of the *Theodore Roosevelt* Carrier Strike Group, whose eyes were bright with the lust for combat. On Juventude's left and across from Chen was Captain Peter Bergstrom, who commanded the three American destroyers in the strike group—a small command for him but all that could be scratched together on short notice.

At the projector end of the table, a captain from Robin's staff took notes. At the screen end sat Zhang Chia-hao—Zhang Heavy, alert and thoughtful.

Robin opened the meeting by summarizing the strategic situation, including the new intelligence that China, per their threat, which some had doubted, was actively considering a blockade of Taiwan timed to prevent the Aegis destroyers from reaching home port.

"How Seventh Fleet might help to foil that is under consideration at several levels of government," she said. "For this meeting, the agenda is to define the escort role of *T.R.* and her group, the optimal track from here to Kaohsiung, and any training between the two countries that might prove valuable. I understand, Cheat, that you and Peter have a presentation for us."

They did, and Taylor's bright black eyes and powerful chest challenged anyone to disagree with it. He had flown himself and Bergstrom here in an F-18 Super Hornet; both were wearing flight suits and had casually parked their helmets on the table (his, with *Cheat* stenciled above the visor, was turned in Robin's direction.

Bergstrom put up the proposed track, a straight shot along the latitude of the Tropic of Cancer, making good a speed of eighteen knots to deliver the ships before the Chinese could act.

Zhang and Chen stared at the table in front of them.

"Commodore Hilty, what do you think?" asked Juventude, who had been watching faces.

"May I reserve comment, Admiral? Until we've heard the rest?"

The rest, in a long slideshow, proposed that the Taiwan destroyers should join Bergstrom's own escorts. Their duties would include acting as radar pickets in advance of the formation, screening against submarines within the formation, and generally getting in the way of any incoming fire like Secret Service agents. In his zeal he had included far too many metrics; these, added up, gave the enemy a near-zero chance of striking the carrier.

Clearly his intended audience was his own boss.

When the final slide came up, a patriotic image of the air wing flying past *T.R.*, Taylor thumped the table, as no doubt he should: no matter what happened to the allies he was supposed to protect, his flagship would be safe.

With a surprisingly supple hand he rubbed Bergstrom's shiny bald head.

Robin said, "OK, thank you, Peter. Very good. Now your comments, Brad?"—arousing him from a reverie that when he had sailed in his first aircraft carrier, the old *Saratoga,* Robin would have been twelve, Juventude nine, and Taylor probably not yet in kindergarten.

"Yes, thank you, Admiral. I should say, as an apology in advance to those who don't know me, that I have an inconvenient tendency to look for fault."

"I dare you to find fault with this," said Taylor.

"Not out of malice, I assure you, sir. As far as it goes, Commodore Bergstrom's presentation is professional and thorough. But here's what occurs to me: I think you've put the cart before the horse."

"If you're going to impress us with your figures of speech, Hilty, why not say *hysteron proteron?* You weren't the only one who took English in high school."

"Aye, sir. But actually I meant it in a physical sense. Your mission is to escort the ships of Taiwan, not the other way around. It seems to me this operation should be just like providing cover for a merchant convoy."

"Except that these are warships, albeit small boys."

"Except that they aren't intended to fight as we do. Taiwan has no aircraft carriers."

"Of course I know that."

"In defending their home islands they must assume the worst case, that China will control the battle sphere. To have any hope of success, these destroyers—please don't call them *small boys,* Admiral—will have to enter into that sphere at mortal risk, conduct their attacks, and withdraw to safety. As far as their training is concerned, they've had no chance to operate with aircraft or submarines or to serve as pickets for an asset like *T.R.*

"On the other hand they are very good at navigation and coordinated targeting—that's where my people have been working with them. During this final leg of the transit, they should be employed as an integral surface action group at some distance from the covering force. The track proposed by the commodore would support that perfectly if it weren't too optimistic."

"Bullshit optimistic. I've checked that track. You just want your independence, Hilty. The book on you is you've never liked working for anyone."

Juventude put his hand on Taylor's arm, and Robin said tartly, "A more moderate tone, please. We're all friends here." But Taylor had no friends, not from his first days as a cocky "nugget" who loved to cut in front of rivals in the landing pattern.

"If you've checked this track, Admiral," Hilty replied, fixing on him a cold look, "you must have been concerned about the easterly trade winds, which, now that La Niña is over, are weaker this year. During launch and recovery, *T.R.* will lose ground to the east, after which she'll have to run like hell to the west to catch up. Her overall progress will be more like fifteen knots than eighteen, with the concomitant delay in arrival."

"Ooh, *concomitant,*" said Taylor, which missed its target, since he had heard such things from Slate all his life.

"Do you want to fly that much?" asked Juventude.

"Opportunity permitting." Which was Cheat-code for *We need to fly that much.*

The meeting was ready to tip.

"I think *T.R.* will want to continue working up," he said to Juventude. And then to Taylor, with an appeasing face, "Sir, you deployed on short notice—amazingly short notice: I've never seen such a response, and I believe I've been following these things longer than anyone here. But of course *T.R.* couldn't possibly have met all her training gates in that time. I've looked at her current readiness report: if she's going to chop to Seventh Fleet anything like certified for fleet ops, she'll need to fly every day. And accepting the slower track—the difference in arrival is about two days—that's a good thing, ideal for training on both sides. Whenever she turns into the wind, my ships can reposition on any number of threat axes. When the last recovery is complete and she turns back, we'll be ready to act as the opposition force.

"As such, we provide you with real-world problems. Can you detect us in a moderate sea state? Can you find us among the merchant shipping? When you're not flying cyclic ops, can you keep enough aircraft aloft to provide long range surface detection? Can the commodore's escorts, with their helos, take up the slack?

"Of course China has three carriers, and they may be our first encounter. But assuming we prevail there, as I'm sure we would, her tactics against our fleet would become very much like Taiwan's against her: hit-and-run raids, surface action groups. These are the very tactics we will show you every night—and perhaps during the day as well. Really, we're a golden opportunity for you."

In the ensuing silence Robin asked for comments from the Taiwan side. Admiral Chen, politician that he was, deferred to Captain Zhang.

"Commodore Hilty and I have had much discussion about this," Zhang said.

"Excuse me, Captain," said the note-taker at the opposite end of the table. "I didn't quite hear that."

Making an effort to speak more clearly, which looked like an opera singer articulating a recitative, Zhang continued: "The commodore has been teaching us about the invasion of Okinawa. As powerful as your fleet was then, you had no answer to the kamikaze. Particularly the radar picket ships, just sitting on the threat axis. I would not like my *Hsinchu* to endure the fate of USS *Laffey*—against hypersonic missiles instead of suicide planes. I doubt if history would allow two ships that would not die."

"Sir, do you agree with that?" Juventude asked Chen. Chen nodded.

"Then I think we have our marching orders. You report to me, Commodore Hilty to Admiral McGill, and we all get along like toast and tea."

"Bring it on," said Taylor. Then, leering across the table, "Be warned, Hilty: I don't take prisoners."

"Aye-aye, sir," he replied. "First round of trash-talking
goes to your side."

"Just keep their hands away from the firing keys,"
Taylor said with a smirk.

Conditional Delegation of Authority

Admiral Chen gave them a ride to the pier. But after saying *gàobié* to Zhang, he beckoned the commodore back into his car and drove around to the drydock where *Luchiang* was being repaired. A large rectangular hole had been cut in her hull, through which the tiny suns of the welding torches could be seen in her engine room. Sparks were falling from the main deck—apparently wherever Cromarty's people had found improvements to make—and teams were working beneath the hull to hydro away the sea growth and renew the sacrificial zincs. Good for them! Good for you, Plumpy!

Sure of himself, Chen waited on the side of the dock, near the great stack of matériel. In about ten minutes Lee, wearing coveralls and a hard hat, came out to see them. This work, with its orderly plan toward a clear goal, exactly suited him. He looked as excited by his prospects as on that first day at the decommissioning, before he had assumed the weight of the world.

"We are here from Admiral McGill," said Chen. "The transit unit sails on Monday."

"*Luchiang* will sail with them."

"No!"

"Yes sir. The equipment is here. The decks are being installed—all new platforms. The main pieces go in tonight, and we start testing tomorrow."

"Yet it seems you aren't quite watertight."

"They have a robot welder that has never failed an x-ray. Thirty minutes to button her up."

"I have lived too long," said Chen.

For a moment they spoke in Chinese, then Chen embraced Lee and said a word in parting that was different than *gàobié*.

The admiral lingered. Perhaps he had more to say, or perhaps he wanted to enjoy this fundamental connection to ships now that he was no longer serving in them. It was a pleasant morning. The terns floated on the easy currents of air, which held in the making tide a sharp smell of lunch; but when the lunch itself failed to appear, they raised their voices in cracking protest. Across the loch the *Arizona* Memorial looked like the empty shell of an exotic white turtle.

Turning to him, Chen explained what he had said. *"Wŏde xīnsuì le.* It means *My heart is breaking*—something you say when a loved one starts a journey. You know by now how highly I think of Captain Lee. One day he will command the navy. When the ships get to Kaohsiung, he will be promoted to commodore of the squadron—in your honored place, my dear sir—and the captain of *Tso Ying,* whose ship will unfortunately be in the yards for several months while her bow is replaced, will command *Luchiang."*

"I'm sure he'll do well."

"His actions in the fire convinced us."

"Yes, absolutely."

"I wish I could be as confident of all the captains."

"Zhang Chia-hao is remarkable, brilliant."

"I wish I could be as confident of all the captains."

He took Chen by the arms and turned him about. Six years of teaching history, of seeing how arbitrary, how unwise, and ultimately how insignificant were the efforts of great men, had given him this freedom. "In many ways Zhang Yu-hsuan is the most talented of the three," he said. "One of my vanities is shiphandling. I've never seen a ship handled better than *Chiai."*

"Yes, talented. I would trade that for a better attitude in a New York minute. If he were merely insubordinate, like Admiral Nelson, it would be one thing. Unfortunately, he despises everyone."

"I've come to the same conclusion. He doesn't like me much either. From now on we cannot afford a maverick. I need to give him closer supervision. When we get underway on Monday, I'll be embarked in *Chiai."*

"Brave man."

"Perhaps I should carry a side-arm."

"Let me tell you about a more efficient weapon. I have brought here two documents signed by our fleet commander. One gives Captain Lee unconditional authority to remove Zhang Yu-hsuan from command. The other gives that authority to you. It requires demonstrated cause, and it must be executed through Lee to overcome the nationality problem. Lee doesn't have to agree with your decision, however, and all of us in Tsoying will support you. Both documents are in the possession of Commander Tsai."

"If it comes to that, Zhang might refuse to comply with either document."

"Yes, but his crew won't refuse. Nor his XO, a subtly ambitious man, who would succeed him. I know you won't abuse this power, Bradford. Zhang Yu-hsuan has many supporters, and Taiwan needs his contribution in some capacity or other. But what the cheat said isn't entirely wrong: we must keep his hand from the firing key."

"That will be my job—and our contractors. By the way, and just for consideration: in the present state of affairs I worry about bringing the ships to Kaohsiung."

"Yes, if the balloon goes up—"

"If the balloon goes up they'll be exposed to the first barrage of missiles without either cover or sea room. A lot like this place on that December seventh. Perhaps there's a secluded port on the east coast, behind the mountains, where we could stash them."

Chen smiled in the recognition of like minds.

"We're looking at that. If you have any spare time you might peruse the *Sailing Directions*. Contact me whenever you wish. Goodbye, Commodore. *Wŏde xīnsuì le.*"

At Breaking Strength

The Problem Child

After they cleared the sea buoy and some coastwise traffic, the transit unit, numbering three ships, stopped to confer. The commodore, the other captains, and the American trainers were boated to *Luchiang,* where before any other business was taken up Captain Lee gave them a tour of the forward engine room.

The change was astonishing. The compartment, down to the bilges, was spotlessly clean; no soot anywhere. The entourage had to wear double hearing protection from the din of both propulsion gas turbines and the gas turbine generator. The control console, around which the engineers stood happily, now showed green lights and properly deflected meters. The decks, flat and new, of high-grade steel, were being painted with yellow primer. Perhaps most gratifying of all, the painters and their supervisors were volunteers from the other departments— the commodore, in an expansive moment in Colon, had peeled potatoes with one of them.

Of course Lee was beaming (news of his impending promotion might be contributing to this, and so too might the shipyard's report that the fire had been caused by a pinhole leak in a fuel line overlooked during the sale— not his fault); and his happiness lightened the captains' meeting. Even (L) praised the speed of the repairs, to which Lee replied, "Why, thank you, Captain. Plumpy is well again."

"Plumpy?" asked (H).

"An affectionate name from another time. Commodore, what do you have for us?"

He nodded; there was much. "I wanted to share with you both and with Tsai Mei-ling"—in her accustomed place on the sofa, taking the minutes—"some information from the pre-sail meeting that Zhang Chia-hao and I attended on Friday," he said.

Without going into the duel with Taylor—(H) could fill them in on that gossip as he probably would the sensitive intelligence—he gave them the general plan, including confirmation that they would be an independent national unit, reporting for convenience to the U.S. Pacific Fleet while receiving dedicated but distant cover from *T.R.* and her escorts.

"How distant?" (L) asked, jumping in.

"Too far for you to shoot at," said (H).

Lee coughed out a laugh, and Mei-ling couldn't help a smile. But (L) was the commodore's own flag captain now, whose vanity wouldn't be curbed by ridicule. The strain was between Taiwanese, but he should step in.

"Actually," he said, "we'll have plenty of chances for that, but only simulated shooting, of course. I have drawn up new safety procedures for all the ships to use. Please look them over and let me know if you see weaknesses. We're going to engage *T.R.* and her escorts every night. There will be a dedicated umpire circuit, so the 'shooting' will consist of radioing the time, the target, and your firing position to the admiral's data collection people. All, of course, with scrupulous honesty."

"The call sign of the admiral is *Cheat,*" said (H). "And he acts like a cheater."

"But we won't cheat, will we, Chia-hao."

"No sir. Save that for the real enemy."

Moving on, he described, as he had at Makalapa, the opportunities for training, the proficiency to be attained in surface action tactics, and the various tactics to experiment with.

"We'll disappear from their plot and go fast to a new point of approach. According to the rules we're not supposed to track each other until sunset."

Lee said, "But they'll know our bearing from our radar emissions. With all those airplanes he can just send a scout to find us."

"Actually, they won't know the bearing," he said, "because we're going to be silent."

"How silent?"

"Completely silent."

"Sonar, radar, radio?"

"Sonar, radar, radio. Satellite, cell phone, TV. We're going to disappear. We're going to learn *how* to disappear, and I promise you, gentlemen, though it might seem strange at first, you will learn to depend on it as you depend on the air you breathe. In a shooting war absolute silence is the key to victory and survival."

Lee was troubled again, (H) was curious. (L), wearing an oily smile, said quietly, "Commander Tsai, leave us now while I speak to your *bānjiū.*"

The blood rushed into her face. Her mouth was a thin line, and her eyes were hard as she stared at (L), who continued to smile. Lee opened his mouth to object but didn't. She rose from the sofa with a deliberation meant to be insolent. When he had transferred his pennant to *Chiai,* she had gone with him. For the duration of the voyage both of them would have to live with (L).

After she had gone (L) stood up and walked around the cabin, poured a fresh cup of tea from the pot she had prepared for him, and, with the cup and saucer in his two hands, stood over his commodore, close enough to spit.

"Let me remind you of your favorite word, Mr. Hilty," he said finally. "Why?"

"Why go silent?"

"Why?"

"To attempt to remain undetected by a very capable adversary," he replied. "As training for the worst case, against another adversary with just as capable sensors."

"Why?"

"I don't understand, Yu-hsuan. Because we need to."

"Why?"

"Now you're just being childish. You will please speak to me with respect."

Whether he would do that remained to be seen, but he did sit at the table again, still holding the cup and saucer.

"How much do these ships cost?"

"I don't know the details of your purchase contract."

"How much did *your country* pay to construct them? A billion dollars each one?"

"Something approaching that. Not quite that much."

"So my question is: Why would you think I would want to risk my billion-dollar baby to play your silly war-game? These ships were designed to operate in a certain way, with all their leading-edge technology. That technology— the best in the world, or so you Americans tell us—gives me the ability to know what is happening around me. I am confident that if I do know this, I will decide correctly what to do."

"But nothing in warfare is certain, and thinking that we do know is a great mistake, often leading to disaster. Look at this monitor. Are you certain that *T.R.* is there? Are you certain that she is heading east and not south-southwest to surprise us with a sudden attack? What if she is sending us a false position already? Why shouldn't she cheat? Her admiral wants to teach us a lesson."

"If my systems are up, I can defend my ship."

"I have said this before, gentlemen," he replied, look-ing at Lee, who would rather not remember. "The Aegis system, capable as it is, is not perfect, even when oper-ated by sailors at the highest levels of training. Look at every battle that has ever been fought, on land, on the sea, or in the air: some portion of every attack always gets through. Always. And with one hit to the superstructure, say from a missile homing in on your radar, you will have no Aegis system."

"Our safety lies in stealth," said (H).

"Exactly. Our safety lies in stealth. The best defense these ships have is built in: their extremely low radar cross-section. That's what we're going to exploit—that, and darkness, and weather, and some ideas of deception that I will share with you, and the fog of war generally. If you learn to do this here in the open ocean, against our most capable combatants, I'm sure that if it comes to it, you will have every fighting chance in the Taiwan Strait."

That should have convinced two of them and settled the hash of the third. After a month of living obsessively with these questions, he had stated the truth, phrase building on phrase, as a mathematician solves a conjecture. They could move on to something else now, of which he had several topics.

(L) spat the bitter tea into his saucer, so that it splashed onto the table. "Not only no but hell no," he said as Lee moved to mop it up. "Never."

(L) took over from the coxswain and turned the boat to the northeast, pushing the throttle to the wall. They flew over the blue waves except for those misfits that doused them. Turning to look at him in the stern, he said, "So we attack *T.R.* now, right? Very stealthy. No electronic signature. Your cheat will never see us coming." Then he put the wheel hard over while they all held the life-rope and steered back to the ship, around which he made three high-speed loops, eyes alight, like a teenager on a jet-ski.

Laying alongside *Chiai's* stern ladder in a perfect approach, he jumped out, ahead of his senior, and flew up the ladder and out of sight. The civilian trainers deferred to the commodore, but he waved them on. He and Meiling sat in the boat, which was rocking gently against the stern, while the three-man crew pretended to be busy up forward.

"I don't understand him," he said. "And that's strange for me. Every other sailor I've led, man or woman, has, at heart, wanted me to understand them—their ambitions, their fears, their resentments, even their guilty secrets."

"You're not the first to bounce off."

"Do *you* understand him? You've spent your career studying morale. Is it him? Is it me? Is it cultural?" When she paused he added, "Is it face?"

[207]

"He is above face. His personality is pure arrogance fueled by self-doubt. And terribly frustrated not to be in charge. Imagine Napoleon as a corporal."

"So how should I approach him?"

"Pick your battles. Make reasonable requests, fully explained. Be patient yet persistent. Document every interaction. I can help you, Bradford."

She meant this in a special sense, that she would help to build a case against a superior officer from her own country. She must know that he knew about the conditional orders she held. It might be in the nature of her duties to recommend that they be executed.

"I don't mind if *T.R.* hands us our heads on a platter," he said. "A few times anyway. It will underscore the lesson I'm trying to teach. It's the P.R.C. I worry about. We learned at the conference they intend to blockade."

"I'm sure you'll find a solution."

"In twelve days."

"What must happen does happen."

"I must keep at it, anyway. What was it that (L) said when he ordered you to leave the meeting?"

"When he ordered me?" In the bright Pacific sunlight the blood was rushing to her face once again.

"Yes. It sounded like an insult. You were angry."

"Yes I was. The word was *Bānjiū.*"

"What does that mean?"

"He called me your turtledove. As if we were lovers."

"I should be so lucky," he said.

"With a duty so serious it's not a subject for joking."

The crew needed to secure the boat for sea.

Losing Battles

The Taiwan Transit Unit would face the "enemy" with all
emitters emitting. That settled, there was no dissent
when he ordered them into a combat V at twenty-five
knots and their crews to battle stations. Following the
new safety procedures, they locked out their weapons systems, and the trainers verified this, notifying him by
phone.

The sun set abruptly off the port quarter, and a cloak-
ing darkness fell that the attackers had declined to exploit. He was divided between excitement at leading the
attack, frustration that it was being made so unprofes-
sionally, and a foretaste of the vindication when Cheat
annihilated them.

In CIC the radar detectors in the electronic warfare
module picked up *T.R.* almost at once. It would take an
act of Congress for an aircraft carrier to go silent while
she had planes up. He made sure that this first report of
contact, from a passive intercept, got the doubter's attention. Shortly afterwards they heard *T.R.* on sonar, for she
was hustling to make up the lost distance: four big screws
at near-maximum RPM. He made sure that (L) knew this
too.

On the tactical display she appeared big and fat and
beyond any doubt. Also beyond their missile range.

"If you had sold us your Tomahawk missiles she'd be
dead now," (L) said.

"Except that she has at least four lines of defense
against them, and she's been alerted that we're coming."

"I should tell them we fired already."

"As you may have noticed, my people are manning the
umpire circuit. I understand that you see no value in
these engagements. However, I strongly recommend that
you don't interfere with them." He looked at Mei-ling,

who was keeping the battle log. She nodded. What must happen would happen.

The fat symbol spawned a brood of aircraft symbols as the ships' radars picked them up. There were twenty, flying directly down the threat radial; soon within range. He issued *Exercise Air Warning Red, Simulate Weapons Free,* and the combat systems people talked the trainers through their firing procedures.

But before Taiwan could "fire" any missiles, the umpire circuit came alive:

"Air-to-surface weapons away, bearing 220, range 115. Left-most of three targets. Four anti-radiation missiles. Closing to release laser-guided munitions."

"I have three on the lead ship."

"Ditto, four."

"Ditto on the right-most."

"Weapons away."

"Away."

The radio was a mob of eager young voices stepping on each other to report their attacks, such a monopoly that the ships had to wait to report any defensive weapons fired. After a few minutes the U.S. strike leader summarized the release of ordnance, a rain of fire. Finally a deep voice from the flagship, identifying itself as Doug Harvey, after the Hall of Fame umpire, announced:

"All three enemy ships sunk. No survivors."

So it was for the next three nights as well. The transit unit came at *T.R.* from different directions. The ships went fast, went medium fast, went at bare steerageway to hide their polyhedronous hulls in the sea return. They attacked in a pack and from widely dispersed positions. They hid, or tried to hide, among passing merchant ships. In every case their radar signatures gave them away. The air wing struck them again and again. Once, when no planes were launched against them and they held their breath against discovery, the three U.S. destroyers unleashed a surprise attack from the void of total silence, the only sign of their presence being a single glimpse of their helo targeting them through the clouds.

Through all the defeats (L) appeared unmoved. "It's only games," he said at one point to his demoralized watch. "Has he no imagination?" the commodore asked Mei-ling. "He should have been in the engine room fire," she replied.

Meanwhile the ships and their powerful covering force continued steadily toward the scene of the crisis.

News from Home

As sailors will who live in the eternal present, the crews of the transit unit adjusted their lives to their circumstances. The nights were given over to exercising at battle; therefore, the days were given over to rest, routine, and recreation.

The training of the individual watch stations was essentially complete. Michael Blaylock reported that all three ships could now pass the U.S. Navy engineering readiness inspection, which included firefighting and damage control.

Having heard that the commodore doubted the wisdom of bringing the destroyers to Kaohsiung—directly across the Strait from China—he and Bill Houy volunteered to look for a safer harbor on the east coast. Both of them lived onboard *Hsinchu* now, where Zhang (H), who had this doubt himself, had offered them his portfolio of nautical charts, his English-language edition of the *British Admiralty Sailing Directions*, and his and his crew's knowledge of the country. And his discretion.

The commodore agreed, although he feared that the existence of the project would get out anyway and cause mischief.

It's an ill wind that blows nobody any good. With uninterrupted access to the satellite, he received a number of communications from the States:

☞ The principal of his high school finally replied that she had hired a replacement for his courses through the fall semester and they could talk about his future employment when he returned. In that light, had he seen a video released by one of his students and now widely viewed in social media in which he appeared to say that the South continued to live in a deluded state about the causes of the Civil War?

☞ Slate Greene wrote that he hoped his friend was having a pleasant vacation and when he returned they must talk about an exciting business opportunity that had come up.

☞ Mad wrote to say that she had signed a contract with the solar guy, who had revised his break-even calculation, making it affordable; that Adam had come for a visit and with his good heart had forgiven his father for driving right past his farm; and that Dustin Parke had been arrested by the British authorities on Jost Van Dyke island for invasion of privacy and falsifying electronic records.

"Have you seen this thing of me supposedly calling the South delusional?" he asked her, taking advantage of the satellite to make a video call. The quality was poor, but he was drawn to her face. Here was home.

"That's what you're calling about?"

"Your email said you've fixed everything else."

"Okay, yes, there's a clip of you saying that."

"But I never did."

"The young lady must have cut and pasted it cleverly, then. It's had beaucoup viewings. A lot of likes too by the way. But the governor took a shot at you last week."

"The governor? Of Virginia? Me personally?"

"He called you—hang on, I've got it here—he called you 'An historical revisionist, an intellectual carpetbagger, a peddler of woke lies, a cruel tempter of our youth, and probably someone with a criminal record.' When a reporter pointed out that you had served thirty years in uniform, he replied, 'And a double-dipper too. The taxpayers are paying him twice to spread his lies.'"

"Why didn't you tell me this before?"

"I wanted to save you from the distraction of it, with everything you've got going on."

"I never said those words. I can prove it: I used a script. I'll send it to you."

"Why don't you bring it instead? I think the storm's blown over anyway. He was just ranting to his base. They're going to do something to censor school reading lists, and he was just putting you up as a *bête noire.*"

"My principal accused me of it."

"No doubt you'll send the script to her, then. Are you really calling just to ask about a girl's cell phone video?"

"Why else?"

"You have no reaction to my last item of news?"

"I'm not surprised. I expect he got what he deserved. It doesn't involve you, does it?"

"I had to give a statement before I left. I told the truth."

Her image, out of synch with her words, looked pained.

"Of course you did. So what?"

"Ratted him out. Snitched. Squealed. Gloria won't speak to me now, which hurts more than I thought it would. I haven't heard from Dustin. Plus there's money involved."

"How so?"

"Nothing happened. In case you were wondering."

"I wasn't."

"The only thing to concern you is that when I declined his offer to add some fun to the trip, I thought I should pay my own way, and that became pricey."

Or she could just have come home.

"How much?" he asked.

"About sixteen thousand."

"That's one month of my Navy pay. Don't worry."

"Plus there's a bill from the lawyer who advised me in the deposition."

"But how much can that be? An hour or two."

"Plus the celebrity couple has threatened to add me to their lawsuit."

"I don't understand. Why didn't you tell me?"

"On several occasions I helped service the drone."

"I could have come to you from Hawaii, Mad."

"The settlement, if there is one, might be expensive."

[215]

The settlement for looking in people's windows.

He said, "I'll need to know the facts."

"Nothing happened. Between him and me."

In one of his favorite novels, Lucy Gayheart rejects a suitor who didn't understand her feelings, who could only be "clubbed by a situation." His wife was like that. She had intelligence, tact, and sympathy, but her ideas about people were situational, judgmental, unnuanced. And now vulgar. But the Navy had taught him to begin with the present facts and work from there.

"I'm sorry the trip turned out badly," he said. "You were looking forward to it."

"He doctored the images to make the women's breasts bigger. I don't care if she won't talk to me. Her brother's a pig."

"I think of him as a goof."

"No, a pig. Be safe, Bradford."

She might have had something else to say, but the picture froze. After he closed the laptop he picked up the phone to dial Mei-ling's stateroom. Before it could ring he hung up the receiver. His hand shook as he held his coffee mug: it wasn't fear but anger—the cords in his neck had that rigidity. He was a little short of breath.

Second-in-Command

Chiai's XO was Lieutenant Commander Huang Tsung, whom Admiral Chen had called a subtly ambitious man. If that was true, the ambition was well concealed by the subtlety. With a pang of guilt, for an unbiased observer might conclude that he was cultivating the XO as a relief for the captain, the commodore invited Huang to a private lunch. Of course he could invite whomever he wanted. And if (L) saw a warning in that, so much the better.

He knew Huang only a little. Besides the occasional passageway encounter, he had sat opposite him at a few meals in the wardroom, during which (L) had been no more than polite to their guest, and his officers, seeing this, were reticent. Huang spoke only if (L) asked him a question or, more often, to criticize the food or correct the white-coated enlisted who served it.

He was certainly serious about his food. Mei-ling said that one of his favorite dishes was shark's fin stew with abalone, to which she would add corn bread muffins with turmeric-infused honey. She supervised the setting of the table and showed Wang how to serve a meal for two; but during the meal itself she stayed away, not wishing, as senior PWO, to seem to be playing a part in it.

Huang himself seemed relaxed about the invitation— or that might be the subtlety.

"In the States," said the commodore, "when two sailors meet, the first question is always *What ships?* You and I aren't strangers, certainly, but I don't know you as well as I would like. So let me ask, then: What ships, sir?"

Huang had no problem talking about himself. "As ensign I was XO of a missile boat—200 tons. As lieutenant junior grade XO of a corvette—550 As full lieutenant XO of a frigate—4,500. Now XO of *Chiai*—10,800. You see: always upward."

"Someday you'll be XO of a battleship."

"Ah, but Taiwan doesn't have these." He turned on Wang with a burst of Chinese, at which Wang snapped to attention, bowed regret, and removed both officers' bowls, although the commodore hadn't finished. This provoked another correction, and his bowl was returned.

"Do you like always being number two?" he said.

"The XO has great responsibility—everything within the lifelines. I have good ability as an executive."

"Do you like tactics? Seamanship? Shiphandling?"

"All those things are necessary in an XO because the captain might be killed or wounded. In such a case I must be prepared to command the ship."

"Certainly, we hope that doesn't happen in *Chiai*— though I'm sure you would do a fine job. But someone who didn't know you might say from your record that you would prefer *not to* command."

"I prefer to free my mind from constantly asking, *How do we look to others?* Like a dog that won't stop barking. When I'm not on duty I'm able to write poetry. I doubt if Captain Zhang has time or attention for this."

Again he turned on Wang, who had just served, quite gracefully, the honeyed corn muffins, glistening in their bowls. Wang took away the dessert forks and pawed through the silverware drawer for two spoons, which in his hurry he laid on the wrong side of the placemats.

"I know why you wish to interview me," Huang continued in a lower voice. "Don't do that," he said to Wang, who was standing at attention by the sideboard.

"Perhaps you would let me correct my own servant," the commodore could not help saying.

Huang stiffened. "I apologize, sir."

"I may be oversensitive," he explained. "But it *is* my cabin, and of course his training is a reflection on me. Please continue, XO."

But if Huang were about to reveal his understanding of a combination against his captain and the conflict between ambition and loyalty which must certainly disturb his poet's peace of mind, the rebuke had cured him of it, and the rest of the meal passed largely in silence and with the promise of further silence the next time they met.

The Cheat's Sense of Duty

With a sudden roar *T.R.'s* helo hovered over the flight deck, while *Chiai's* flight deck crew remained in the hangar. A rescue collar descended by hoist, and the commodore, wearing the one extra cranial helmet to be found in the ship, fought his way into the downdraft and pulled the collar over his arms and head, giving a thumb's-up to the air crewman in the doorway. Amid acrid puffs of jet exhaust, he was lifted like a sack ever higher as the destroyer receded beneath his feet until, level with the door, he was hauled inside.

He had expected a jump seat, but the crew, with all their other duties, had taken the time to reconfigure the cabin for a VIP. The crewman exchanged his cranial helmet for a real one with the "Eightballers" logo on the front and an audio system which he plugged in for him.

"Welcome aboard, Commodore," the pilot said, looking aft with his visor raised. "I could have put her down on the deck, even without the certification."

"I'm sure you've been thrown out of better bars than this one," he replied, a bit of camaraderie rewarded by two clicks of the mic.

The message had come in after midnight, and Mei-ling had awakened him with it. Admiral Taylor would like to confer with the commodore at his convenience. A helo would be over *Chiai* at 10:00 a.m.

"We've got a treat for you," the pilot said. "We happen to be flying right down the International Date Line."

"Fantastic. What were the odds?"

"I know! Look, now it's Thursday." The helo jinked to port. "Now it's Saturday." More jinking. "Thursday—Saturday—Thursday—Saturday. What do you think?"

"I don't know whether I'm more impressed that you can fly the date line so precisely or that you're so excited about it. You do know that every time you cross ahead of the line you add a day. At this rate you'll be my age when we land."

"Never that old," said the happy young voice.

He rewarded this with a double click, the airedale version of a *Like.*

The last time he had crossed the International Date Line, going home, Mad had been in labor with Adam.

They had to cross the line twice more because *T.R.,* steaming west as the transit required, reversed course to launch her next event. The Eightballers flew into a holding pattern off the carrier's starboard side, which allowed the pilot to narrate the launch, with all its wonderful choreography. Once, years before, the commodore had known all colors of the life vests.

When the last plane had been catted off, making that thrilling dip toward the sea before pulling up confidently as if to say *Fooled you,* the helo stood on its side in a sharp turn toward a landing spot aft of the island. It touched down lightly, and the crewman slid open the door. The air smelled instantly of jet fuel, and the roar of jets turning up was loud in his Mickey Mouse ears. The ATO, air transport officer, in his white vest—that was it: white were safety personnel—brought him along a narrow path to a watertight door in the island, where the helo crewman relieved him of his helmet, and the admiral's aide in his working aiguillette brought him topside to the flag bridge. Even within the ladderwell the sound of jet engines dominated.

"Commodore Hilty, sir," the aide announced like a butler at a doorway. Taylor was sitting in his chair with a captain, also aiguilletted, standing by his side.

"Greetings, Commodore," the admiral cried. "Welcome to Paradise."

"Thank you, sir, and it might be Paradise if it weren't for all these goddamned airplanes," which received the requisite grins. Good old American trash-talking wasn't like him, but in his years as a civilian teacher, enjoined to be solemn, he had missed it. So it was with memories.

"The chief of staff has orders to your old squadron," said Taylor. "DesRon 22."

The captain looked modestly pleased—probably to be away from Taylor. "Yes sir. Very fortunate. Any tips, Commodore?"

"That was fifteen years ago, Chief of Staff. You'll be something like my eighth descendent."

"It can't be all that different, Commodore," which had been his own mantra these past few months.

"All right, here's a tip: you can solve any problem you want—you'll have the power, both by regulations and the bully pulpit. But you can't make *all* the changes you want, so you'll need to pick and choose."

"You can't do better than that, Brian," said Taylor in the tone of voice that wants to end a phone call. With a nod the chief of staff left them.

Four Super Hornets flew up the port side not much higher than the flag bridge and one by one peeled away in a racetrack turn to separate themselves for the approach. Off the ship's quarter, the leader continued the tight turn, straightened out directly on glide path, and landed plunk on the flight deck, trapping the optimum third wire. Pulled aft a few feet as the wire retracted, he or she gunned the engine to taxi up to a spot in the bow. Almost at once the next Super Hornet landed. Then the next. In good visibility a well-trained carrier and air wing could recover an aircraft every thirty seconds. *T.R.* wasn't far from that goal. And what joy to be in those cockpits.

Taylor picked up the phone. "Excuse me for a minute. I've got to make the captain shit his pants. —Hey, Red Dog, this is a drill: sudden onset of fog, ceiling and visibility zero. Make all appropriate responses. —There, that'll unstop him."

He said this with a wink. Then he collected himself. The athlete's chest filled with air, and the voice was loud and angry: "Hilty, what in hell are you people doing down there? Are your ships even *trying* to attack us?"

"Well, sir—"

"They're sitting out there like sinkex targets."

"Yes, I agree, but—"

"You're making it so easy we're not getting any train-ing out of it. We'll chop to Juventude and still not know how to fight the Chinese."

He waited.

"Your face tells me there's another side to the story," Taylor said in another voice.

"Yes sir."

"Let's have it."

He profiled each of his captains—Lee competent, pro-gressing; Zhang Heavy the brilliant warrior; Zhang Lite a riddle wrapped in a mystery inside an enigma. Taylor missed the reference—he must not have read Churchill in high school—but as one of the Navy's chosen statesmen he intuited the political constraint.

"And you can't just tell him to turn off his radars?"

"A month ago, despite my orders, they slowed each morning to fish"—feeling a pang as he said this because those had been Mei-ling's decisions. "Every order I give is subject to ratification by the captains. The only time I felt certain of my authority was when I guided them around the hurricane."

"What about the exigencies of battle? Can you fire his ass? Can his people fire him?"

"There's a provision for that—even I could do it—but it would probably cause an international incident, his XO isn't ready to succeed him, and I don't know enough Chi-nese to assume command myself."

"All right, then. As they say, you can't solve every problem, but you sure have to solve this one. Before push comes to shove."

"Is that going to happen?" he asked.

Taylor bellowed "Flag Lieutenant!" who appeared at once. "I've arranged for you to have an all-sources brief by my spook. The aide will take you to him. When you're done, come back; I'd be grateful for some advice."

In all of this there had been no sign of Cheat who didn't take prisoners; only of Admiral Taylor who knew his duty.

On the flight deck the remaining planes aloft, having marshalled in the "fog" at a procedural point miles astern of the carrier, began to appear one by one at the ramp under radar control.

In the relative silence interrupted by *T.R.'s* fog whistle, and in the hushed atmosphere of the carrier intelligence center, where the past and the future counted for more than the present, Lieutenant Commander Rick Moore was waiting for him, a handsome, well-built man who looked as if he belonged in a squadron ready room but who spoke in the fluent purr of the academic.

"There have been some interesting developments," he said. "A great many national resources have been dedicated, and we have more visibility into the intentions of China and the likely response by Taiwan, military and political, than we've ever had. Before I start, Commodore, may I ask: are your clearances up-to-date?"

"They were in 2012."

"Oh yes, no doubt. But am I right in thinking that this is 2018?"

"I believe so."

"I see: a needs-of-the-service briefing, then. Are you a loyal U.S. citizen, sir?" His puckish face said he could cut corners as well as anyone, and with pleasure.

"Not according to the governor of Virginia."

"What does he say about you?"

"I'm disloyal to the South, purveying the false claim that the Confederacy wasn't about the Lost Cause."

"That was you in that classroom?"

"Apparently. I haven't seen the young lady's video."

"You should. Even without computer analysis the lacunae were obvious. And of course your thesis is correct."

"Thank you."

"We won't ask the governor, then."

"Thank you."

"Yes sir. On to the briefing. Here's what the Chinese have done in the last forty-eight hours, and here's what we think they're planning."

The intel was remarkable, if it was right. The Chinese were carrying out a large-scale training exercise with two phases. In the first phase, going on now, many of their combatants had sailed into the Taiwan Strait, and their strategic forces—the "Second Artillery"—were firing ballistic missiles into the South China and East China Seas, including one generally toward Okinawa.

"Missiles or aircraft over Taiwan itself?"

"Nothing as yet. There's been a debate on that within the P.L.A.—the People's Liberation Army."

"Yes."

"Their Nanjing Military Region. Some say they should wait to see whether the Seventh Fleet shows up, in which case an overflight would test our reactions."

"And act as a rehearsal for a full-scale air assault."

"Yes sir. And that's the question about the second phase of the exercise. Merchant and amphibious ships have been arriving in ports along the Strait. It could be part of the training, or they may be gradually massing an assault force, *so* gradually we won't notice—a Birnam Wood-to-Dunsinane sort of thing."

But that was about fulfilling the witches' prophesy, ostensibly by hiding an army with camouflage. Here Shakespeare sacrificed realism to artistic device. Macduff didn't need a stealthy approach: he outnumbered Macbeth. And why, even more egregiously, has everyone since then confused this passage with gradualism, a useful tactic?

"How many ships so far?" he asked.

"Something like a full battalion's worth."

"At this rate, how long before two army corps?"

"And support them? Weeks and weeks. But the slow buildup would work to their advantage: first, they know what they intend and we don't, despite good sourcing; and second, even if they decide not to land, the pressure on Taiwan to cut a deal would be enormous."

"They could assemble and load and even sail the ships, but without command of the battle space it would be a massacre, like the Spanish Armada."

"That's how our guys see it. The buildup of assault forces would be slow enough for us to watch and evaluate. It's the surprise attack that makes us nervous."

"Hence the term *surprise.*"

A grin. "Yes sir."

How he loved being back!

"And what about a Chinese blockade?"

"Nothing new. They continue to discuss it. Actually deploying one would carry few risks as long as they didn't enforce it."

But no blockade was legal unless enforced.

"And Taiwan's thoughts?"

"All over the spectrum. Strategically, there's a divide between the political parties on whether to accommodate the Chinese or defy them. Accommodation ranges from promising not to declare independence to offering themselves for annexation. Defiance is mostly to keep their heads down, survive the first assault, and wait for the Seventh Fleet."

"And tactically?"

"For several years they've been building hardened shelters on their east coast and in the Chung-Yang mountains. Given sufficient warning they would move their most vulnerable assets—aircraft, artillery, missile systems—into these shelters. They don't drill at it for fear of revealing the locations."

"But surely not their semiconductor manufacturing."

"No sir."

[227]

"You say they're all over the spectrum. In your opinion what's the national resolve to defend themselves? Scale of one to five."

A slow grin. "What does one mean?"

"No resolve at all. Cave at the first sign of pressure."

"Yes sir. In my opinion, Rick Moore in my little intelligence bubble in my well protected keep, if it comes to an attack, they'll be a four, maybe even a five. History tells us that people defend their homes way beyond expectations."

"It's a comfort to hear you say that, Commander."

The intelligence officer brought him to flag plot, where Admiral Taylor was hearing from Commodore Bergstrom, his bald-headed crony, about the superb readiness of the three U.S. destroyers. Bergstrom greeted him respectfully and cordially without mentioning, as a example of their readiness, the thrashing his ships had given Hilty's—essentially an equal force.

"If I could change the subject," Bergstrom said, "I wonder if you could tell us about the fire."

"The fire: *Luchiang's* fire, of course. Forward engine room, all three turbines running. The fuel supply line to the generator has a flange at the base plate. The neoprene gasket in the seal developed a pinhole leak, and the ties on the flange shield came loose. It was probably in that condition when the ship was sold. Eventually the leak turned into a spray, and the fire spread into the lagging."

"NavSea has copied us on your report. Every snipe in the Navy has been checking gaskets and flange shields. But what about firefighting?"

He admitted that he and Captain Lee had led hose teams into the compartment and extinguished the fire.

"Yikes. And may I ask your age, sir?"

Several junior officers had come over to listen.

He smiled. "Old enough to know better. The real feat was our female political warfare officer, who put on her first OBA and broke up all the lagging with her axe."

He was about to add the rest of it—*And gave me her own air to breathe after I passed out*—when Taylor, pulling rank, steered him into a corner.

"Now that you've heard from Moore on the intel, tell me your thoughts on the rules of engagement. If the Chinese look like they're going to attack your ships, do I wax them?"

"I would think, sir, you'd be bound by the doctrine of self-defense, just as with our ships. There's a very good chance that the P.L.A. would test you right to the limit. Particularly if they don't really intend to fight. A preemptive attack by us would only strengthen China's position. Also, and I know we haven't shown it yet, but I think the Taiwan ships will give a good account of themselves."

"I concur that you haven't shown it yet. All right, the ROE are clear enough. At Pearl you mentioned something to Juventude about stationing the carriers. I wonder if you'd share that with me."

It wasn't criticism for jumping the chain of command: he sincerely wanted to know. Or perhaps Juventude had asked his strike group commanders for recommendations.

"I told him to put you east of the island, Admiral." He listed all the reasons. "By the way, that's the same advice I've given to Tsoying: limit their vulnerability in the west, counterattack from the east."

"Got it, thank you. Thank you for coming over today. Now go forth and do better."

The aide and he trotted down the ladders to the flight deck. By the door the same crewman was waiting with a helmet and a white vest with the commodore's name and rank stenciled on it, and the ATO was ready to take him across the deck.

The jet blast deflectors rose, and the first aircraft launched with a roar. Besides the beauty of the thing, the perfect integration of time, space, machines, and human beings, carrier flight operations were as iconic of American values as the Capitol or the Statue of Liberty. You didn't have to squint very hard to imagine Torpedo 8 taking off from the carrier *Hornet* in the Battle of Midway seventy-six years before, never to return.

In the cabin of the helo he plugged in his audio jack and spoke over the hum of the engines to the pilot.

"When you said you could set down safely on our uncertified deck with our untrained flight quarters team, you weren't just being polite?"

"No sir. Piece of cake. We won't tell the FAA."

"What's your name?"

"Tom Daly, sir. Lieutenant Daly."

"Do me a favor, please, Tom Daly. Get the ATO back here. I need to talk to the admiral again."

The Difference between Authority and Power

There was no exercise that night. The next morning Tom Daly brought his helo back and landed it on *Chiai's* deck. The crewman came into the hangar with helmets and life vests. Moments later the three captains, Mei-ling, and the commodore, keeping their heads down, walked under the whipping rotor blades and went onboard.

At the aircraft carrier they were greeted by the admiral, the commanding officer of the ship, and the commander of the air wing; asked a few cursory questions by a doctor; given a safety briefing; given a mission briefing; outfitted with flight suits and other helmets; and brought back to the flight deck. The three captains then boarded an E-2C Hawkeye early warning aircraft and were strapped in, two of its three operators having stood down to make room for them. There was not enough room for Mei-ling, but she wound up with the grand prize, for CAG, the commander of the air wing, put her in the back seat of his Super Hornet.

With a tiny throb of envy and a large influx of pride, the commodore watched them launch. The Hawkeye, accelerating from zero to 140 knots in about two seconds, looked with its size and its radar dome too ungainly to fly, but once airborne it rose gracefully enough to its departure altitude. The Super Hornet, on the other hand, looked as if it had been bred to the catapult: when clear of the bow, CAG put it into a vertical climb like a trip to the moon.

Ninety minutes later, the two planes caught their arresting wire with that sudden stop which always felt as if your heart would keep going right through your chest. As intended the guests returned to earth better informed, high in spirits, well disposed toward their hosts, and slightly disoriented.

This was followed by lunch in the flag mess: a filet mignon so tender it must be lying and a cheese souffle so light it floated above the plate. The admiral made an agreeable speech; Red Dog, the captain of the carrier, presented the guests with framed Tail-Hook certificates; and CAG and the aide helped each of them into a leather flight jacket with their names on the chest patch. He was especially charming to Mei-ling, his "guy in the back," who was delighted with this entire day.

After lunch Commander Moore took them to the intel center for a sanitized version of the briefing he had given the commodore, and when the briefing was over, as if by magic *T.R.* was between launch and recovery cycles and the helo was waiting. Tom Daly contributed to the entertainment by buzzing the three destroyers, whose crews had crowded topside to wave at them, before landing and debarking everyone on *Chiai.*

The commodore wouldn't have used the term "softened up," but it did seem like a good time to hold another captains' meeting. They followed him into the inport cabin, where Mei-ling, as she served them tea, emoted about being upside-down and weightless.

A few minutes of such small talk helped to digest the adventure. The mood of the company was lighthearted. Presently the men took their places with him at the table, and Mei-ling took hers on the couch with her steno pad.

"We do have two serious items still to decide," he began. They waited to hear what these were, although certainly they had guessed them.

"Today we saw the surveillance capabilities of just a part of the *T.R.* strike group. I wish I could have taken you to your American sister ships as well, to see how they conduct surface actions, which, frankly, have been so superior to ours, but we ran out of time. I can arrange this if any of you are still unconvinced."

"Unconvinced of what?" (L) said.

"Of the pressing need, with less than a week before we arrive in contested waters, to learn, finally, how to operate in complete electronic silence. Of the need to gain proficiency and also confidence that by operating this way, we have a very good chance of winning any battle."

"Yes, I am unconvinced," (L) said.

"Very well. Would a visit help?"

"I am unconvinced by anything you say."

The others stirred. Just raising his fingers from the surface of the table, he cautioned them to let (L) continue.

"You cannot teach me anything. And since you're not in my navy I don't have to obey you. You may be ignorant and stupid for all I know. Filled with wrong ideas. But you are unlucky, that is demonstrated. Disasters follow you like the Pigpen. Our ships—*our* ships!—will not begin to do well until you leave us."

"You are wrong," Lee said, perhaps embarrassed by the Pigpen reference, which could only have come from him. "If it were not for Commodore Hilty, we would have driven right into the eye of a hurricane."

"You might have. I would have crossed ahead of it."

"You said there were two serious items," (H) reminded Hilty after a silence. "What other?"

"The other is our destination. My people and I have done some research"—as if (H) didn't know this—"and we think that Kaohsiung would be a dangerous place to bring the ships. It is too vulnerable to air attack, not to mention having to transit the Strait."

"What better port, then?"—a leading question.

"Somewhere on the east coast, tucked behind the mountains. Su'ao looks ideal, with its infrastructure already in place. At least as a temporary stop, until the situation is clarified. What do you think, gentlemen?"

He looked at Lee, their future commodore.

"I agree about electronic silence. I agree that we must practice this against the *T.R.* strike group. I will have to think more about recommending a change in port, when our families have already moved to Kaohsiung."

"Captain Zhang?"—meaning (H).

"I agree with Captain Lee."

(L) was tensed behind the table, ready to spring. "I don't agree with anything you say. It's much too late to change our port. Could you do this in America? I think you must be senile."

To the others he spoke in Chinese, perhaps insisting that any decision must be unanimous.

"Any decision," Lee said quietly in English, "will be made in tones of respect and with appreciation for the help we've been given."

"My point exactly: help from foreigners."

"Perhaps we should take a break," he suggested, at which (L) strode from the room.

"I apologize," Lee said. "I am deeply embarrassed."

(H) said, "I am embarrassed and also concerned. He is unfit to command. Better now a sharp knife."

Clearly he knew about the documents.

Mei-ling, who held the documents, physically and perhaps morally, said, "I heard Zhang Yu-hsuan say *I don't have to obey you.* To me that also means *I don't have to but I choose to obey you.* Our objective should be to reinforce that choice."

"I'm not sure about Su'ao," Lee said. "We bought a house in Kaohsiung."

"First priority is radar silence," (H) said. "His refusal gives cause."

"He would say it was about Su'ao," Lee replied.

"It's about national defense," (H) insisted. "And there's not a moment to lose. This is why you have the letters."

"Will *you* make this decision?" Lee said to Hilty.

He looked at each of them in turn. Mei-ling was confident of her powers of persuasion. The disagreement between (H) and Lee pitted alarm and perhaps exasperation against self-doubt, self-interest, and perhaps the desire to evade responsibility.

Knowing the answer felt like flying. "I would make such a decision in the heat of battle, and certainly he's given cause. Personally I don't think it's come to that yet. As a foreigner I shouldn't be involved in what is otherwise an administrative matter affecting your officer's career.

"But let me remind you of the difference between authority and power. Kuan-lin, it's no secret among us that you have the authority to relieve him simply because you've lost confidence in his ability to command. But the *power* to do that needs something more. Far better for the three of you to reason with this highly intelligent officer who, above all else, wants your respect. I'm sure you can bring him around.

"I'm going to the bridge now and leave that to you, however you can manage it. We need to settle both questions right away and also get a promise from him for a more cooperative attitude going forward. I'd be particularly grateful to all of you for that."

Of course this was not the first time he had left a problem for subordinates to solve. But after so many years away from command he had forgotten how good it felt, how courageous, how essentially human: embracing the risk that they might fail while accepting accountability for the result. Yes, he loved being back.

He arrived on the bridge in time to see a section of Super Hornets flying past, the western sun golden on their wings. As the planes broke off, the ships sailed on, alike and different, toward the unreachable horizon.

Bānjiū

Mei-ling came into the cabin with a bottle of champagne inside her leather flight jacket. As the door closed she kept her hand on the knob, and there was an extra click. Without looking at him she went to the sideboard, took down two glasses, and brought the wine on a tray. By then he had moved from his desk to the couch beneath the tactical display, which showed the tracks of *Luchiang* and *Hsinchu* close aboard and the *T.R.* strike group some miles away to the northeast, spilling aircraft symbols.

Standing in front of him she slipped out of the jacket and sat on the couch, far enough so that they might turn toward each other but close enough to clink glasses.

It was two p.m. on Friday, August thirty-first. Tonight they would rendezvous with the main body of the Seventh Fleet, consisting of the *Reagan* and *Nimitz* strike groups, a logistics group, and the fleet command ship *Blue Ridge*. Tomorrow they would dock in Taiwan. It would be a long night, and he had planned to sleep this afternoon to be ready for it. Mei-ling had known better than that.

She and the two captains had brought (L) around. No one would be fired. The ships had learned to turn off their costly electronics, sailing by instinct and with whatever hints of the enemy the sea and the aether gave them. The first night they had been waxed by *T.R.* anyway. The second night had been a draw. The last three nights they had done the waxing. The master of *Henry J. Kaiser,* their oiler, had verbally winked at the commodore during their most recent refueling, and Cheat Taylor had sent him a congratulatory message with copies to Seventh Fleet, Pacific Fleet, and Taiwan. The ships were ready. The ships' companies were proud.

"You did it," she said.

"I think *you* did it. Starting with the fishing."

She smiled at the fond memory, once so fraught. "What are you feeling now?"

"I'm trying to hold the flood back, like the Dutch boy at the dike. I'm happy with how the month has gone, I'm pleased by my part in it, I'm grateful to you and the others who helped so much. But I'm disappointed too. Sad and empty. What seemed impossible a month ago now seems unimportant. Why did I care so much? The way it is with all dreams once we realize them. Mostly I don't like it that this terribly interesting time is ending."

"No," she said quietly, "it hurts."

"I suppose, also, I'm afraid of the future. I'm sure the Navy will want to retire me again. Some wicked student at my high school faked a video of me saying incendiary things about the American South, and now everyone from the governor of the state to the local school board wants my head. I'm going to have to learn a new profession. My friend Slate Greene has something in mind, but it's in business, and I'm not sure I want to soil my hands."

"You will be the first compassionate rich person."

"The other thing you know about. I've told you."

"Your wife, Madeleine."

It was charming the way she pronounced her name.

"I'm at a loss to explain it. I don't know what she wants—or what I want. Are we just tired of each other, or are we sick and tired? Do I care? When we've been apart emotionally for so long, except for a joking sort of irritability, would it be so awful to live apart for good? Am I up to it?"

"Of course you're up to it," she said. "What must happen does happen. I learned that after my husband died." She smiled to see the past again. "It's not out of the question," she continued, "that you would find someone else."

"I'm rather difficult to live with."

"As if I wouldn't know *that,*" she said.

"I'm also going to miss my friends," he said. "Miss you."

To this she had no answer.

"What will you do next?" he asked.

"But that's what the champagne is for, Bradford. I've been promoted. Or I will be tomorrow. Tsai Mei-ling, Commander, Republic of China Navy. My sister the president will be so proud."

He rose and refilled their glasses and clinked again. She was pleased, with shining eyes. "Wonderful news! Terrific! No surprise at all. Someday you'll be an admiral. Will you have a ceremony? Will you let me be the one who changes your shoulder boards?"

"Yes, you can be my bridesmaid."

"Promotion. And then what?"

"Something in the Ministry of Defense as a PWO. I'll be able to buy an apartment in Tsoying. Two bedrooms and a study. Room for a king-sized bed in case a king wants to lay his head there."

"As certainly one will."

"And a sound system," she said as if she hadn't heard him. "You don't know this about me, but I love music. All kinds of music. I'm going to buy one of those systems where I can just pop my cell phone into its hole and— poof!—I sit in the audience. Wireless too. Now that I've learned Aegis, I can learn Spotify."

"And you'll be ashore from now on, Mei-ling?"

"Unless you guys sell us an aircraft carrier. All ashore from now on. Plenty of stability for me and my king."

"I'm so happy for you."

"No, you couldn't be happier. But you could."

"I don't see how."

"May I tell you something? A secret?"

"This would be the time for it."

She moved closer to touch him just above the knee. Her pulse beat in her lovely throat. In her eyes tears were brimming. "I would like you to come to Tsoying. To stay as long as you want. Meet my Chowa. Maybe make a home there—my home or some other home. You could learn Chinese. Here:"

From her flight jacket she took a paperback book, *Chinese Is Easy,* and turned the pages for him. "Most people know maybe ten thousand characters. In Taiwan we tell foreign speakers they can get by with four thousand. If you—Bradford Hilty, so smart!—learned only fifty characters a day you would know our language in just three months. Fifty characters! Three months!

"This is Top Secret Eyes Only Burn Before Reading: Admiral Chen wants you to join his staff. As a senior consultant—that means well-paid consultant. You say you worry about the future: here is a future, Bradford. In a beautiful, beautiful place, where you will be honored as prophets never are in their own land. Where no one will alter your speeches. After this crisis we Taiwanese will return to our foolish pursuit of pleasure, of living and loving. No war, great happiness, great coffee: I know you will like it. Let's change each other's shoulder boards."

She was weeping now, letting the tears run down her cheeks. His heart ached. Such a leap for her. Taking her hands he brought her to her feet, and they held each other. At first as friends who have shared an adventure, then gradually as something else. She fitted against him, her cheek against his, her chin soft in his neck; her breasts, her hips, her thighs, even her feet. Her arms encircled him. With a word from him she'd be his. One word would be as much to her as a marriage vow.

She murmured in the embrace, "I'm such a hypocrite, busting Lieutenant Wú for loving an American."

He thought, Foreign speakers.

He held her while her dream faded. Gradually her arms relaxed. He looked into her eyes and saw disillusionment.

"It would be all that you say, Mei-ling. I could like it very much. If I weren't leaving behind so many questions. So many years. So much trust."

"I know. Bradford Hilty, always fighting entropy. Oh, my dear man." She embraced him again with a tenderness that might still make a claim on him if he would unbend just a little. "Imagine: in one month we have come to know each other. Really know. And always, from the first, there has been something between us. Maybe— don't be shocked—maybe love! I have studied this. Not a mistake. Not boss and secretary pulling off a big deal. Not the fool's gold of a shipboard romance. (L) wasn't wrong. *Bānjiū*. I want to find out what it means."

"I feel it too. You can't know how appealing it is to think of running away with you. But I'm trying to look ahead. In the future I must know that I did the right thing. And that I decided it myself, without debts to pay."

"I am going to believe, then, that you will freely do the right thing. And be hopeful."

"Mei-ling, I don't see how," he said; an exaggeration as things blurted out tend to be. But once the words were in the air between them, they sounded true, and above all there must be no false hope. "Tomorrow my old life will claim me. We'll be ten thousand miles apart."

"I know. *Wǒde xīnsuì le,*"she cried. "My heart is break-ing to see you go."

Home Away from Home

About an hour before sunset, the tactical display began to fill with symbols, and Commodore Hilty went up to the bridge. The main body of the Seventh Fleet was coming down the east side of Taiwan, the *T.R* strike group was sailing north to meet them, almost thirty ships were involved, and the coming maneuver would be like a motorcycle gang making a U-turn on the interstate. *T.R.* was flanked on her port side by the Taiwan destroyers in one column and on her starboard side by the American destroyers in another. *Chiai* was last in her line.

Over the radio an unhurried voice read the long signal.

A diagram was posted with the many stations involved.

Students of tactics might be pleased that the main body—the three carriers, the logistics group, and *Blue Ridge*—had been ordered into a circular formation, something hardly seen since World War II. Students of cover and deception might be pleased that around the main body all eighteen destroyers had been ordered into a circular screen, which would then be rotated several times during the night to present any snooper with an impossible shell game.

The signal was executed, with every ship for herself.

Captain Zhang, whatever his resentments, had been on the bridge from the beginning. He got his officers together and correlated the diagram with what they could actually see: identifying the southbound ships, pointing out where each joining ship must go, warning them about those whose tracks must take them close aboard *Chiai.* He understood it all, and when the conning officer turned to the new course at a higher speed, it was obvious that the ship was sailing true. This was (L), who seemed to take nothing seriously, who had never made such a complicated maneuver.

Coming at them, bigger every minute, from left to right were *Blue Ridge, Reagan,* and *Nimitz. T.R.'s* station was to the other side of *Nimitz.* As she sailed north on the reciprocal course, she must time her maneuver to fall in with the oncoming traffic while allowing for the enormous turning circle of an aircraft carrier.

It seemed that all hands on *Chiai* wanted to judge this turn. They were standing at the lifelines with their shadows long upon the waves, excited by the ship's speed, by the occasion, by the naval power on display. They yelled in delight when a wave coming over the bow drenched them with spray. Their Chinese was entirely plain: *T.R.* would certainly miss her station. By the time she completed her turn she would be miles astern of *Nimitz*—she would be somewhere in the East China Sea—she would be in Okinawa asking where the Seventh Fleet had gone.

The moment came. The American destroyers, taking their separate courses to the outer circle, had gone ahead. The Taiwan destroyers were passing safely astern of the carrier before proceeding to their own stations. As last in the line *Chiai* had a clear view of it all. Not enough room! The tone on the bridge was both scornful and uneasy.

Glowing in the red rays of the sun, *T.R.* began her turn. As she heeled, her island seemed to duck under the horizon like a man with a tall hat under a low doorway. She carried ninety aircraft plus trucks and other wheeled equipment. The crew would have had to double the tie-downs. But the turn!—more ambitious than the observers thought, it kept exceeding expectations. She snapped into place exactly on *Nimitz's* quarter, and when *Chiai* passed her on her way to the screen, the two companies waved and cheered, and the commodore had the signal-man hoist "Wow" in the rosy light.

Night fell, a black moonless night. The reinforced fleet continued south, often turning east so that *Reagan,* the duty carrier, could launch and recover. The destroyers were constantly following each other around as their circle spun back and forth.

꿈 꿈

The adversary knew they were coming. As Juventude concentrated the fleet, and as the "bandit" destroyers of Taiwan drew closer to home each day, the public warnings of the P.R.C. had darkened, and its preparations for military action had accelerated. The naval exercises expanded. The amphibious ships began to load. At hard-to-hit points along the coast, mobile missile launchers moved into position.

Under the circumstances, then, the Seventh Fleet was ready when, about midnight, a Chinese Yùn-9 maritime patrol aircraft approached them from the south. *Reagan's* CAP intercepted it at two hundred miles and escorted it over the formation. From the bridge of *Chiai* the several aircraft could be seen moving faster than the starry backdrop, sometimes passing through wisps of night cloud as, indefatigably (the Yùn-9's endurance was more than ten hours), they wove up and down and back and forth. In a video conference the commodore had discussed this possibility with Taylor and Juventude. From their collective knowledge of China's spy-planes, it seemed like a good thing.

The midnight rotation of the screen left *Chiai* in the rear, with *Hsinchu* to starboard and *Luchiang* to starboard of her. Ahead, if one counted them, were the twenty-four stern lights of the fleet plus the three carriers lighted up like a tent-city in the desert. There was nothing to do for the next few hours but turn east periodically for the cyclical launch and recovery and then back to the south. The commodore, with no responsibilities except as the author of the plan, could go to bed or at least could catch some sleep in his chair. Instead, he went out to the bridge wing to stand under the stars with (L).

The air was warm with a gossamer touch of dew; it smelled clean and salty like kelp. An easy sea, scattering reflections of starlight, rolled under the ship.

From out of the darkness (L) said, "I'm sorry for treating you so badly. You didn't deserve it."

Certainly he hadn't deserved the additional stress: the cords in his neck, which drew tight with every new problem; the jagged breath when he imagined speaking to (L); waking up in a cold sweat with a pounding heart.

"Thank you. I forgive you. I wasn't sure if you were angry at me or just angry period."

"Maybe a little of both. I didn't understand how you could care so much about affairs that don't concern you."

"Perhaps it's easier that way. But that was then—"

"So you admit you didn't care what happened."

"I was going to say I didn't know your country then. Now I am committed to your success, heart and soul."

"And now we will slip into Su'ao, like Abraham Lincoln traveling to his inauguration disguised as a woman."

An embellishment of history, but the thought wasn't wrong. He let it go. "What made you decide to work things out with the others?"

"Your *bànliú* had the documents to relieve me, which you know. Zhang Heavy, as you call him, threatened to arrest and confine me. Lee was prepared to do all those things. For once there was no softness in him. My fort was invested and the siege batteries were in place."

The word *bànliú* caused him pain, as it had done the first time (L) had used it; as no doubt it always would do. Someone worth loving actively loved him.

"It was good to keep it quiet," he said.

"Yes, quiet. Quiet has been the whole point, hasn't it. So quiet that they confiscated my cell phone and forbid me to use the radio."

"I don't understand. Who would you contact?"

But Admiral Chen had told him that Zhang was supported by powerful officials.

A few minutes passed. With a broad stern-wash the ship turned and the heavens revolved. High aloft the masthead traced a figure eight among the stars.

(L) patted the bulwark.

"It doesn't matter. I'm going to resign my commission."

"You can't mean it, Yu-hsuan."

"As soon as the mooring lines are doubled."

"You can't possibly do such a thing."

"Why not? It's a free country, so they say."

"If nothing else—and I don't suppose you care—it would make me feel guilty."

He looked at him with a smile. "Not so long ago I would have done it just for that reason. But now that we've kissed and made up, I'll tell you: I will do it as a matter of principle. All resistance to China is not only futile, it's immoral."

"Go on."

"What is Taiwan? Not a nation—a refugee camp that got lucky. What are the people of Taiwan? Ninety-five percent Chinese. Ethnically, spiritually, morally, historically, geographically, we are an administrative unit of China already, and annexation would only codify what already exists."

"Except you're free and they're not."

"That will come if it's meant to. I'm not so sure it's a good idea anyway. Freedom, market capitalism—what have they done for the Earth? Are these things really worth fighting for? Killing people for? Destroying the life's work of so many generations? Wouldn't it be better just to live, Commodore?"

At the *Arizona* Memorial she had suggested this.

"I agree with you about the goal," he said. "If human life is going to survive, the boundaries between nations will have to disappear. But how to get there?—always the question. Right now there *are* boundaries, there *are* tyrants. The president of China doesn't want you to live your life: he wants you to live the life he dictates for you and which incidentally keeps him in power."

"I don't care about him."

"Let me continue. Since you've confided your intentions to me, let me, as your elder, beg you to hear my reaction. You have exceptional gifts, Yu-hsuan. Your country needs them. The world needs them. Do not, whatever hopelessness you may be feeling now, do not give up this position you've achieved: put your gifts and your energies toward changing the system from within."

Another smile, in the form of a show of teeth. "That old cliché. Don't worry, Commodore, I won't leak your plan to the P.L.A., even if I could. I'm curious to see how it turns out. It is your plan, isn't it?"

"My idea, anyway."

"It's quite impressive. But what if China, in establishing the blockade, has already laid mines?"

He looked at (L) as a sudden wind blew through his gut. "Do you have any knowledge of that? Tell me now, Zhang, before it's too late."

"No, no, I just wanted to surprise you with something you hadn't thought of."

But he had thought of it. At this moment four minesweepers were sanitizing the approaches to Su'ao. Only Lee had been told.

"I don't suppose you would knowingly expose your ship and all your people to a minefield," he observed.

"Oh, but I would," (L) replied. "If the end justifies the means, of course I would."

Turn east and turn south, over and over. After hours of this *T.R.* and her American escorts turned south while the rest of the fleet turned north. The Yùn-9, unable to clone itself, chose the shorter route home, which must have coincided with Chinese intel that Kaohsiung was the Taiwan destroyers' destination. *T.R.* put up a section of CAP to take over the escort.

At sunrise the strike group rounded the *Nan Wan* peninsula and entered the Strait. The Yùn-9 had just time to make a low pass and verify the Taiwan sunburst flying from the masthead of each of the destroyers before her time expired. With one extended launch *T.R.* put up half her air wing, which blanketed the southern third of the Strait all the way to the Penghu Islands.

Alerted by the spy-plane, the Chinese ships at their fleet exercise went to battle stations and set a course to Kaohsiung. It was four hours before their leading ships reached the twelve-mile limit, where they must turn back or commit their nation to war. By then anyone could see that the destroyers had entered the harbor at the southern entrance, proceeded along the fairway, bypassing the piers, and exited at the northern entrance, simultaneously hauling down the flags of Taiwan and breaking the flags of the U.S.A. The reconstituted strike group, at battle stations themselves, then continued north to demonstrate the right of passage in international waters.

Across the island, radar silent, the Taiwan destroyers were detached from the screen at dawn as the Seventh Fleet sailed past them. Happy messages were exchanged by flashing light, including one to the commodore from Juventude. The fleet was withdrawing to a position to the northeast from which, with three carrier air wings *(T.R.* would rejoin by day's end), plenty of sea room, and some number of submarines, it would command the Strait. China, which could count the ships by satellite and suspect the submarines, now understood their adversary's resolve. For Taiwan the question of *When would help arrive?* had therefore been answered: if war was coming, America was already here.

Once detached, the ships made best speed for Su'ao, covered first by CAP from *Nimitz* and next by F-16s from

Hualien. The pantomime in Kaohsiung had lasted long enough to bring the prize unmolested to Cape Houhou, which marked the southern side of the harbor channel. At the sea buoy, lined up in order of seniority, they turned to the west-northwest.

Here was a moment of tension, known only to the commodore and Lee. The minesweepers had found no mines, but were they buried in the channel mud, waiting for the right pressure signature or for a spy in the hills to trigger them? Had (L), seemingly so open now that he and the commodore were soon to part—had he been *entirely* truthful? If his ship blew up, if lives were lost, would he care? Only zealots believed that the end justified the means, and the proverb was itself a flimsy justification. Could his resignation from the service come in the form of a deadly underwater explosion?

On the other hand, it was hard to tell this anxiety from the excitement the commodore always felt when making landfall and from the suspense of ending the voyage and seeing the results of his plan. The outer port was protected by two breakwaters with a narrow opening on the north side, across from which ships were loading and unloading at the commercial piers. The naval base lay beyond a crooked breakwater to starboard, where the largest berths, along the quay, had been cleared for their arrival.

The harbor itself was "surrounded on three sides by high ground," as the *Sailing Directions* laconically said. The ships at their berths would be hard to hit, but any attempt to do so would tear through windows and walls. Taiwan was the most crowded country in the world. War at home must be unthinkable.

Ignoring the harbor pilot, (L) was conning the ship himself. His jaw was set as though to kill, and the veins stood out in his forehead. *Luchiang* had already landed at the quay and was doubling her lines. *Hsinchu* was easing into her berth an inch at a time, as befit her name and her captain's prudent sense of the occasion. *Chiai's* captain had his own sense of that. So much adrenaline quickening the blood was unbearable when ships moved so ponderously. His ship must moor first. The commodore went out to the bridge wing, though there was nothing he could do.

The berth came up shockingly fast and at too flat an angle for a second chance. (L) gave a command into the speaking tube and also pointed through the door at the man on the throttles, who knew what was at stake. The transom shook as the reversed propellers, at full power, dug in. The shaking traveled through the entire hull, followed by a surge of water that carried into the berth ahead and pushed *Hsinchu* away from her mark. *Chiai's* own berth was coming up too fast, still too fast, a little slower, slower, very slow, the ship was almost stopped and (L) must take off the enormous backing bell before she gathered sternway. The batter's decision to swing must be made as the ball left the pitcher's hand.

He nailed it. The ship simply stopped in her own turbulent water. The lines were handed over—an easy exercise since she was already alongside—and doubled while *Hsinchu* was still correcting her position. From the fo'c'sle and the fantail came whoops and cheers. On the quay a small crowd, mostly in uniform, witnessed the godlike skill.

Though triumphant, (L) managed a comical eyebrow in his direction. The commodore shook the captain's hand, patted his shoulder, and proposed that tomorrow they make up the dinner they had missed in Panama. The response was an unreadable smile.

He went into the bridge and called "Well done!" to the watchstanders, who knew they had done well but were wondering what came next. XO Huang gave him a thumb's-up. Opening the door, he left the bridge—probably forever—and walked down the passageway.

At the end of the passageway was a radar room; no one would be there now. With a practiced motion he pulled the long lever that undogged the door. The hum of electronic equipment enveloped him. Even at her berth, the ship would remain ready to fight. But that wasn't what moved him now. Nor was it satisfaction at the success of his plan. It was relief after forty-two days of constant nerve-strain. His hands were trembling. His mouth was dry, and the chilled air he gulped wasn't enough. He stepped over the combing, switched on the lights, stood on the brightly colored insulated matting, and sobbed until the vital strings holding him together let go.

The End of Act Two

Statecraft

The next morning, wearing jeans and a T-shirt, the commodore walked into town. Beyond the main gate of the naval station, guarded by soldiers with automatic weapons ready to fire, the road climbed under a jumble of power lines and billboards, whose language was just as mysterious to him as when he had joined the ships. Only a few characters a day, she had said, and he would be fluent—this place on the other side of the world from his home, from his sixty-year continuing education in avoiding mistakes. This foreign place. As he climbed, the billboards kept growing: however high the roofline, images of beautiful young people saying presumably clever things dominated it. In fact billboards stood all over the city like some advanced energy-collection system. Most of the products advertised were American.

But here and there were billboards advertising something else: national resolve. On these, though each had its commercial message, a lookout platform had been built, and camo-clad figures were watching the skies. This certainly evoked the Battle of Britain, but against a threat that could travel more than twenty times as fast as a German bomber, what kind of warning could they give? The Aegis ships could give that warning, but probably not when blocked by a mountain. Perhaps (L) had been right all along. Perhaps the ships should have taken their chances in Kaohsiung. But in that case, why had everyone listened to him?

The working day had started, but people were everywhere on the streets, going everywhere. They wore casual Western clothes. One woman in a Taylor Swift shirt handed him a pink brochure. Underneath the block of characters was English:

Stop the mad thinking!
With only a hammer, all problems look like nails!
Promote peace and reconciliation!
Welcome our Mainland brothers and sisters!
Taiwan the 23ʳᵈ Province of China!

The brochure felt like counterfeit money. As soon as he was out of sight he crumpled it up and threw it in a trash bin. An old man watching him laughed, pointing at his own head. The commodore hurried on.

Around the corner was an open-air market. In the narrow aisles between tables the number of shoppers seemed like the "before" picture of a crowd crush. But after so long without food—he had been too tired to eat last night, and this morning neither Wang nor Mei-ling had appeared in the cabin, her great day after all—his stomach was a hardened knot. He made his way into the crowd, rubbing (both) shoulders at once.

At an attractively organized table a young woman was cutting the tops and bottoms off a yellow fruit whose grain looked like that of pineapple. The pieces were star-shaped, and the sign, in English, said *Starfruit.* He stopped and smiled and nodded when she looked up. She put the three slices on a paper plate and handed it to him. He tried a bite as Slate Greene or Robin McGill would, to praise her, and was lost in the sweetness. The expression on his face did the praising. He offered her money. Shaking her head, she filled a bag with fruit—a papaya, a guava, a shriveled-looking rufous-colored wax apple, a green sugar apple with warts all over, and something called a durian, a large jaundiced thing covered with thorns that smelled like an oil lamp. *Yes, yes, it's good,* she urged as he stood fearing poison if merely touched it.

While this was going on, people pressed against him. For a moment he thought they were beggars. A gray-haired woman gave him a container with jumbo shrimp in black bean sauce. A woman who must have been her sister offered eels. A boy gave him a pastry like a

[256]

chocolate eclair with honey instead of chocolate. A willowy beauty in tight jeans poured out a bowl of Wulong tea. He drank while everyone watched. It was delicious, it tasted as if it knew him—how could he not have tried Mei-ling's tea this past month? When he handed back the empty bowl the beauty refused to take it; a gift. Nor would any of them take money. They pointed at their heads as the old man had done. When he didn't understand they pointed at his red ballcap with the white Taiwan sunburst. The boy waved his fingers like scrambled eggs over the bill of his own cap and stood up straighter to mime importance.

"You're American," said the gray-haired woman, whose lips parted to reveal whitened teeth.

"Yes ma'am."

"You arrived yesterday."

He nodded.

"You brought the ships." She pointed down the hill to the harbor, and for this her countrymen gave her space. "To protect our free nation." With her two hands she reached for his.

"Indeed you did," said a confident voice. A tall man, another American, had joined the crowd. It was Slate Greene.

"Is that really you?" he asked.

"Shall I text you a code?"

"What are you doing here?"

As the shoppers slipped among them, they were talking over their heads.

"I want to offer you a ride to Taipei."

"I didn't think I was going to Taipei."

"Indeed you are, as directed by the combatant command through which you may be traveling. Come get in my car. I assure you it's safe."

The car was waiting a few hundred feet from the entrance to the market. A Taiwanese driver in a coat and tie opened the doors for each of them. Slate too was wearing coat and tie, an expensive light gray summer suit.

"Aren't I underdressed, Admiral?"

"Your charming *bānjiū* has taken care of that. Before we call on the president you'll change into dress uniform at the residence."

"What the hell is going on?"

"As far as you're concerned, I have all the particulars. Regarding world events, that remains to be seen."

The car ride was probably the strangest hour he had ever spent with Slate, but that was his own fault. He wanted answers, like the man who sought the guru on the mountaintop. After an arduous journey (lasting forty-two days), he reaches the summit and finds the guru, who waits to be asked the meaning of life. But instead of asking, the man only talks about himself.

Slate listened patiently with a smile of pleasure on his face for twenty minutes, through a narrative, mostly studded with technical details, of the hurricane, the accidental missile shooting, the engine room fire, Robin McGill's kindness, the breakthrough in training, his own brilliant gambit to fool the Chinese, and the strange behavior of Zhang Lite...until, with a palm upraised, he said gently, "You must tell me more, but right now I have to work up some talking points for the meeting with her nibs." And he bent over his phone, making notes with his two thumbs like a teenager, ignoring both his company and the landscape.

For about twenty miles the road paralleled the coast, close enough to show a blue ribbon of the East China Sea, and then angled toward the interior, climbing through a barren mountain range until it descended onto a plain where a great metropolis waited. Even though he knew these were advanced people, the city surprised him with its density, which he might have expected, but also with its extent, spread across a wilderness. This was Taipei, with New Taipei City surrounding it: urban sprawl in three dimensions. On the broad hilly streets tall build- ings were everywhere; their rooftops formed a generally regular skyline hundreds of feet high.

Except in one regard: the skyline was dominated by a giant teal-colored tower twice as high, which looked as if it had been set in place to rule over them.

"What is that building?" he asked the car.

Slate was absorbed, but the driver replied, "Taipei 101." He was a moment understanding that this was its actual name, not some call for the foreigner to take an introduc- tory course in geography. "World's tallest green building. Hundred and one stories. Made like bamboo stalk. Eleva- tor take you to the top so fast you puncture your ear- drums."

"You're having fun with me, of course," he said.

"I'm sorry, mister, I can't hear you."

They arrived at a modern building whose façade, with a setback, was made of gray steel plates with tall win- dows between them. The building was too big to be the residence of a single family, too small to be an hotel. Be- fore he could ask about it the driver turned down a ramp to a basement garage and drove under the low concrete overhead to the back entrance, where two men waited.

"What shall I do with this food?" he asked the car.

"Leave it for my hungry family," the driver replied. "Thank you." Reaching beside him he picked up a handgun and slipped it into his waist band as he got out to open both doors.

Slate, putting his phone in his pocket, said, "This is the Blair House of Taiwan. The government guest house. You and I and two others will share the grand suite, fac- ing the rising sun."

"When did you get here?"

"Last night, after an all-day video conference on *Blue Ridge* with a bleary-eyed White House Situation Room and a tireless Robin McGill and her people. Ed Juventude should have arrived by now. Along with the ambassador we're going to present the U.S. position to President Tsai. And we're going to present *you,* who will endorse and personify that position. So shower if you need to and then a quick change into your uniform, which is ready. We're expected in an hour."

"You've met Mei-ling." The reference to his *bānjiū*.

"I have. She and two other ladies unpacked your cruise box and hung your vast panoply of medals."

"I must thank them."

"As no doubt you will. One of them was my wife. The other was yours. All four of us are here in the suite."

She was waiting for him in the living room, holding her hands at her waist. He was blinded by the light behind her. The sun streaming through the windows was so bright he could hardly read her face. No doubt he himself was lighted up, warts and all.

They hugged and kissed, both of them temporizing.

"I can't believe you're here," he said. We have so much to settle, he thought. So much has happened.

"Yes, I'm here, long trip, brains jumbled, but you don't have time for that now, you have to get ready to call on the president."

"Surely I can take a minute."

"There is not a minute to lose," she and Slate and Julia Greene said in unison, and laughed. Julia had hugged and kissed him too, with greater confidence.

In the bathroom he had an impression of the relentless attention to detail that helped Taiwan become the world's largest chipmaker, and then he was standing in the bedroom in his T-shirt and boxer shorts as all three of his suite-mates dressed him. His uniform fit perfectly, and yet he envied Slate his casually athletic bearing, broad-shouldered, long-limbed, head beautifully set, as he supervised from the arm of a couch. No one in the president's office would even look at the naval captain.

[260]

To signify that he was ready, and perhaps that things between them were properly conjugal, Mad patted his cheek.

"Listen," Slate said in the elevator. "It's a short walk to the palace, and we have a few minutes in our pocket. I want to solve the problem of Bradford Hilty before we get there—it may be our only chance to talk. Tell me truly: are you in love?"

They walked into the street, accompanied by the driver and the two plainclothesmen. Their little formation sought the palace by inference, like starlings.

"I might be," he replied. "I don't know. I do love her, if that makes any sense."

"Perfect sense. She seems like someone easy to love. Truly a good person. Happy. Shall I tell you what I think?"

"Of course."

"It won't be worth it."

"What won't be?"

"The euphoria of feeling that kind of love again. The excitement of foreign adventure, of rebelling against convention. Not to mention getting your beans snapped. None of it. Not when the cost is giving up your life."

"Or taking it in a new direction."

"You're too old for that, old friend. Look at it another way: you've earned your golden years: enjoy them."

"I'm not sure."

"I know whereof I speak."

"That much is true, anyway," he said.

In the balm of the morning all things seemed possible. A hum of some kind of positive energy filled the streets, not unlike the sounds of a ship when sailing sweetly. And without acrimony: no grinding diesels, no rebuking air brakes, no angry horns.

"What do you think of Mad and me?" he asked.

"I've told you that: married for life, an inspiration to all your friends."

"But I bore her."

"You bore me—sometimes. Mostly you make me laugh."

"She irritates me."

"Welcome to blissful married life."

"You think I should go home and make this work—regardless of the other thing?"

"Not regardless: *because* of the other thing, which either a) cannot work, in which case you'll be miserable in a foreign country; or b) might work, but with so many compromises you'll be miserable in a foreign country. And then think how that will be for Tsai Mei-ling, who will have given up her future."

"That's why you, loving Robin, stayed with Julia."

"Partly. Mostly it's because I saw that I lucked out with Julia. But I didn't travel out here to save your marriage, or at least not primarily. Besides averting a war, I have an exciting business proposition for you, one which, I admit, might affect your decision about Maddy. Are you listening?"

He was. Slate talked faster as they crossed the street and were saluted by the gate guard. A small reception committee was waiting for them across the parking lot.

The Company had lost another commercial aircraft. The cause was the same—bad software—and there was no denying it any longer. The NTSB report was conclusive, the FAA was ready to punish, heads were going to roll. Among them was Joc Philip McCracken's head, the CEO on whom Magister Hilty had made such an indelible impression at the Greenes' Fourth of July party, correcting him about our founding documents.

"He was wrong, that's all."

"No doubt. But I need to finish this."

They had stopped among the cars. Slate had turned to him to show that he was making a point; still the reception committee must be getting restless.

"Very well, move on."

"Don't make me beg, you asshole."

"Beg for what?"

"You know perfectly well. Beg you to ask me who's go-ing to replace him. You've already guessed it: I am."

"Of course you are. Well done, Slate." They shook hands, and he added, in case his joy at the news hadn't been suffi-cient, "The Company will take off now. I'm buying stock."

"Which might send us both to jail for insider trading. But thank you, Brad. I do think I can do the job, unlucky as it's been. That's where you come in. I want you to be my senior vice president for quality assurance."

They were met by the committee and conveyed inside. In between pleasantries and out of the corner of his mouth he scoffed, he protested. He was unqualified. He had no business experience. He had never built anything. How many people and how many manufacturing sites? One hundred and forty thousand people at sites on four continents? He couldn't do it.

"Au contraire, you'd be perfect," Slate murmured.

"I stopped nitpicking entropy years ago."

They were climbing a grand stairway. "Not that: I'm talking about real leadership. You've just made an island nation believe they can fight a superpower. This, by com-parison, will be cake."

"You're talking about another deployment. I'd have to do it 24/7. Madeleine would divorce me for sure."

"Or she might enjoy Chicago's remarkable culture and the lifestyle your income would provide for her."

The president of Taiwan was waiting in the doorway.

"Will you do it?"

"Now? You want an answer now? You're asking me to interview one hundred and forty thousand suspects in a murder mystery. One of them has his hand on my throat."

Slate laughed. "Nice one. Yes, I want to know today. —Madam President, it's delightful to see you again. May I present my dear friend, Commodore Bradford Hilty of the United States Navy?"

卪卪

He felt as if he knew her, one of those people from our past whose name we have forgotten. A teacher, perhaps: that pleasant oval face, with mild, intelligent eyes behind rimless glasses; a small presence that might be mistaken for easy-going and harmless. On her father's side the family was Hakka—indigenous. She owed nothing to China. She was defending her ancestral home.

Responding to Slate, the president laughed in a high titter and gave him both her hands as the woman at the outdoor market had done. "A new acquaintance but an old friend. Even without your splendid uniform I would know that you were a hero—and now a hero of Taiwan. I am very, very happy to welcome you here. And, personally, to thank you for your kindness to my sister."

From behind her the sister stepped out to be recognized. It was Mei-ling.

His grin was meant to be jocularly accusing.

"I asked if she was your sister."

"Half-sister, same father. I was the afterthought."

She was in uniform, with her two and a half stripes. The president gestured to this and said that all the family was proud of Mei-ling's success, which, overcoming an early tragedy, she had earned herself, without influence.

"I can well believe it," he said. "She's probably the most capable person I've ever met."

That titter. "Much more capable than me. Come in, gentlemen. The ambassador is already here, and Admiral Juventude. You have news. We have a lot to discuss."

The office was wide, as the palace was wide. It sat on the eastern side of the rotunda—facing the rising sun, for the architect had come from the Japanese empire. Our bombers had heavily damaged the building in the last year of the war. No doubt the Japanese governor-general had had a basement to shelter in. No doubt the present administration did too, though hypersonic missiles wouldn't give them much time.

[264]

As with the Oval Office, the furnishings suggested col-
legiality. The president's desk was at one end of the room,
a conference table was at the other, and in the expansive
middle was a large seating area, chairs and sofas. As she
brought them inside, everyone already seated—in the in-
ner circle Juventude and the U.S. ambassador, whose
name was Gillette, and the ubiquitous Admiral Chen, up
from Tsoying—rose to attention. She sat, with her official
interpreter in a folding chair at her shoulder and Mei-
ling at her side. He and Slate sat beside Gillette. Behind
them sat perhaps a dozen deputies, none of whom, if Taiwan was like America, would speak unless asked for information.

Gillette opened by giving the state of play, deferring to
Juventude for military developments. China was in a position to conduct a limited attack on Taiwan—not a sus-
tained bombing campaign but selective strikes, aiming
both to damage critical defenses and infrastructure and
to send a warning of worse to come. Their combatant
navy was mostly at sea, still firing training ammunition.
Since the arrival of the Aegis destroyers, however, and in
response to back-channel communications, they had
paused their amphibious buildup. The situation, therefore, was still extremely dangerous but now at a point
ripe for diplomacy.

Tsai glanced at Chen, who nodded his agreement.

"So," she said, "thanks to the wonderful intervention
of the United States Navy, China has second thoughts."

"That's right," said Gillette.

"But still a diplomatic and policy impasse."

"Yes ma'am."

"And they want control of their twenty-third province."

"Certainly. That's a constant."

"So, Mr. Ambassador, what do we do?"

Gillette shifted his weight forward and put his hands
on his knees, signaling that here was his pitch. In his
place the commodore would have sat quietly with his
hands in his lap, relying on reason and that Ivy League

voice. "As we've worked through the policy choices, we've come repeatedly to the example of the Cuban Missile Crisis: a superpower confrontation involving other states."

"Client states, you mean."

"One certainly was. But remember that West Germany and Turkey were involved as well as Cuba."

"So who am I, Cuba or the Turkey?"

This was actually a pun. Pleased with it, she looked to Mei-ling for approval. The president was his own age. Growing up she might have been a second parent to Mei-ling, especially if the girl had felt alone in a cobbled-together family.

Gillette went on: "That crisis turned on some subtle language by Khruschev in an otherwise threatening letter to Kennedy. The president ignored the threats and focused on the subtlety. The Soviets were willing to withdraw their missiles from Cuba provided that they received certain guarantees, which might be kept secret."

"So I'm Turkey," she said. "I give up the missiles." By that she meant the national sovereignty of Taiwan. She looked at Slate for clarification.

He replied for Gillette in the voice a family doctor might use to a patient whom a specialist has offended. "China will propose a bi-lateral summit with the U.S. She would exclude Taiwan on the basis that your country is already her own province. We will counterpropose a regional working conference—a dozen nations, including Taiwan—to discuss all the outstanding issues on the table—Taiwan, North Korea, China's false claims of sovereignty in the South China Sea, and the dangerous harassment that almost sank the destroyer *Tso Ying*. But the real purpose will be to freeze the military buildup and normalize the diplomatic process, which can then take as long as it will—the longer the better."

"If I give up the missiles."

Gillette said, "Your own contribution would be to stop calling for independence."

"Ah-ha, gentlemen! Now we come to it. Of course it's impossible. The goal of independence is a fundamental tenet of my party, supported by a great majority of our citizens. I couldn't do it if I wanted to."

"Again, ma'am, it would be secret."

"There are no secrets in public life. It would be obvious in my face, my body, what I say, what I don't say, who I meet, who I don't meet. Perhaps you forget, Ambassador Gillette, that our national language depends on intonation. We are very good at reading subtlety."

"Taiwan would be free and independent and growing ever more prosperous," he said, "under the ambiguity of One China, which might last for a century. It's in no country's interest to force a resolution of this issue. With your agreement, my government will provide Taiwan with further assurances of security and other material assistance. Since we've made China accept the Aegis destroyers, there's no reason why the military sales shouldn't continue, bit by bit, Birnam Wood coming to Dunsinane."

"Slate?"

"I believe there's one more point, ma'am."

Gillette nodded. "At the same time, my president is prepared to say—in his off-the-cuff way—that the U.S. will not support an independent Taiwan."

"Then you would stab us in the back."

"Not at all, ma'am. We want to avoid World War III."

She was upset, even at her level. She needed a moment to compose herself. She said something to Mei-ling and received a soothing reply, but she wasn't soothed. Her eyes looked all around for help.

"What do you think, Commodore Hilty?" she asked.

Here was a headline: *Hilty Starts Nuclear War.* But besides that what did he have to lose? Another outcome was his becoming the president's national security adviser, speaking in a foreign accent of persuasive erudition, like Kissinger or Brzezinski. This was another of those moments when a door opened and he could choose to walk inside. Just now all the doors in the corridor were springing open and slamming shut again.

"I think you must feel this as unwelcome pressure," he said. "A narrowing of options, which seems like exactly the wrong response to a crisis. But the real challenge of a crisis, and the easiest thing to get wrong, isn't *what* must be done but *how much time* do you have to decide it. In this case I would advise you not to be rushed. The Chinese have paused. In my judgment it would be ruinous for them to attack you. My country can wait—the Seventh Fleet has lots of fuel. Take your time and be sure."

This pleased no one in the U.S. delegation, but each would react to it differently. Juventude probably thought about the expense of further operations. Gillette that an amateur had undone in one stroke hours of high-level decision-making. Slate, though he liked the idea of secret agreements, chuckled at the chutzpa of his friend.

The president was visibly relieved. "I like this man!" she said to her sister. "Any other thoughts, Commodore?"

He had gone this far, he might as well make a new enemy. "Just for Ambassador Gillette. Sir, Birnam Wood was about using camouflage to conceal an attack—which was hardly necessary anyway since Macduff had superior forces—not about effecting change so gradually that no one notices."

The president liked this too, not because she knew the reference but because the bearer of bad news, with his cultured self-assurance, had been put in his place. Slate's reaction was apparent by his chuckle.

Honors and Promotions

Something more was planned, that was clear from the sidelong glances. But the president wanted a word with her advisors, and the Americans were asked to wait outside. The ambassador left, probably in a huff. Juventude, Slate, and he made eyes at each other as staffers rushed past them full of their brainstorms.

"You have no idea what's coming, I suppose," Juventude asked with his pleasant half-smile. King George VI had said this to Winston Churchill after summoning him to Buckingham Palace to become prime minister, and the commodore, like Churchill, carried on the silly joke:

"No sir, I couldn't possibly imagine it."

"This is Taiwan's show, or I would have liked to do a double ceremony. But you should know that Uncle Sam will recognize your performance with the DSM."

"Good heavens, that's too much." The Distinguished Service Medal was almost never awarded below flag rank; only the Medal of Honor and the Navy Cross were senior to it, both of which required actual heroism. It was such a high award that he would be proud to wear it in his civilian buttonhole, if that was the door he walked through. If he could still find that door.

"I wish we might do it on *Blue Ridge,*" Juventude said.

Pretending to miss the reference, he replied, "Or you could mail it to me before you change your mind."

"But that's the question: where should I mail it?"

"Probably to Leavenworth for insulting an ambassador."

Juventude had run out of sly introductions to the subject. He said, "I'd be honored to have you on my staff, Commodore. However this turns out with the Chinese."

"And you'd be lucky to get him," said Slate.

"Yes sir, I believe it. Cheat Taylor also wants you. And your friend at Makalapa. And—for all I know—this lady. Everyone wants the man who saved Taiwan."

"That's not even close to being an accurate description."

"Wait and see, Commodore."

"I feel like I'm being dismembered by horses," he said. "At this moment I can't tell you what I'm doing tomorrow. Unless we're at war, which might be a relief."

An aide came out of the office and escorted them to the rotunda. They ambled through the corridors and trotted down the stairwells. A vast space opened before them within which the layout of the presidential ceremony—a dais, two rows of chairs for the audience, a place for the media with their lights and cameras—seemed like someone's private party. The tourists moved freely behind a velvet rope. He hoped they'd been screened. How ironic if his next choice was made for him by an assassin's bullet. But would he even know?

Slate took a seat between Mad and Julia in the first row of chairs. Juventude and he were on the dais along with Admiral Chen and a heavy-set man who was probably the Minister of Defense, though he had sat with the other aides at the back of the office. In front of the dais the interpreter from the meeting stood next to an interpreter of sign.

None of the tourists looked dangerous. The members of the media looked as if this was only a routine ceremony and hardly worth their time, despite the crisis. Among their equipment, of course, a gun could be hidden.

Julia's look was happy and expectant.

Mad's look, as Slate chatted her up, was distant.

The president came out smiling confidently, followed by Mei-ling holding an ornamental box, and they walked up to the audience—an odd positioning which reduced the dais to a backdrop. She began in Chinese, pausing for the interpreters. After a few remarks she turned and looked back at him, a nearly affectionate look but with a sock of coins in it: *Thank you for saving my country and*

I will happily welcome you to my family but if you are trifling with my sister I'll have you murdered.

He understood that he was to get up, squeeze past Juventude, descend the steps, cross the floor, and stand beside her while everyone waited; a maneuver almost impossible to achieve in a gait both natural and dignified and with always the possibility of a fall. He did his best, keeping his shoulders squared. Mad, close enough to touch, looked up at him and the two women as if she wondered what was happening. Mei-ling read a citation, which she translated herself. Amid the camera flashes, the president with a sure hand hung on his chest an elaborate red, white, and blue medal overlaid by an ivory-colored cameo in the outline of a dragon. She said something as she did this, and he nodded as if he understood: *Tortured first then murdered.* They shook hands. The audience, because the presentation was so close to them, thought fit to add only a smattering of applause. The tourists kept their eyes on the president.

"Commodore Hilty," she said in English. "I thank you from the bottom of my heart. The transit of the ships you commanded—so important to my country—has written a saga that the people of Taiwan will never forget. As you will see! For once you have learned Chinese, you will read about yourself in our history.

"Now sir," she went on after Slate's chuckle, "I have seen myself that you know words to suit an occasion. Wise words, which I will think over carefully. On this new occasion would you give me the pleasure of hearing you again?"

It was always right to share the credit, of course. He said that the medal was the most beautiful he had ever seen but that it gave him a prickly feeling because the honor belonged to the ships' companies—he named each ship and her captain in case the Minister of Defense was keeping track.

"I worked hard," he said in a loud voice, "to understand your culture under trying circumstances. The more I gave

[271]

to this effort the more I wanted to give. And the more I learned. I learned in practice what you told me, Admiral Chen, at the Bahá'í Temple: that your country deserves our support, not only because we have promised it—and, as I think you'll agree, we have delivered upon that promise"—he turned to receive the obvious nod—"but also because your values and our values are so much alike. Those of you who have visited Liberty Island in New York, where a beautiful lady holds aloft an eternal torch, may remember words much wiser than any of mine. They stand for an ideal, an aspiration, not yet fulfilled in any country. This past month I have seen that they apply just as keenly to the people of Taiwan: like us, Madam President, you yearn to breathe free. May your yearning come true. It is mine for you as well."

Here an unbiased observer would say that the brilliant politician put her foot wrong. The occasion was about him, and the emotion he had evoked was just right to end with. Moved by it too, she extended it to her family. An aide carried her sister's new shoulder boards. Perhaps the commodore would help with this...? Chen and the Minister of Defense came down from the dais, leaving Juventude by himself. People in the second row—all Taiwanese, no one he knew—stood up with their cell phones ready. Despite the presidential command, he himself wanted to sit, but Mei-ling restrained his arm, reminding him that he had promised to be her bridesmaid. So he replaced one of her shoulder boards, and then to make his situation even more difficult he kissed her in front of his wife. Mei-ling's eyes turned to him as he brushed her cheek. That the president replaced the other board with a kiss afterwards hardly lessened the blunder.

When he returned to his spot, standing straight to face the audience with his new medal while the media took his picture again, his wife looked away.

Love at Twelve Hundred Feet

The president left the rotunda, and the velvet rope was taken away. Several of the tourists, not having read the saga of Hilty yet but understanding that he was famous for something, came up and examined his medal. One man got him for a selfie, and then others had to have theirs.

"That dragon is particularly nice," said Slate.

"Isn't it," said Juventude.

"I would have gone for an asp," said Mad.

Julia was silent on the subject.

Admiral Chen approached, with the new commander. Hilty presented them to Mad and Julia, but Mad interrupted to say that of course they had met Mei-ling—didn't he remember that she had brought his clothes to the residence?—and congratulations to her for the promotion and also for putting up with her husband for a month.

Though actually it was forty-two days.

"May we borrow the commodore for a few minutes?" Chen asked. "Some unfinished business from the transit, if you please."

"Offer to give him command of the fleet," Slate said. "He'd know just what to do."

"I'm sure he would. So we'll stay in touch today, gentlemen, in case the president needs us for her decision."

"Speaking for Julia and me, it will have to be today, Admiral. I turn into a coach mouse at midnight."

"And I'm returning to Tsoying tomorrow on the high-speed train. By then I hope...."

"Nail a gold doubloon to the mast," Slate replied. "Come to our party tonight in any case."

Just off the rotunda was a break room for the security guards with a wooden table and some chairs. No one was there now. Chen had them sit, then he shut the door. The walls were lined with sound-proof tile to which some posters and printed notices had been attached with pushpins.

Chen said, "I understand that Mei-ling has given you a book on Chinese, my friend. Contrary to western belief, our language is easy to learn, especially if you know how to sing."

"You should hear me in the shower."

"I'm sure you're a veritable Pavarotti. As well, most employees of the Ministry of Defense are fluent in English. I say this to assure you of a warm welcome and a seamless transition. You wonder: transition to what? I would like to invite you to become a senior member of my staff, working closely with the fleet command and the other services."

"To work and live in Tsoying?"

"That's correct, sir. To make a meaningful contribution to the defense of our country, to which you have already showed so much devotion, and of which you spoke so eloquently to our president. As a civilian, causing no conflict with your own navy. I understand that your job in Norfolk may be somewhat up in the air—not because of your service to us, I hope."

"I've been libeled by a schoolgirl and defamed by the governor of Virginia. It does look like my teaching days are over." But of course Chen knew this from his spy.

"Then teach *us*. This is so easy for you—a reflex. I'll bet you a month's pay you have already thought about how to defend the ships from missile attack in Su'ao, and how you would get them underway, and where you would send them. Now haven't you?"

"Always allowing for the danger of surprise."

"Share this gift with us."

"Tell me, Admiral, where is Captain Zhang? Zhang Yu-hsuan. He was absent from *Chiai* this morning."

"Yes. Zhang Yu-hsuan. Defected to China, it seems. He came here yesterday afternoon and flew to Beijing last night. He called his sister from there."

Mei-ling nodded; she must have seen the intercept.

"That's a disaster, then. You said yourself the navy needs him. Certainly *Chiai* does. Plus his knowledge."

"He will tell them something about these ships. But his real value to them is propaganda. We haven't had a defection since the K.M.T. went out of office."

"I have to say, Admiral, just before we arrived in Su'ao he made a passionate speech for appeasement. And for annexation. I—well, I tried—"

"You wouldn't have been able to stop him. He has always been contrarian."

As he himself was. Then perhaps (L) was right.

"But now, Commodore, you can help us repair the damage, if you will. Join Commander Tsai and me on the train tomorrow. Everything else will fall into place."

"Of course my wife is here."

With a glance at Mei-ling he went on smoothly. "Yes, of course she is, charming lady, I just met her. Forgive me. What the foolish admiral *meant* to say was, Enjoy a few days while you make up your mind—take your time, as you so profoundly advised Tsai Ing-wen. Visit our beautiful country, see our progressive people. Give that famous intuition of yours a chance to work. Then come to us. Your wife too may want...."

But Chen wasn't sure what she might want, which was too bad because he and perhaps Mad too would like to know.

"It's a flattering offer, sir."

"I too can wait, beyond the present crisis. This is an investment in the future, for both of us. I think you'll find what you want here, Bradford. Beauty, kindness, vitality. Respect for traditions along with eagerness to innovate. Most of all, we yearn to breathe free." He turned to Mei-ling. "I'll leave it to you to persuade him." He tapped her shoulder. "Four stripes if you succeed."

༻ ༺

"We're going to talk," he said. A question not a statement.

"If you please."

"But not here. With you, about us. In a sound-proofed room. I may be sitting in a chair where the powerful tortured their enemies."

"Perhaps tortured them with kisses."

"I want to go to Taipei 101. Have you been?"

"So high? Actually, never. I've always wondered if I would get vertigo."

"Are you willing to find out?"

But when he went back to the rotunda to tell his companions that he was needed for a couple of hours, they were gone.

She was waiting in the corridor. "You're sure about 101?"

"This will be like landing on the aircraft carrier. How can we not make a good decision with our brains scrambled?"

It was easy to get there. A Metro station south of the palace connected to a Metro station in the basement of the tower. On the ground floor the ticket-taker let them in because of their uniforms. *Thank you for your service* meant something in the U.S., whose wars were nearly constant and in distant places. It meant something else here where the prospect of war, at home, so unfamiliar, was every hour in the mind.

The elevator, which happened to face China, had observation windows. Mei-ling made a gulping gesture when the door closed. Whatever they meant to say to each other, it seemed all right to join hands as the floor catapulted them upward. The sense of speed was in his knees and also in how fast the perspective of the skyline changed. His ears crackled. Before they hardly knew they were high they were very high. The outdoor observation deck was on the ninety-first floor, more than twelve hundred above the ground. The elevator slowed smoothly and yet suddenly, and their first steps were like those of sailors long at sea finally walking on dry land.

The doors to the observation platform protested the change in air pressure. Outside was no city place; rather an aerie, a dreamscape upon an alien civilization, unreal and somehow less important. Admiral Chen, assuming that he really wanted him, would never have let him see the Taiwanese so small.

The railing was fifteen feet high with an inward curve and with no sense of an edge: they were safe. Mei-ling waved her hands to mock the vertigo she wasn't feeling then dropped them lightly on his shoulders with a laugh then embraced him.

It seemed all right to hold each other if only to acknowledge the painful position they were in. His medals dug into her soft chest, which had no decorations of any kind. She pulled away from the pressure while longing for more. It seemed all right to kiss. He closed his eyes, and felt her striving lips, and wished he knew what to say with his: but the only word he knew was *yes* when the word he needed was *help*. The kiss pushed their caps askew. They laughed and restored appearances.

A few other observers were watching: the handsome couple in uniform, on the brink of war perhaps.

"My sister would like to kiss you as well," she said. "Maybe I should be jealous."

"She's just about my age, too."

"I shouldn't joke. This is my crisis. And my crisis is more urgent than hers."

"I don't know what to do," he said.

"You could start slowly. Birnam Wood comes to Dunsinane—I know, I know, wrong metaphor. Take the train with Admiral Chen and me tomorrow. Be honest with your wife. Say you need to see more before you decide on something so important. It's fair, from what you've told me about this summer." Fair, she didn't say, after his wife had gone off with another man.

"But what more do I need to see?"

[277]

"Me, naked."

"With pleasure. In that case I'd have to touch you."

"Good, that's what I want. We can start here, on this platform. Only six, seven—seven people would know, out of three million down there, and none of them will talk."

"I told you my mind would be jumbled."

"And I am drunk with love, with wanting you. It gets worse—better—more powerful—each day. This morning I made love to you in the shower. It was so powerful I had to stuff a towel in my mouth and scream."

"I want you too, more than a fantasy life, more than just to have you. Do you think, if we commit to each other, we'll feel the same way five years from now?"

"When both of us will have given so much?"

"Yes. When you will have given everything."

"Of course we will. We get along."

"We have the same values. We do tell the truth."

"You are maybe better at that than I am."

She was leading up to a confession.

"Did you think Zhang would defect?" he asked.

"You want to know this?"

"Yes. Tell me the truth. I'm testing you."

"Personally, I did. With a little encouragement."

"I'm sorry? Was this some sort of stratagem?"

"Perhaps I would call it a *preference.* I'm telling you what I shouldn't so you will trust me and find the courage to make a new life, Bradford."

"Your side *preferred* him to defect? But why?"

"For that you'll have to stay with us for a while and be read into a highly classified program. But that is step five or six in your recovery. Step one is get on the train tomorrow and let step two make you deliriously happy."

Twelve hundred feet in the air, the prospect of making love to her seemed not only clamant but inevitable. He wanted her as he had never wanted any woman. Nothing else seemed important—family, friends, career, money, even honor. Against the enormity of step one, more

[278]

kissing now was exciting, joyful, generous, excusable, and surely without harm.

Seeking Peace in Peace Park

He returned to the residence to find Julia alone. Slate was at the embassy on a video conference. Mad had left for a walk. Reading from a tablet, Julia provided this information without looking up, with none of her former friendliness.

"Do you know where she is?" he asked.

"I think the park across the street. If you want to talk to her you ought to wait here. I'm going to disobey all the rules of jet-lag and take a nap."

"Are you unhappy with me, Julia?"

Now she looked. Her look was direct and unflinching, pained and angry.

"As you said in Chicago," he reminded her, "we're old friends. You can tell me."

She spoke slowly, in her minutely inflected voice. "Have you any idea, Brad, how hurtful it was to watch you put shoulder boards on that lady?"

"I was called to do it. By the president of the country."

"Your whole manner around her. You weren't simply carrying out an official duty. It hurt *me* to see it. Imagine what Mad must have been feeling."

Tears had welled in her eyes. She put her hand down by her hip to steady her. She had the gift of empathy. Yet above all she was honest and fair-minded.

He said, "Since you and Slate share everything, you know that Mad and I are not getting along. I won't point to her conduct this summer, which you also know. What you allude to about me and Mei-ling involves true and deep feelings which we are trying to work out unselfishly. Both of us. I have to decide what to do—several things all at once—decide today! Do I accept a job with Slate? Do I accept a job in Taiwan? Do I stay in the Navy and work for Ed Juventude or some other admiral? Do I return to Norfolk and fight to get my job back? Do I try to persuade my wife to seek a reconciliation, or do we separate, which seems to be the path we're on? Do I sever myself from my old life for someone who, if you knew her, you would believe to be as good as gold, as honorable as Julia Greene, or do I risk letting her and this prospect of real happiness slip away from me? Please know that I'm not a young sailor falling in love with the first foreign girl he meets. I want to do the right thing for everyone. Which, as a departure from my usual practice, also includes me."

"Then as a friend I feel for you," she said. "As a woman, old-fashioned and narrow-minded perhaps, I'm offended. But as someone who has had to make difficult choices about her marriage too, I'd advise you to wait."

"I've given that advice myself today. In my case, I'm not sure I have your patience."

"Think big picture, Brad. Nothing really needs to change right now—except perhaps your job prospects."

"One of which affects my romantic prospects."

"Well, yes. So much for my advice. But maybe turn it around. Make everyone else wait while you put first things first."

She rose.

"Now, if we're going to give a reception tonight, I really have to sleep. Mad's across the street. Peace Park, I think the name is. It has a date as well."

228 Peace Memorial Park. The number meant as much to the Taiwanese as 9/11 to Americans. It was short for February 28, 1947, on which date and in the days following, the Nationalist troops of Chiang Kai-shek, called in to quell a hopeful resistance movement, lost themselves to blood lust and murdered thousands of their fellow citizens.

It wasn't a large park, but it took him a while to find her. Whenever they went on vacation (not often, not often enough), she wanted to know the history of the place—or perhaps he did and she went along—so he began at the

memorial museum, which used to be a radio station occupied by the dreamers until so many of them had been
slaughtered. She wasn't there. Outside was a vertical
banner in Chinese and English: *Pray for peace.*

Then he tried several small lakes, where water lilies
grew and willow fronds hung down, where peace could be
known or at least prayed for. Then a free-standing trip-
tych gate with an inscription about the massacre and its
lessons in unity and tolerance. Then a temple, then a
bandstand, both in the pagoda style. No Mad.

Several modern sculptures stood in the park at strategic spots. Their meaning wasn't revealed to him either by
experiencing them or by their Chinese placards. Mad was
sitting beneath the least accessible, an open-air steel
structure where the merits of peace might be felt except
that its top was pointed like Bismarck's helmet. She was
sitting alone, staring into space.

"Madeleine."

She turned her head. "I've been imagining where you
were. It's a bad habit. I'm going to give it up."

"I wasn't surprised to find you here," he said. "This is
the kind of sculpture that Adam makes."

"How serious is she, Brad? Someone important to you?"

"She's someone I admire, certainly."

"Is there love?"

"Yes, maybe. I don't know what kind of love."

"I'll bet she doesn't have that problem. She's fifty?"

"Forty-eight."

"Single?"

"Widowed. Adult son."

"And pretty. Fresh, wholesome, just what you like."

"Also funny, smart, courageous, and honorable."

"Also the president of Taiwan's sister. You're made in
the shade, boy, as long as the K.M.T. don't come back."

"I was hoping you'd be—not so much fair as thorough.
You and I have been growing apart, without much complaint by you. You live the way you want. My work as a

teacher you seem to find ridiculous when I don't bore you otherwise. You took off on an adventure with another man, knowing how I would feel about it. I accept your description of the circumstances, but what made him think he could proposition you? For that matter what did the celebrities see in your relationship to include you in their lawsuit? And why did the police depose you?"

She thought about this. A squirrel came up to beg for food, then, seeing the mark was preoccupied, skittered away. At the temple a flute drew a line of notes on the air. Like the art, the phrase made no sense.

"Yes, let's be thorough," she said finally. "I don't condemn you. I was in love too, but not how you think. I was in love with his energy and sense of fun. It was fun when Gloria was with us, and then it was crazy fun after she left. Dustin doesn't take anything seriously; it's all pleasure, even working. He's irresistible that way: we're put on this earth to enjoy ourselves: he just goes after what he wants. I ask myself if I would have slept with him if he had pressed me, if I hadn't seen what he was up to. I honestly don't know."

"Fortunately, neither of us is committed that way." He frowned as he said this, which would have offended Lucy Gayheart.

"Yes, I'm clubbing you with a situation. Unfortunately it's now: you have to choose. It's too bad for both of us because you have other decisions to make as well, and here's a tip: you don't like complexity."

As if he didn't know that. But the only decision that mattered was the present one. Nationality aside, Mad and Mei-ling were nothing alike. The choice was almost too complicated to think about. Continuity versus stimulation. Boredom versus excitement and grief. Forty years of memories versus everything new and all the past to be explained. Two dear faces, one like love and the other like home. Regret either way. He didn't trust his judgment.

Perhaps the wise thing would be to leave them both.

But that would mean getting used to himself.

"It's more complicated than you're implying, isn't it," he said. "I can't assume you still want to be married."

"No you can't. How hard for you."

"Is that even a possibility now?"

"Do you think I would have come all this way if it weren't?" So saying she got up, and they walked back to the residence.

Hints, Inferences, Kindness, Decisions

Both of them needed to rest. Their room had a couch as well as a bed, but the bed was big enough that they could lie down in their clothes with as much room between them as at home: surely that wouldn't compromise his decision. Neither did Mad object.

Instead of sleeping they talked in fits and starts and stared at the molded ceiling with its incomprehensible figures.

"Myself, I'm open to it," she said. "If we could work out the settlement I'd be okay with a divorce. Not ecstatic but okay. Grateful for the time we've had. We'd both continue to be excellent parents to our wonderful children, with no taking sides. I'd still care about you, wherever you were."

"Thank you."

"I believe it would be different for you, however. The idea of scandal horrifies you."

"Doesn't it you?"

"Wanting to be happy isn't a scandal—or shouldn't be. These days people don't think twice how a marriage ends as long as no one's hurt. But *you* would feel it."

"I might. I'm more concerned about being so far away and having to learn Chinese."

"When we unpacked your cruise box we saw that book *Chinese Is Easy,* and Julia and I looked at each other."

"Only fifty characters a day and you can be Shakespeare."

"The question is how would we be happier," she said. "Myself, I don't think it's possible that you could change the things you do that bother me. They're you. You say I'm bored. I'd say I'm just worn out. I don't think I can offer you a whole marriage anymore."

"Not that it's been whole for some time," he said.

"All right. But I need to look to myself."

"Would you want to go to counseling?"

"And spill my secrets to some yoga teacher?"

"That's not you," he agreed. "Or me."

They were silent for a time.

"Do you want her that much?" she asked.

No answer was an answer.

"You should know," she said. "I hate the images."

"I understand."

After a long silence,

"We fell in love once, Bradford. Or at least we had a romance. It won't happen a second time. I won't feel again
with you that astonishment, that pleasurable discovery: *so
that's what someone else thinks about life.*"

"It's all right." But had they not been in love when they
conceived Sarah? No, probably not: they were just on a
path that both understood was leading to marriage. But it
hurt him to think that if he hadn't been in love, she hadn't
either.

"If that's what you want," she said, "you should be with
her, if you want it so much, all that newness."

"Or maybe I'm meant to be celibate."

"If you think you'll like her after the newness is over."

"That's just it."

"Or someone else later. It doesn't have to be her."

"Or for you as well."

The reception was called "dessert," justifying its nine p.m.
start. Besides a ceremonial cake there were other sweets
plus enough savory hors d'oeuvres to make a meal. Plus
a well-stocked bar. Drawing on the embassy's rolodex,
Slate had filled the residence: various foreign diplomats,
officials from the ministries of foreign affairs and defense, business people, a couple of influencers. Most people spoke English and Chinese interchangeably. The commodore and Mad, at the door along with Slate and Julia,
had a few seconds to greet each person and try to

memorize their name before they moved on into the crush, striking up instant conversations.

"I'm indebted to you for correcting me on the Scottish play," said Gillette, the ambassador, as he shook hands. "Though it heaps shame upon my head, since I did my master's thesis at Oxford on the bard."

"You were a Rhodes scholar, sir," he said.

"The now obliquitous Cecil John." Mad snorted at the epithet. "I contrasted Shakespeare's uncanny insight into human behavior with his profound stupidity about politics. Speaking of which, and I mean no invidious comparison: you may have been right today, Commodore, and certainly I'm sympathetic to President Tsai's position, but I'm afraid you cost me another four hours with the White House this afternoon, gone from my life forever. What do you think, Slate?" For Slate had shut down the receiving line.

"I think he made it easier for her to take the bitter pill. There's nothing like getting to the heart of the matter, which we, the greatly washed, often forget."

"Or we just like to hear ourselves talk, the gods be thanked because it keeps us employed. This has been a tough couple of weeks, but I don't think I've ever enjoyed myself more. Such a difference when diplomacy really matters! Think of it: war and peace! War between superpowers! The president's not here yet? No. I'm hoping she'll drop a hint tonight. Or someone from her staff may know her leanings."

He was ready to roll up his sleeves and join the crush.

"Before you go, sir," Hilty asked, "what would you say was Shakespeare's most telling insight?"

"*Lord, what fools these mortals be.* Good evening to you—good evening, Mrs. Commodore," he added above the din, "and good luck at home."

"Nice fella," Slate said. "Maddy, what can I get you?"

ฅ ฅ

"A bit of admin for you both," he said, returning with the drinks. By then Julia had joined them. "Our check-out time is tomorrow morning."

"You're going back to *Blue Ridge?*"

"*Au contraire,* I'm leaving questions of war and peace to all of you. The company's announcing me in about two hours. Tomorrow morning this young lady and I are flying to Jakarta. And the president wants her residence back."

"What's in Jakarta?"

"The families of crash victims. My first act as CEO will be to apologize. Ethiopia will be next. I'm going to grieve with them and let them call me all kinds of a monster. The silver lining is that our legal types are horrified."

"That's exactly the right thing to do!" he exclaimed. "Slate, I'm proud of you."

"So join me, Bradford, in my noble quest. Maddy, you too, as Vice President of All Things Good."

"Wouldn't that be nepotism, if *he* joins you?"

"Only if you're still married," Slate said with a wink.

President Tsai and her sister walked through the doorway. The politician was ready to be pleased as she turned the corner and saw the crowd. Mei-ling, holding her arm, smiled by rote like a dutiful wife whose thoughts were far away.

The four Americans shook hands with the president, Slate kissed Mei-ling on the cheek, and then he had to follow. Her cheek rose in response, and he thought he heard her whisper, "Don't leave me." If the women shook her hand or kissed her he wasn't aware of it.

Looking at the president, Slate tilted his head comically to imply the obvious question.

Tsai put him off with a grin. "Commodore Hilty," she said, "I was concerned to hear that Admiral Chen and my sister gave you the third degree after I left. In that place where no one can hear you cry for help. She won't tell me what it was about"—given the closeness of the sisters, this had to be a politician's fib—"but I am very curious to know."

Rows and rows of possible replies rattled through his mind like those flight status boards that rattle like a breeze blowing through venetian blinds:

☞ I'm going to learn Chinese in three months.
☞ I accepted an offer to command the Taiwan Navy.
☞ I'm going to divorce my wife and marry your sister.
☞ I'm going to roast coffee with your nephew.
☞ I'm going to dance to music all day.
☞ I see that you yourself are about my age....

As with the status boards he wasn't quite quick enough to see how the mechanism worked, and he shut his mind to the image before the board could say *Flight Canceled.*

"I was giving them my evaluation of the outstanding officers who command your fine new destroyers, ma'am. One in particular, Zhang Yu-hsuan, highly talented, but who seems to be having a crisis of conscience."

She studied him for a moment to know his game.

"I have heard of him, Commodore. As you say, highly talented. A crisis of conscience? I believe he is visiting his sister, an unfortunate invalid, in Beijing now."

"I hope you can get him back."

"That would be something else to talk about at the working level meeting proposed by the United States."

She looked at him as her mouth widened into a smile.

"Good for you, Madam President," Slate said.

She gave a confirmatory nod. "Our neighbor to the west has ordered his ships back to port and begun redeploying his soldiers. I wish Admiral Juventude were still here so I could thank the Seventh Fleet. But Ambassador Gillette will do, and new CEO Greene, and our new friend Commodore Hilty. I feel ten kilos lighter. Don't I look it?"

Arms raised, she turned a circle and laughed. "Now, where is this famous dragon cake?"

She waded into the crowd followed by Slate and Julia and made a point of praising the arrangements before the organism of the party ingested her. Mei-ling stayed behind, with the Hiltys.

They were the only people near the entrance. The crowd within was as tightly packed, as noisy, and as fragrant as at the open-air market today—this morning!—but more people kept coming in. The word must have gotten out that the president was here, uncordoned. Politicians, diplomats, military officers, perhaps a clubber or two. Since the Greenes had abandoned their posts—across the field of heads and shoulders Slate gave him a shrug—there would have been no one to welcome the newcomers if the commodore hadn't done it. He smiled and shook hands with every person, all of them strangers (though several acted as if he should know them); and handed them off to Mad and Mei-ling, thinking to himself, and in one case actually muttering, "This is my wife, and this is my girl friend." The two women performed their duties willingly enough, notwithstanding the frequent interruptions, or perhaps they welcomed them.

Mei-ling, hugging herself otherwise, looked frightened and yet determined. Oddly, it was he she seemed frightened of and Madeleine she seemed determined to talk to. As a new guest passed on, she touched the other's arm.

"Thank you for coming such a long way. Isn't it odd that we left from the same place. For me, coming by ship, it feels like a *very* long way."

"Well, of course I flew. But it does seem long."

"Six weeks traveling. And months of training before that. I haven't seen my country since the new year—our New Year, in February," she smiled.

"That's as long as a deployment—oh, for God's sake, Bradford," she said as a young man in a shiny blue suit launched himself through the doorway with a shouted greeting in Chinese that meant, "Good news! I'm here!" Mei-ling stepped in front of Hilty to perform the welcome and, with voluble Chinese in the same celebratory tone as his, injected him into the party.

"Over here," Mad said, taking up a new station behind the opened door, where Hilty and Mei-ling joined her.

"You've been gone—" "I was going to say—" the two women began. Mad relented, and Mei-ling went on.

"I wish there was a better time and place to speak. I wish I knew you better. But this will have to do, and I will trust that your heart may read mine over all this noise.

"What I feel for Bradford is real, Madeleine, and I tell myself I've done nothing to be ashamed of. This is true, my conscience is clear. During the trip I had occasion to teach him the Chinese idea of face. I feel no loss of face in loving him, in wanting him in my life. I've done nothing to be ashamed of—nor has he—and I tell myself that you and he may be unhappy together. Still, I must seem a threat to you, to your freedom of choice if nothing else.

"You should know that I will not have him if it hurts you. You may believe that. Now that we have met, you are an important person in my life. You carry great weight with me, even beyond this temporary fear I have. I don't know what will happen or what is best for all three of us, but I do know I must never hurt you. If we make this decision together—or certainly if you make it and my only part is to be informed of it—I will do nothing to cause you pain or to lose your respect."

Her face was pale but composed. For a moment her eyes looked calm and perhaps pleased with herself as she waited for the response. Then they were shining and the teardrops, tiny and whole in the lamplight, were actually falling onto the tile.

Three more people came in, three women. One of them, looking for their hosts behind the door, glimpsed the private moment and moved her party on.

Mad held both of Mei-ling's hands together within her own. Another step closer and the magnetism would have drawn them into an embrace. He himself could feel it. Her small chest filled with air, and she said, "I see only a good person here, Mei-ling. Someone troubled like me. I don't think of us as rivals, and I do wish you happiness. Whatever comes from this will be two sets of decisions: Bradford's and my own, and yours and his. Separate decisions. We self-respecting women would never allow a man to choose between us, isn't that true?"

"No, never," Mei-ling replied with a thick voice.

"Then if the situation is painful—painful for all of us— it's just life and no fault of yours. And no fault of mine or Bradford's either."

"Thank you, Madeleine."

Mei-ling turned away and dried her eyes with a handkerchief. When she turned back she said, "You are very kind. Very kind. Now I must not stay, or my sister will keep me up all night. Good-bye, and I wish you happiness too. Good-bye, Bradford. I'm on the train tomorrow. I'll see Chowa. Think how happy. Good-bye." She and Mad had an oddly formal handshake, then she took his wrist and leaned forward as if to kiss him then decided not to. He swung the heavy door wide open, and she left, turning again as if she had more to say, shaking her head twice quickly, and the doorway was empty.

"Who is Chowa?" his wife asked.

"Her son, a barista in another city."

"Will you be on that train?"

"Does it seem even possible that you and I could make this decision so quickly?"

She looked as if she had just put her hand into a pocket and found a lost set of keys.

"Not from where I stand," she said. "We've only just defined the problem. Deciding what to do about it *tonight* would be like throwing darts."

"Why did you travel all this way?"

Her famous snort: "I was suckered into it. Slate said, 'Oh, come to Chicago.' Then, 'Robin wants us in Pearl Harbor. You come too.' Then, Slate and Robin and Julia: 'Help us represent your country in Taipei—see the good work your husband has done—don't worry about that little matter of the war.' I did get a tail-hook certificate out of it, and it was nice to see *Blue Ridge* and think of *Mount Wonderful.* We have a great country, don't we. Sometimes my heart aches so much for it I could die. So here I am, literally a third wheel."

No, figuratively one. "I'm glad you came, though."

"They told me about the fire, Bradford. You old fool: what did you think you were doing?"

"Making a point to the captain. Also saving *Plumpy.* Also, maybe, straining my own heart a little."

"Your heart? Is it serious? Have you seen a doctor?"

"When we get home. I'll have a retirement physical— it's fine, probably just a murmur"—lest she insist on calling for an ambulance.

"Does *she* know about it?" Her soft blue eyes looked up at him. Despite her confident talk she was tremulous with the uncertainty.

He shook his head, which was true only because Meiling had never mentioned it. Either (H) or his corpsman had probably told her. After she had saved his life, and while she was nursing him, it would have been natural to learn his condition.

He would keep all that to himself. She wanted to believe him, and the headshake was as good as a dart.

"The naval hospital in Portsmouth has a very good cardiology service," she said, adopting a pragmatic tone.

"As does Evanston Hospital, where I was born."

"So: Chicago, not Norfolk?"

"I'm going to take the QA job. That much seems clear."

"I think you're right. You're perfect for it. If you want me to join you, I'll be your plus-one again. While we sort out the rest. We could buy a house on the North Shore. This might be a second act for you. In your old hometown."

Of course she would welcome the lifestyle.

"A third act, at least. When will you fly back?"

"Next week. I didn't come all this way and risk my neck in a war not to see the sights."

"That's our first problem, then. When I don't get on that train tomorrow, all of Taiwan will feel like a war zone." In fact it felt like an engine room fire already. "I can't stay here."

"I understand. I'd feel the same. In any case you need to have your heart checked. If you left tonight you could be in Chicago tomorrow."

"With the International Date Line I can be there to-day," he said, but when she frowned he was too tired to explain it. He changed the subject. "So what are we going to do about your problem in the British Virgin Islands and mine with the evil student, the craven school administration, and the lying governor?"

"Sue them all," she said. "Sue the pants off them."

"That's the American way," he replied with a smile.

Acknowledgments

I am indebted for Commodore Hilty's opinions about the founding documents primarily to Kermit Roosevelt III, *The Nation That Never Was: Reconstructing America's Story* (Chicago: The University of Chicago Press, 2022). For the causes of the Civil War I drew primarily from the research for my novel, *Decoration Day* (Philadelphia: Bernice Feigenbaum, 2022).

Descriptions of the hurricane came from my own experience, informed by Nathaniel Bowditch, *American Practical Navigator* (Washington: U.S. Naval Oceanographic Office, 1966). Bowditch also describes these clouds as "mare's tails," a term widely used by sailors. He is responsible too for my depiction of the green flash, a phenomenon I only wish I had seen.

For the Gatun Locks I drew from David McCullough, *The Path Between the Seas: The Creation of the Panama Canal 1870-1914* (New York: Simon and Schuster, 1977).

The heroic story of USS *Norman Scott* was told me in 1991 by one of her officers and refreshed by Wikipedia. USS Laffey's toughness is extant in naval history; again, I used Wikipedia for a refresher.

The references to Shakespeare came from *The Yale Shakespeare* (New Haven: Yale University Press, 1923).

Willa Cather's memorable scene, in which the heroine understands of her suitor that "a feeling meant nothing to him, he had to be clubbed by a situation," is from *Lucy Gayheart* (New York: Alfred A. Knopf, 1935).

The description of the harbors of Su'ao and Kaohsiung, neither of which have I visited, came principally from the Royal Navy Admiralty, *China Sea Pilot* (Somerset: U.K. Hydrographic Office, 2019), vol. 3. For Taipei I relied on my own visit in 1974 and on Wikipedia and other sources.

Acknowledgments

Finally and most important, for their enthusiasm and encouragement I thank my children, Heather, Matt, John, and Patrick—all Corcorans, each so gifted—and with my whole heart and once again, my wife, Linda Perry, who may be even fonder of Hilty than I am, if that's possible.

About the Author

Thomas Corcoran entered the Navy in 1972 and retired in 1993 as a captain, having served during the Vietnam War and Operations Desert Shield and Desert Storm. He commanded two ships and was selected for command of a destroyer squadron. He lived in Navy ports on both coasts, including Norfolk. Besides sixteen years of sea duty, he served in the Pentagon as Special Assistant to the Chief of Naval Operations and as Military Assistant to the Secretary of Defense.

Commander Hilty's Second Act, the second in the series about this quixotic character, is his fifth published book of fiction.